TANGLED ROOTS

Jessica Brodie

Praise for Tangled Roots

"Jessica Brodie reaches in and grabs hold of the reader, refusing to turn loose. You can't help but love and relate to her characters. For a memorable read, check out *Tangled Roots*. You'll be glad you did."

Cindy K. Sproles, bestselling author of Appalachian novels *Mercy's Rain*, *Liar's Winter*, *What Momma Left Behind*, and *Coal Black Lies*

"I know that only in Christ do happily-evers really happen, and this is the secret weapon behind Jessica Brodie's narrative—Christ. Far from the formulaic, just-believe-in-Jesus-and-your-problems-will-go-away stories that soft-pedal reality, between page one and the happily-ever-after, *Tangled Roots* leverages real-world scenarios to point people to our only hope."

Lori Hatcher, bestselling author of *Think on These Things*, *Refresh Your Faith*, *Refresh Your Hope*, and other devotionals

"Jessica Brodie isn't afraid to write characters who struggle with real issues, and she does so with authenticity and grace. *Tangled Roots* presents an intriguing blend of Southern fiction, romance, and character depth."

Jennifer Slattery, multi-published author, speaker, and founder of Wholly Loved Ministries

"A relevant story that tackles tough issues, delivering a hope-filled message that our lives don't have to be defined by our pasts, *Tangled Roots* promises to stay with readers long after the final page."

Natalie Walters, bestselling romantic suspense author

"Jessica Brodie's *Tangled Roots* hooked me on the first page."

Ginny L. Yttrup, Christy-award winning contemporary women's fiction author

Book Two in the Dahlia Series

TANGLED ROOTS

a novel

Jessica Brodie

VALOR
PUBLISHING GROUP

Valor Publishing Group, South Carolina

Copyright © 2025 by Jessica Brodie

First published in the United States of America in 2025

Library of Congress Cataloging-in-Publication Data
Tangled Roots
p. cm.

Cover Design by Hannah Linder Designs

ISBN 979-8-9929008-2-8

*To Matt, whose patience holds me steady
so I can quiet all the churning and express what's needed.
Thank you for being my rock. I love you.*

CHAPTER 1

BENEATH THE CAFÉ TABLE, Tiff's crossed ankles clenched so tightly she thought they'd break in two if she didn't release them.

She took a slow breath and sipped at her ice water, her dark eyes on Bobby's as if her mind was anywhere but a million miles away. The news she'd gotten not an hour prior sliced through her like a knife, and inside, her heart thudded.

James was coming. Her brother was actually coming. *Oh, dear God.*

The lump in her throat got bigger, so big she thought for sure Bobby could see it through her skin, but he didn't seem to notice.

"You really think a hundred people?" She forced herself to ask it like nothing was wrong, to smile at her fiancé.

Bobby leaned back and gazed at her, his face open and kind.

"Baby, a hundred at least." He squeezed her hand gently, his calloused thumb somehow soft on her skin. "It's our wedding day! Why, I think a hundred with just my family alone, and then there's friends, and coworkers, and—"

"Now you're starting to freak me out." Tiff gave a nervous laugh, and he brought her hand to his lips, winking in a way that made his dimple quirk. Her stomach tumbled, and not entirely from nerves.

1

"So that's what's bothering you tonight. All the people? Tiff Lacey Steadman, you have no reason to feel shy. I'll be right there by your side the whole time. I promise you."

"But I—"

Bobby shook his head. "No buts."

She looked around and realized they were the only ones left in the restaurant. Just him and her and the waitress. The candle in the green glass votive burned so low she could see the tiny metal square that held the wick in place. Around them, she could picture their town, Dahlia, like a cozy blanket wrapped around her shoulders, the cute little gazebo right there in the square, the rows of trim clapboard houses reminding her of childhood storybooks. Safe.

Nothing like where she and James grew up, where fighting and broken liquor bottles set the scene. But she'd gotten out, run so far and fast she never had to look back. Except for sometimes—times like tonight.

Tonight, it all felt like it was closing in on her, and everyone would see her as the broken, no-good fraud she felt like, way down deep in her darkest places.

Bobby's voice grew soft. "I love you, Tiff. You made me the happiest man in Dahlia, in the whole world, when you said you'd be my bride. And I want all our family and friends to be with us on our special day. All those prayers wrapped around us . . . I can't think of a better way to start our life together. You don't need to be nervous about one single thing."

She readjusted her legs beneath the table, gritted her teeth. If only that were it.

Tiff fiddled with her engagement ring—a full carat, which still shocked her all these months later—and leaned in. Her eyes caught Bobby's in the candlelight, and for just an instant she thought she could do it, blurt it out then and there.

I've lied to you, Bobby. I've lied, and it's big. There are things you don't know. Things that might just make you change your mind. My family isn't good, like yours is. I've got a jailbird brother, for starters . . .

But her mouth was on autopilot. "I—I love you, too, Bobby. With all my heart."

It was the honest truth, at least. She'd never loved anyone in all her life like she loved him. She loved him like a fairytale, like sunshine sparkles in the creek she used to play in when she was a little girl, before the fear and shame and secrets got the better of her.

Bobby reached out, tucking a lock of dark hair behind her ears.

"I just wish your folks were still around, wish you had some close family nearby. It's got to be kinda weird, I bet, planning your whole wedding without your mama."

No way. Her mama would've turned her wedding into a first-class disaster.

"I've got yours." Tiff's lips felt tight as she tried to smile. *Just say the words! He'll understand. He's going to be your husband. It's not like you can keep it from him forever.* "Your mama seemed really excited to help, didn't she?"

Bobby's eyes lit up. "She sure did. I don't think I've ever seen her that happy."

Tiff wouldn't exactly call it happy, but Mrs. Smathers did take her upstairs, show her the wedding gown she'd saved in the large cedar hope chest all these years.

Still, she'd seen the shadow cross Mrs. Smathers's face when Bobby announced the news. It was so quick Tiff probably wouldn't have caught it if she hadn't been looking for it. But she always looked for it.

When you grow up a Steadman, you know that look well.

"She does have three boys. Four, if you count your dad." Tiff smiled, pushing the look on Mrs. Smathers's face aside. "I imagine she's positively craving some girl time."

Bobby laughed and pulled out his wallet, placing a few bills beneath the check.

"I like the sound of that. My two ladies." He stood, offering a hand, and when she rose to him, she felt as light as air.

They walked to Bobby's car hand in hand.

Tomorrow. She'd tell him tomorrow.

Why spoil a perfectly good night?

When he dropped her off, Tiff stood in the dim light of her living room, watching Bobby's pickup back out and bump gently over the dip in the driveway. The cat knocked against her leg, and she picked him up, stroking his orange fur absently as she sagged against the front picture window. Waiting. For what, she didn't know, but she couldn't bring herself to move just yet.

James. She could still hear her brother in her head, still hear those three little words that had turned everything haywire.

"I'm getting out."

At first she didn't think she'd heard him right. James, calling her? From prison? She thought maybe it wasn't even him at all—a wrong number, or a twisted joke. She knew better, of course. Knew it would one day catch up with her. It always did.

But a girl could hope.

Six weeks, then her world would change forever. And once again there was nothing she could do about it. Not one tiny little thing. Her heart pounded just thinking about it. And her head, for that matter.

"I'm getting out," James had said again, when she hadn't responded. She hadn't trusted herself to respond. A clatter came, and she could tell James was clutching the phone, leaning in close. "Come on, Tiff. Say something. I can hear you breathin'."

She tried. But the words just wouldn't form. They'd hung there in her mouth, giant blank balloon bubbles as the seconds ticked by, turned into minutes, and she could hear the prison guard or whoever it was standing next to him tell him to wrap it up 'cause Sanger needed to make his call, too.

James had let out a long, slow sigh.

"All right, Tiff. I'll let you go. I know it's been awhile—hush it, Sanger—so you just let it sink in a bit. We've got some time. I'll call you again tomorrow. Around six."

He gave her a date of his release and some details, waited a beat, but again she said nothing.

"Love you, sis."

His words were quiet, tender like they used to be when they were kids and he'd huddle with her under the blankets in her twin bed, as if the soft cotton would somehow protect them from Mama and Daddy railing and drinking and who knew what else. As if it were just the two of them, Big Bro and Lil Sis, against the whole wide world.

She swallowed and nodded as though he could see her over the line. When the call finally went dead, she was surprised to find her eyes were wet.

James was actually getting out. Getting out and coming home.

Well, coming here. If you could call here "home."

Standing at her front window, she shook her head, wanting to rattle some sense into it. Bobby's taillights had disappeared into the darkness a good five minutes ago, and she made herself turn both locks, then slid the chain and padded into the kitchen.

Peaches meowed, and she set him down. She moved on auto-pilot to the cabinet, pulled down the cat crunchies and the tin of herbal tea.

When the kettle whistled and the tea bag was steeping she paused a moment, looking at the lavender mug cradled between her palms. The Future Mrs. mug, with the red hearts the girls at work had given her when Bobby'd proposed. The mug was hot, almost too hot, and she stayed as she was, letting the heat sink in, forcing herself to be still. To endure the heat. She imagined her palms turning as red as the hearts themselves.

Why now? Why was he getting out of prison now, of all times, when everything in her life was starting to go right for once?

A tiny bubble of you've-got-to-be-kidding-me laughter threatened from somewhere, and she took a sip of the tea, staring out the kitchen window toward the dark night beyond.

She remembered when James first went in, all those years ago, how she used to wish with all her might that somehow, somebody'd gotten it wrong. That James hadn't actually done that bad thing at all. That he'd been framed. That one day the news would come out that someone else had really done it and James was free to go. Once she'd even run out in the middle of the night in her thin pink summer nightie, ran all the way to Aunt Lula's grave so she could pray in front of all those pretty gray stone angels, sure they'd get the message to God faster than Tiff could possibly do on her own.

Please get my brother out of prison. Please bring him home.

But the wishing went away as the years passed. And now she'd do anything to keep him where he was—safely gone from her life. The life she'd tried so hard to build on her own. The life here in Dahlia, South Carolina, where no one knew she was kin to them no-good-Steadmans, where all people knew was what she told them. It was all the truth: small town girl, college scholarship, hard worker, looking to settle down in a town and make a life of her own.

It was what she hadn't told them—what she couldn't tell them—that she planned to do her level best to keep far, far away.

Of course Bobby needed to know. Of course he did. She'd be the worst wife in the world to walk down the aisle with that secret still in place, to let him find out after. When it was too late to change his mind. That was something Mama would've done.

Of all the things Mama'd done in her life, the one good thing she'd given Tiff was the example of how not to live her life.

No, she wouldn't do that to Bobby. Not in a million years. Not even if he decided she wasn't worth marrying when he knew what kind of people she really came from.

Tiff glanced at the phone and swallowed. Six o'clock tomorrow. She'd hear James out, hear what he had to say.

And then she'd talk to Bobby. Tell him everything.

For his sake, and for hers.

CHAPTER 2

James

JAMES SAT IN THE PRISON CELL, the dog-eared New Testament smooth between his palms, the faint cracks so worn they were almost soft. On the fleshy part of his right thumb he could barely see the lick of black, so subtle if he swiveled his wrist inward an inch the tattoo would disappear entirely.

Instead he swiveled it out, stared hard. As though the staring would change things.

Tiff hated that tattoo. Had shamed him up one side of the creek and down the other when he'd showed her that first night. He could still remember that night. All the details, the real ones and the ones he'd invented over the long, long years to pass the time. If he thought about it hard enough, he could still taste the bourbon, too, the sour stench that ran through his hair and his clothes, left its mark on the soles of his feet. Tiff swore the cat could even smell it on his fingertips, one of a dozen reasons she'd said the three-legged fur-trap steered well clear of him. He had no use for mangy cats anyhow. At least he didn't then.

Two thousand six hundred forty-five days sober. Two thousand six hundred forty-five days locked up. One and the same and yet, somehow, different. Distinctive. That was the word Pastor Chad

had used last week, and it fit.

"All up." The guard's voice made him flinch even though he'd been expecting it.

James set the Bible on the bed and rose slowly with his cellmate. Enrique was quiet today. Usually a bad sign, though James tried not to think much about it. His countdown was on, and all he needed to do was keep his head down and focus on Re-Day. Release Day. Only five weeks and six days left.

He wasn't convinced it would actually happen, though the attorney and his pastor both insisted he'd be set free. It wasn't a faith thing that caused the doubts. It was more that he'd been in so long he wasn't even sure he could handle thinking beyond the cell, beyond the correctional facility that had been his home for about as long as he'd been a full-grown adult.

Enrique was muttering under his breath by the time the guards got to their cell, and James was sure the double set of black boots would stop in their tracks, turn, and force them both out into the corridor for a lesson on respect. But the boots kept on. Either they didn't hear him or they didn't want to.

James knew what that meant. Busy day today. Maybe the governor was visiting, or the group that brought cookies from the church.

Tiff. He tried to picture her as he turned back to his bed, carefully tucking the Bible atop the stack of other books on the bedside table. Did his sister still look the same? Skinny as the cat, long hair, dark scolding eyes. He imagined she did, though maybe she'd cut her hair now, or wore it curled. If he were her, he'd want to look nothing like their past.

Scolding eyes—better than scared eyes. He'd seen those too many times, didn't want to see them ever again. He liked Scolding Tiff far better than Scared Tiff.

He wasn't stupid. He knew she didn't want him coming around, messing up her life. He didn't intend to mess it up. But he knew they were right. It looked better—heck, he knew it was better—if he settled anywhere but where he'd been raised. He'd leave the state if the judge would let him, go clear up to Canada or Vermont, even. Someplace cold, where he could wear turtleneck sweaters to hide the scars and the ink of his past and really start fresh. Reboot. Rebuild.

Dahlia would do for now. He didn't want much, just needed to stay off the radar and do his community service, try not to bug Lil Sis any more than absolutely necessary.

He just hoped he didn't have to see those other eyes, the eyes she'd had that last day she'd visited him in prison, seven years ago. Empty, cold, locked up tight.

Those he couldn't bear.

CHAPTER 3

Tiff's heart thudded in her chest as, the next night, she perched on the worn beige couch in the tiny living room of her rental house. The phone lay heavy in her lap. All she could hear was the tick of the wall clock, which sounded like it was beating time with the whoosh of pulse in her ears. Would James call or plumb forget like he used to? She half wished he wouldn't. Then everything could go back to normal.

No such luck. The phone rang at five-fifty-nine, and suddenly the world went from far-off and fuzzy to sharp, cold, and clear. She wasn't seventeen anymore. She was a woman, full-grown and about to get married. If she couldn't handle this, her own flesh-and-blood brother for Pete's sake, how in the world could she expect to handle anything else life threw at her?

Oh, but it took her back.

It had been seven years, but his voice still sounded like it'd been yesterday—that mix of salt and honey, of climbing trees and sneaking into the barn way too late at night to hide under blankets and let their good-for-nothing parents drink past the witching hour. She could almost hear him mutter, "It's all right, Lil Sis. They're too fogged up right now to remember they even had kids," as she'd shivered from fear Daddy'd find her, pull out the belt again, drag her into the laundry room, and—.

"You there, Tiff?"

She blinked and gripped the phone.

"S-sorry." She cleared her throat, tried to make her voice hard. Adult. The past couldn't touch her now. No one could. "You said early release? I didn't even think that was possible. Not after . . ."

"Most'a the guys here are in for far worse." James's voice was low, somber. "But me, I haven't been in solitary, not once. Didn't hurt that Mickelson ended up coming clean about his part in the whole bit."

A million questions swirled as she tucked her legs beneath her on the old couch, making room for Peaches to nestle in the crook of her arm. His purring was loud in the silence of the room, and she focused on it, on the steady tick of the wall clock, on the cool metal of her engagement ring, the small diamond catching the side lamplight just so.

"Aren't you gonna say anything?"

No. Best to keep what she really wanted to say inside. "I just don't know what to say, James. I mean, it's been years."

Seven years and one month, to be exact, since she'd walked out of the visiting room the September of her senior year in high school and never looked back. Not once.

The purring stopped, and Peaches pressed one claw gently on the back of her hand to remind her he was still there.

"Five minutes, Steadman," came a voice, and James sighed.

"Look, Tiff. I'm really sorry. I know the last thing you want is your big bro on your doorstep, invading your new life. It's just till Easter. The probation officer said I needed to log three hundred hours of community service, stay put for three months solid, hold down a steady job, and check in again. He said it'd look especially good if I'm staying with family, but, well." She wasn't sure if the sound he made was a sniffle or a snort. "My pastor thinks I should get as far away from the old neighborhood as I possibly can, and the only person I could think of in the whole world was you, Tiff. You're all I've got."

She almost choked. "Your . . . pastor?"

"Like I said, sis. I've changed. I've, well. I've become a Christian now."

"You've got to be kidding me."

James, who'd once called himself a hillbilly skinhead, who had more tattoos on his left arm than she had fingers, who'd once said faith was for the weak and mindless sheep of the world who had nothing else going for them, a Christian? She tried to imagine him at her church, where the guys wore polo shirts and khakis, where the little girls donned big white bows and didn't look like they'd been dirty a day in their life.

"I figured you'd be happy about it, Tiff. I mean, you were always going to church as a kid, sayin' your prayers'n all before bed . . ."

Her chest felt itchy and hot, and her mouth went dry. Cool it. "Is that why they're letting you out early? Because you decided to pretend you got religion to look good for the parole board?"

"Tiff." He sounded hurt, but she didn't want to hear it.

"James, you're my brother. We have a history, and I'll always be grateful for what you did when we were kids. But I've gone through great pains to remake my life here. No one knows I have a brother. No one knows a thing about my family, my past—"

"—and they don't have to!"

"James." She pressed a hand to her temple. "Please."

"Come on. I can bunk on the couch, walk to work or hitch a ride. I won't tell a soul we're related if you don't want . . ."

"It's a small town. And you don't exactly blend in with the locals."

His voice got quiet. "Please, sis."

Her sigh, when it came, was resigned.

"Just give me all the details. What you need me to do on my end. And give me a few days to think it through."

"I'm really sorry to be putting you through all this. I know it's a lot all at once."

She barely heard him. All she could see was the look on Bobby's face. The one she'd get that evening, when he saw her with new eyes.

Mrs. Baker from back home was right. The past always does catch up with you.

When she dreamed that night, she dreamed of the old barn from back home, the creek just beyond, the frothy black water rising past the surface and spilling out.

Flooding them all.

Chapter 4

Tiff

"Aren't you gonna answer it?"

Tiff blinked, forgetting where she was for a moment. The din of the newsroom swirled around her. Dinah the sales rep cracked her gum, the pop oddly loud amid the noise. Her boss, Rebecca, was on the phone, some big news story with the county sheriff, and Millie the receptionist stared at her expectantly, giving her that oh-Tiff look she always got whenever Tiff got spacey. Which these days seemed to be more often than not.

Three days.

Three days since she'd talked to James. Three days, and she hadn't even told Bobby yet.

A coward. That's exactly what she was.

"Sorry," Tiff told Millie, picking up the phone at her metal reporter's desk. Even though she'd been promoted to editor over the summer, nothing much had changed. The one-room brown-paneled newsroom was still four desks and a bunch of paper racks, the front door still smashed against the window frame when the breeze took it just right, and her tiny desk and chair still sat exactly where it had the day she first took the job, straight from college.

To be honest, some days that was exactly why she loved it—

though the stories changed and the weather changed, she could always count on coming to work where everything would be exactly, one hundred percent the same. The scratched-up gray desk, the rolling chair with one wheel slightly askew, the placard above her head that listed her name and title. Reminding her who she was, lest she ever forget.

"Well, hey there, pretty lady." The long drawl over the phone line made her giggle. Old Mr. McMasters, of the side-swept hair and long earlobes, who she'd befriended her very first week on the job. Zeke McMasters wasn't exactly old-old, but he talked old and dressed old and acted old. He was also one of the nicest people she'd met in town, introduced her to the pastor of her church, even, and eventually to Bobby himself. These days he was calling himself the matchmaker, though Tiff knew it was really that day at the grocery that sealed the deal, how she'd grabbed the orange from exactly the wrong spot, and they'd all gone tumbling down in a catastrophic mess. Bobby told her that on their fourth date, said he'd never seen anyone so frazzled—or so adorable—over making such a disaster.

"Hi, Mr. McMasters. Got another batch of collards for me?"

His laugh sounded like sandpaper and sawdust, and her lips curved.

"Shoo, girl, you know you don't care one bit for collards. Sure you're even Southern?"

That made her laugh.

He got to the point, told her about the issue—his sister, Mamie Louise, had taken a bad fall and gone to the county hospital, and could she maybe run a story asking for help?

She bit her lip. "Are they doing a fundraiser or something?"

Rebecca would never let her run a blatant appeal even if she wanted to. Though the citified publisher had softened considerably since she'd moved here, Tiff's boss had been in the business a long time, and like she always said: "Ads were ads, news was news."

"Why yes, ma'am. The Hosten Brothers are bringin' their guitars to the community center next Friday night, and we're gonna throw a fish fry."

Tiff arched a brow. That could work. "All righty, well, let me know what time, and I'll swing by, take a picture."

"You got it, sweet thing. You give that man a'yours a big ol'hug when you see him next, hear?"

"Sure will, Mr. McMasters."

They hung up, and she held the phone a moment. Thought about Bobby, about how she'd begged off the last two nights. Said she'd had a bellyache and had to go to bed early. Bobby'd been so good. He'd asked no questions at all, even offered to bring her chicken soup, which made her feel downright rotten.

Deep down, she knew her bellyache had nothing to do with real sickness and everything to do with nerves.

And deep down, she also knew there was only one way to get rid of those nerves: stop being a darn coward and talk to her future husband. Once and for all.

"You okay, hon?" Millie eyed her from across the room like she knew exactly what was running through Tiff's mind.

"Yeah," Tiff said, reaching for her cell phone—and what she knew she'd needed to do from the start.

"Love you," she texted Bobby. "Can we get together this afternoon?"

She had it all planned out—what she'd say, how she'd start, the shift from small talk to deep.

But it all went out the window the second she saw him, standing there beside his truck at Dahlia Community Park. It was a pretty day—blue skies, leaves hinting at the buds to come, though spring was still a long way off. No one was in sight, not even mamas and their chunky-legged toddlers, chortling on the swings or whizzing down the slides.

Just him and her.

Dear goodness.

"What's wrong?" He cocked his head at her just so.

She lost it like a crybaby, and then the story began to spill out in gulps and ugly hiccups. All wrong, all unplanned. An onslaught of words and sighs and tears. Even she couldn't figure out what she was saying.

"Oh, baby." He wrapped his arms around her, held her close as her sobs slowly subsided and she finally peered up at him. Her long bangs were wet, and she wiped at her face. Bobby didn't seem to mind, just waited till she caught her breath, looking at her like he could see into her very soul.

"Tell me," he said.

What else could she do?

Leading him to their bench, she sat, ankles crossed tight. And told him.

Everything.

"A brother. Tiff . . ." Bobby gripped her hands, looking out at the trees. His jaw was tight, as if his teeth were clenched, and a thrum of fear rose in her chest, flickered and fanned.

A long moment passed, and they sat that way—him looking at the woods, her watching his jawline until finally he took a breath and swallowed. When he spoke again, his tone sounded wounded.

"Why didn't you tell me?"

It was her turn to sigh, to stare at the trees.

"I guess—I thought if I pretended long enough and hard enough I could forget everything. But, well." A shuddery sigh came, not even affected, her shoulders sagging beneath the shame.

He held her then, and she leaned in to him, held on tight, like he was a sturdy log and she was being tossed this way and that in the writhing, frothing riverwater.

"When does he get out?" Bobby's voice was quiet.

"Five weeks, give or take." Her hands felt cold in his. She risked a glance, and the look in his eyes was off somehow. Guarded.

"And he'll come here?"

"That's what he says." Her eyes shot to his. "He said his probation officer doesn't want him going back to where we—he. Used to live before."

Bobby's brow creased, and he nodded. "Makes sense."

"It does?" She blinked.

"Yeah." He glanced over, the guarded look gone, and squeezed her hand. "Patterns. Influences. Like, when I used to hang with the Peters brothers, and they'd get me all riled up over stupid stuff, remember?"

The Peters brothers—Mickey and Rook—were known for starting fights in town. Bobby had stopped hanging out with them shortly after he and Tiff became a couple.

"I forgot about them. I suppose you're right."

"Mama always says, 'Bad company corrupts good morals.'"

She swallowed. No telling what Bobby's mama would say about James. And the kind of people Tiff came from. "She's right."

Bobby wrapped her in his arms again, pulling her close.

"It's going to be okay, Tiff-Almost-Smathers." He put his finger to her chin, tilting her face to his for a soft kiss. "I wish you'd told me about your brother. But I get it. I do."

Tell him about the rest. The voice tugged at her, pleading.

Now or never. It would be so easy—there's something more, Bobby. Something else you should know. Something I've been wanting to tell.

Mama. And Daddy. The drinking and the rages. And how she'd

left it all in the dust, never once looking back.

It's all in the past.

They were dead to her. Well, Daddy was, but as good as dead, in Mama's case. Maybe even was dead. For all she knew, Mama could have drunk herself into a stupor years ago.

Better to leave it all as it was. Safe in its box.

Locked away for good.

No one really needed to know. Did they? Wasn't the pastor at church always telling them to keep their hand on the plow and move forward, not back, like Jesus said?

Kissing him back, she breathed in deeply, letting the late afternoon air swirl around them like a blanket.

"I'm sorry I didn't tell you, Bobby."

He cupped her face in his hands. "We'll face it all, sweet love. Together."

And closing her eyes, she let herself believe it.

CHAPTER 5

THE LETTER ARRIVED IN THE MAIL a week later. Tiff knew it was from James even without the "inmate mail" stamp—he still wrote in all caps, and she could still see the indentation of the letters on the envelope. When they were kids, he used to press down so hard he'd accidentally break off all the tips of her mechanical pencils till she'd finally started hiding them from him, made him use a regular soft-lead or a ballpoint.

"You just want everyone to know you mean what you say," she'd tease him back then, and he'd always give her that puh-lease look.

She cringed as she slid the mail from the box, wondered what the mail lady must be thinking. She wished he hadn't used her given name, Tifyni. No one called her that. She didn't even spell it that way anymore, had changed it with the courts years ago on her nineteenth birthday. Normal Tiff, just like everybody else.

The letter stayed on the coffee table until she'd fed Peaches and charged her iPhone, changed from her fancy work heels and wrap dress into her cozy-comfies. Bobby was helping his dad and brother restock—Friday night at the grocery was always prep night for the weekend, but that didn't bother her, even though Bobby said just about every week he wished he could take her out on a Friday like a regular couple. Having a night alone gave her a chance to relax, to bum around in sweatpants, and besides, she was usually tired at the end of the week, her energy spent from phone calls and interviews and dealing with people all day. Bobby said that was the introvert in her, and he was probably right. Tonight, she'd planned to cook some chicken, make a healthy green salad, and open that bottle of high-end vinaigrette dressing her boss Rebecca had given her, maybe take a bubble bath and do her nails.

Now, none of that sounded remotely appealing. Instead she made herself a bowl of cereal and flopped onto the couch.

She eyed the letter with each bite, made herself finish the cereal before she reached for it. Peaches settled warily at the end of the sofa, pretending to be asleep.

When she opened the letter, the envelope tore. But her hands didn't shake once.

> Lil Sis,
>
> I'm sorry for begging you to let me come there for a couple months. I feel real bad about it. I don't want to mess up your life none. It's just I have nowhere else to go. But if you tell me no, I will respect that. I could maybe go find some other place. You don't need your Big Bro tearing down all the hard work you put in there to change your life and leave the old days behind. I guess what I'm asking is can you pray about it. And then write me back or call me here at the prison and tell me your choice. If you want to call my pastor, you can.
>
> Your loving brother,
> James Wallace Steadman

He'd drawn a cross in the upper-right corner, shaded it so it looked like it was casting a shadow, and printed the name and number of a Rev. Chad Barwick at the very bottom of the page.

Tiff sniffed. Call his pastor? Pray about it?

James used to poke fun at people who said that stuff. Even at Tiff herself, till it got to the point where she was careful not to talk too much about religion to him. It became her own private thing. And now he'd written her a letter from state prison asking her to pray?

This had to be a con. Didn't it?

Some Bible verse tugged at her, something about how when people ask for help we shouldn't ask whether they need it or whether we should help them but just do it, no questions. Well, that sure was easy when it was a panhandler asking for money or Miz Trudy two doors down asking for a favor. But when it's your convict brother pretending to know Jesus and claiming he's turned his life around? What then?

She crunched up the envelope and tossed it across the room, startling Peaches, who jumped off the couch and scurried off somewhere safer and quieter.

Fine. She squeezed her eyes shut, bowing her head.

But the prayer, when it came, felt false on her lips. As if she was praying toward God, in his general direction, rather than a conversation. Even sinking to her knees on the living room carpet didn't help.

Finally she gave up and flopped onto the couch again. From the kitchen her phone chirped, and she padded over. Bobby usually checked in around now, making sure she'd gotten home safely.

But it was a text message from her boss Rebecca, not Bobby. "You coming tonight?"

Tiff had completely forgotten—she'd told her boss she'd help out at the Friday Night Giveaway, the weekly food and donations ministry at church. She and Bobby had only started going to Dahlia Community Bible Church recently, after Rebecca joined. It was still new, but so far Tiff liked it much better than Bobby's mama's church, where she always felt on display and like people were more interested in her hemline than her soul. Dahlia Community Bible Church was more of a come-as-you-are type place. Plus, Rev Bryant and his wife, Marla, were super sweet, and she got to spend time with her boss on a different level.

She'd die of embarrassment if Rebecca knew it, but Tiff would pretty much turn circles like a lap dog to soak up some more Rebecca time. Tall, confident, and beautiful, her boss had that "been there, done that, got the T-shirt" vibe. In the eight months or so that she'd known Rebecca, Tiff felt like she'd grown a million percent as a writer just from being around her. Best of all, you could tell her anything and she wouldn't bat an eyelash—the big sister she'd always wanted. She'd just hear you out and you'd be set straight again.

Even something like a secret brother about to be let out of prison probably wouldn't faze her.

Tiff looked at the letter, still on the couch where she'd left it, considered lugging the Heavenly Hash ice cream out of the fridge and parking it on the couch with some bad television for the rest of the evening.

Before she could cave, her fingers slid over the keypad. Wallowing never did her or anyone else any good.

"Be there in fifteen."

Rebecca's forehead creased as they stood together at the clothing table, her at one end, Tiff at the other. "He really said that? He's become a Christian?"

Tiff dug the letter from the back pocket of her jeans and passed it over, then started folding some long-sleeved T-shirts. "Even gave his pastor's name and number."

"Wow." Rebecca bit her lip as she read the letter.

Around them, the basement at Dahlia Community Bible Church was bustling with giveaway volunteers—Mr. Mike on their right with the shampoos and mini soap bottles, Mrs. Martha by the door with her clipboard, a few teens from the high school running trays of spaghetti and salad from the kitchen to the long folding tables on the side. Two people knelt with towels, mopping up what looked to be an entire pitcher of sweet tea that had spilled.

When Tiff looked back at Rebecca, her boss had her hand over her mouth.

"Oh, Tiff."

Tiff knew what that meant. Rebecca had that I'd-be-crying-if-I-cried catch to her voice, and if she wasn't mistaken, the woman's eyes looked moist. It was the same look Rebecca got when she was writing one of her tearjerkers, like the series she'd done in the fall about the family living in their car.

Only James wasn't some story. This was Tiff's life.

"I know what it sounds like. I know what he wrote in that letter. But if you only knew what he did, how he was . . ."

Rebecca cocked her head, her eyes still soft. "That bad?"

"Rebecca, he's got a giant black swastika covering his entire forearm." Tiff's voice was low, but she still felt like she was shouting: Hey, everybody, guess who's kin to a racist?

Her boss looked down at the letter. Tiff couldn't tell whether she was rereading or just couldn't look her in the eye.

"People change," Rebecca said.

"I guess."

"But you think he hasn't?"

Now Tiff could feel Rebecca's eyes on hers, but she didn't want to meet them. Instead, she reached into the big cardboard box, digging out another sweatshirt. This one was pale yellow and had been washed so many times it felt like a baby blanket.

"Maybe he has." Tiff set the folded shirt on the table, reached for another. "It's just—people are going to see the skeletons in my closet."

Realization flickered in Rebecca's eyes as she passed the letter back over. "Bobby's mama."

"Not to mention the entire town."

Tiff folded the letter into a tight square and shoved it deep into her back pocket once again. The bulge pressed in hard, uncomfortable, a pea beneath her mattress she shouldn't have been able to feel but did nonetheless.

Silence fell over them as they folded the rest of the items, then tucked the box beneath the table. Tiff could hear the buzz of voices from the guests, dozens or more of Dahlia's needy, who lined up outside the church every Friday for a meal and other basics. Some of the guys had been in prison themselves, she knew. She'd talked to a handful of them. It wasn't prison itself that was so bad, not that she wanted half the town to know their reporter had an ex-con brother. It was embarrassing enough they knew she was getting married into the Smathers family, what with the questions about had they set a date yet and what was the holdup and did they plan to start a family straightaway. As if that were anybody's business.

"Look, Tiff, I'm not the best example of how to get along with family." Rebecca leaned against the folding table, her voice so low Tiff had to lean closer to hear. "I spent half my life keeping as far as I could from mine, at least until I became a Christian. But sooner or later it always catches up with you."

Only, wasn't that exactly why Tiff had run so far and fast—to get away from anything and everything Steadman, James included? She was counting on her past not ever catching up with her. Not to knock Rebecca, but her boss came from some upper-crust

Virginia family where her daddy was some big-shot government lawyer and her mama played tennis and shopped too much, and they quarreled over things like "expectations" and "empathy." She'd met her once, Rebecca's mama. The lady had those perfect white-tipped fingernails that gleamed like firecrackers in the office fluorescents. Wore one of those big gauzy scarves. Smelled like lavender and baby powder and called Tiff "dear" and sailed in and out like she owned the place. Nothing at all like Tiff's mama, who favored purple glitter fingernail polish and skintight acid-wash jeans. Who liked to brag she could drink like a sailor and curse like one, too. Who she saw go toe-to-toe with Daddy on more than one occasion till they were both sprawled drunk and battered on the couch and sported black eyes like badges of honor. No wonder her older brother had ended up a jailbird.

As far as Tiff was concerned, the past could try its hardest to catch up with her. If she had it her way, it never would.

The bell rang out then, sharp and clear, and the guests began to pour in. A rail-thin mom with her two stringy-haired kids in tow made a beeline for Tiff's table, picking over the sweatshirts while the kids jabbered at each other until the piano started up and they couldn't hear well enough to fight properly. Tiff watched as they moved to the food line, saw the older one, a boy, snag a plate for the younger, a girl, then helped her pile on the pasta.

A flash of James hit her without warning—the night the thunderstorm had knocked out the lights and Mama and Daddy had passed out early, and they'd snuck back in the house and James made them peanut butter and jelly sandwiches. They ate them right there in the kitchen, legs crisscross-applesauce on the linoleum floor, scrunched up near the window so they could see their food from the glow of the porch light. They knew better than to turn on the house lights after Mama and Daddy had gone and passed out. She must have been six or seven then, in school for sure, and James not all that much older, but old enough to cut off her crust and help her set her plate in the sink so it didn't clatter and wake anyone up.

That was the night she'd cut her foot on the glass from one of the shattered bottles, and James had to wrap it up tight with the dishtowel and some duct tape when the Band-Aids wouldn't hold. Cut it so bad the school nurse had to take her to the real doctor the next day and stitch it up right. Funny now, looking back, she remembered none of the pain, just how good it felt to sit there on the kitchen floor with her Big Bro and eat her sandwich like she was one of the Tolsen girls from down the street, the ones with the swing set and the lunch bags that matched their backpacks.

Tiff watched the kids make their way through the food line and follow their mama around to a table in the rear. Watched the boy ruffle his kid sister's hair.

Tiff leaned down to pick up one of the socks that had fallen, and the letter in her back pocket poked at her hard. Of course she needed to do the right thing. Of course she had to let him come here. She didn't like it much, but she knew right from wrong, knew after all James had done for her growing up that she needed to reciprocate.

But just because she took her ex-con brother in didn't mean she needed to spill all her secrets, did it?

CHAPTER 6

James

"STEADMAN, JAMES WALLACE."

James knew it was coming—the unit guard had told him, and Pastor Chad, and the gray-suited attorney—but he jumped anyway. Hearing your own name over the prison loudspeaker wasn't something a body could get accustomed to hearing. At least, not him.

His stuff was all ready, had been since two nights prior. Wasn't much. His Bible, the picture of him and Tiff tucked deep inside. The clothes he'd worn coming in. Three journals he wasn't sure he wanted to keep, though Pastor Chad made him at least promise to take them. He could decide later whether to burn them or toss them or save them. Save for what, he didn't know. As far as he was concerned, the only good thing to happen in these seven years was coming to know the Lord. The rest he'd just as soon forget. He knew he deserved the punishment, though it was hard enough forgiving himself for what he'd helped do to that boy. But like Pastor Chad had said, all sins are equal sins against God, bought and paid for by Jesus Christ our savior on the cross. If God could forgive a liar and a thief, he could sure enough forgive James Steadman.

"Leave the past in the past, J." Chad's eyes had been sad that day, there in the prison chapel. But behind the sadness he'd reminded James of a tiger, fierce and wild and ready to tear into him if he turned and ran from the truth he had to give. "Hear me? When you become a Christian, you get a brand-new life."

James could only nod, but Chad's eyes got all squinty, and he wouldn't let James off that easy.

"Second Corinthians," James finally mumbled.

They said it together, quiet but still audible enough that the other guys in the chapel glanced over: "If anyone is in Christ, the new creation has come. The old has gone, the new is here."

Every day since then, James had said it, trying his level best to believe it.

New creation.

He felt their eyes on him now, the collective stares of the entire cellblock, as two guards walked him past the gate and down the twisted hallways to a cold fluorescent-lit room, where they had him change from the jumpsuit into his old street clothes. The basketball-style sneakers felt too tight on his feet, the arches too high, like he was encasing them in bubble wrap, and he half-wanted to leave the shoes there in the room, piled up in a heap with the beige uniform, and just slide back into the cotton inmate-issue slip-ons. But he left the sneakers on and tried to walk as normally as possible, like it was natural to wear Nikes and jeans and a T-shirt and hoodie again.

They ushered him to the front counter next, signing forms and inking and pressing his fingerprints into neat black-bordered squares. He wanted to ask if he could wash his hands, but he was afraid to say the words, as if speaking would break the spell and they'd stop, turn on their heels, and take him right back in. Instead, he held the Bible and journals in the creases of his fingers, careful not to touch his inky fingers to their covers.

He paid no attention to the actual leaving part, through the prison gates and shuttling the four miles to the bus station in the squad car. All he could see was the fading evening light around him, catch the smell of grilling meat on the air. Hear the bustle of cars and trucks and some female's high-pitched laughter. Thousands of people all around him, and no one seemed to have a care in the world.

His heart beat steady and sure beneath the soft cotton T-shirt. He held onto that sound, tried to focus on it, tried to breathe. In and out. Out and in.

On the bus, he asked for a blanket from the driver. She gave him a pillow, too, small and squishy, like it was filled with tiny birdfeathers. Curling his long body toward the window, he stared out at the Gervais Street Bridge, the black river water below, the first smattering of stars just beginning to twinkle in the night. He had no seatmate tonight, didn't know if that was luck of the draw or standard for prisoners just released. He swallowed, breathed, focused again on his heartbeat.

There now. If just the noises would settle down. The noises and the smells. He'd forgotten about the smells. Meat and warm bodies and women's aerosol hairspray and some sort of coconut scent.

Surely his fingers were dry now. He glanced down at the Bible and journals in his hands, not an ink smudge in sight, and carefully flipped to the back of the New Testament. Ephesians, and the picture of him and Tiff.

Flipping on the light above him, he stared hard at the picture, as if he hadn't fallen asleep with it in his hands every single night. He wasn't sure exactly what it was about the picture that drew him—no, that was a lie. He knew. He gazed at it a moment, studying it afresh. Tiff's black hair fallen over one eye, a missing tooth giving her face a lopsided, spunky appeal. Her pale-yellow tank top with the darker yellow smiley-faced sunshine front-and-center. The mangy cat she held up, so close it looked like it wanted to be a million miles from there, its legs stick-straight and its fur all tattered and scruffy at the neck. And James himself, looking like a kid in his blue T-shirt. Smiling his real smile. He was a kid, then, fourteen at most. Her, maybe ten.

He remembered that day—it was at the town fair, and Tiff had been helping that animal shelter lady with the cats, and he'd gone looking for her and found her in a pile of unwanted kittens with their flea-bitten, skin-and-bones mama cat. That animal shelter lady had been taking pictures of the cats for her flyers and she'd snapped this shot of the two of them, given the photo to Tiff. Tiff presented it to him on his first day of high school, sealed tight in an envelope.

"So you can remember me when you get to be a big shot," she'd told him, sticking her tongue out and swatting his arm.

So young. So innocent. Both of them.

If only he could erase everything that came between then and now—the dark days, the bad crowd he'd fallen in with, the drinking, the lies. The hate.

Swallowing hard, he glanced at his sister's face, the open grin and missing eyetooth, and suddenly felt cold all over.

What if she wouldn't take him in? What if she took one look at him and couldn't stand the sight?

He slipped the picture back into the Bible, then flicked off the light and huddled under the thin blanket, staring out at the dark night behind hooded eyes as the rumble and hiss of the bus bumping over the highway lulled his tight muscles into submission.

No choice now. Nowhere to go but onward.

CHAPTER 7

THE VEIN IN HER HEAD THROBBED as Tiff sat in her small blue car at the bus station, hands gripping the steering wheel. Soft music played, but she couldn't hear the words, just the sharp thrum of the drumbeat pounding along with her head and heart. She jabbed the radio off.

Hers was the only car in the lot at this hour—apparently eight on a Friday night wasn't the regular time most people caught the bus from the capital. At least, most people visiting Dahlia. She had the heat on, just the floorboards, and the headlights cast a hazy glow on the bus station's concrete wall.

Her eyes stayed glued to the door, waiting. Any second now, James would walk out. Would she recognize him? Surely she would. Her ears began to itch, then her throat. She fished for the water bottle in her backseat and took a sip, dribbling some of the liquid onto her sweater. As she twisted the cap, she realized her hands trembled.

All of a sudden she regretted telling Bobby she'd be fine, that it was better for her to pick James up by herself. It was his busy night at the grocery, she'd said, and besides, she and James had some catching up to do. Only now, she'd give anything to have Bobby there beside her, squeezing her hand, making her laugh with some corny joke. Anything to keep her mind off this.

Maybe it wasn't too late to back out. Maybe James would get here but have to turn right back around—his parole officer had made some mistake, really he needed to stay in Columbia, couldn't leave the boundaries of the city, some other red tape.

Her left eye twitched, and she rubbed at it, checked her watch again. Eight-oh-four.

A loud hiss and the squeal of heavy brakes came from somewhere behind the building, and she cracked the window, heard the rumble of a bus motor idle, then pull away.

And then the door to the bus station swung open and a tall, thinnish man with shaggy dark blond hair and a hoodie and jeans pushed through, canvas duffel slung over one shoulder.

James. Her heart did a flip-flop, like the catfish she'd landed in the river, only instead of belly-flopping onto the murky surface, it did a tumble. Straight down into her core.

She could see him scan the lot and look her way. Before she lost her nerve, she flung open the car door and flashed her lights, said his name.

The word came out almost like a cough, but he heard her. He strode over, all six-foot-who-knows-what of him, and she was looking up at him like he was a stranger or a celebrity or both.

James. Her heart flipped back up on its imaginary fishing line, smacking down hard on the water's surface.

James was here.

She couldn't see his face till he was almost right in front of her, all covered in shadow and mystery, but the eyes were the first to hit her. She'd know those anywhere. Still dark, still wide—like almonds, Mama used to say—though the trace of laughter that used to run through them was decidedly absent. Haunted, that'd be the way she'd describe them now. If she had anyone to describe him to.

Anyone who knew him when.

She didn't. She'd shut those doors long, long ago.

The rest of his face was skinny and drawn, like he'd aged fifteen years instead of seven. The way he wore his hair, neck-length and unbrushed, made him look like an overgrown rock star.

The tattoos were nowhere in sight, at least till the streetlight caught up with his wrist. That's when she saw it, the telltale black stripe barely poking out from under his sleeve.

His arms lifted like he was going in for a hug, stopped. Hung in midair.

Don't. She wasn't sure at first if she'd said it or just thought it. The word, caught on her lips, trailed off into a sigh.

They stared at each other, her with one hand on the car's doorframe, him shifting his weight from one foot to the other like an unsure kindergartner deciding which seat to take on the first day of school.

Seven years. Everything had changed.

Nothing had changed.

She almost wanted to laugh. *My brother the jailbird. Come after all these years to live with me.*

"You look good," he finally said, his voice at once too loud and far too quiet in the cool winter night.

". . . Thanks."

She bit the inside of her cheek hard. Everything she wanted to say felt strange on her lips—how was the trip, where'd you get the clothes, what happens now, what'd they do to you in there—so she said nothing.

A moment ticked by, then another. On the street behind them, a car passed slowly, kept going. Finally he gave a little shrug and stepped to her, the hug stiff and smelling like Dial soap and stale air conditioning. She didn't even have time to put her arms around him—it was over as soon as she could blink.

He threw his duffel in the backseat and climbed in, leaning the seat back. She tried not to look at him, at the faint ink she could see on his collarbone now that he had his head tilted back, at the way his cheekbones looked high and tight like he'd been through a war and not seven years in prison. Instead she just trained her eyes on the rearview as she buckled up, backed the car out, and turned onto Dahlia Highway.

"It's not far." She kept her eyes on the road, expecting him to fill the air between them with endless chatter like before. This new James was odd and silent, a ghost walking around in her brother's skin.

Next to her, she could feel him flick his eyes to the window, watching Dahlia cruise by. She peered out in the silence, trying to see the town as he must—the cutesy streetlights like some too-perfect store-bought Christmas village. The old-timey village square and main street with the ice cream parlor and ninety million churches instead of some dingy pool hall or check-cashing operation like back home. The gazebo by the rose bushes something out of a squeaky-clean movie—the spot, in fact, where Bobby had proposed. All of it surreal, like nothing they'd grown up with, yet so familiar to her.

"That's my office." She pointed at the newspaper building when they got to the red light. He scooted up in the seat a little, gave it the once-over, blinked.

"Looks nice."

"It is."

They drove in silence the rest of the way. Even Peaches didn't meow when she turned the key in the lock and ushered them inside, just took one look at James and darted into the kitchen.

She showed him to his room, white down comforter on the bed with its just-from-the-package crease, guest sheets fresh and crisp. Flicking on a light, he sat on the bed, gave a small bounce.

She watched him a moment, wanting to be angry, wanting to hate him, hate what he'd done, what put him away all those long years, but coming up empty.

As if reading her mind, he looked up at her. She couldn't read his expression.

"Tiff, I just want you to know how much I appreciate—"

"Oh, it's fine—"

"No." His voice was firm. "I meant what I said on the phone and in the letter, Sis. I won't be no trouble. None at all. I just got to put in my time, do what I've gotta do, and get back on with my life. Let you get back on with yours. I'm just grateful you let me stay. It can't have been easy."

She was surprised to hear the gentle tone to her words when they came. "It's all right, James. You're my brother."

They stared at each other, years looming between them like a barrier. Finally, she gave a half-shrug and gestured to the dresser, where a stack of towels sat folded neatly.

"Help yourself to the shower and kitchen. I've got eggs and bacon, and there's plenty of shampoo and stuff in the bathroom. I've got to be up early for work, and I'm beat. Bet you are, too."

He rubbed his eyes. "You work Saturdays?"

"Covering the volunteer fire department breakfast. But I'll be around after awhile. Just make yourself at home. I'll show you around tomorrow afternoon."

"You don't have to."

But she did. She would.

She went to bed hugging herself, wishing she could cry or scream or just forget it all. Sleep, when it finally came, was restless and sporadic, dreams filled with broken bottles and pool sticks and bloody dishtowels.

And the big white village square gazebo—only instead of rose bushes all around, there were rusty old tools, broken-down pickups, and a neat line of prisoners with their arms crossed, standing guard.

When she woke up, he was gone.

CHAPTER 8

THE NEXT MORNING, Tiff huddled in her ice blue jacket outside Dahlia Volunteer Fire and Rescue, snapping pictures. The sun felt entirely too bright for a cold February morning, so bright the rays seemed like daggers piercing through the camera lens as she tried to zoom in on the firefighters flipping sausage patties. Laughing parents and kids and old folks clustered at folding tables slathering butter on biscuits.

It was getting tough to feel her fingertips. She wished she'd worn her thick gloves instead of the super-thin stretchy ones. But she was taking pictures, and she couldn't mash the button right with puffy forefingers, so it was thin gloves or no gloves. Besides, she didn't need to stay long.

Not that she wanted to get back home anytime soon. "Job hunting" read the note James had left next to the coffee maker. But who could tell how long that meant. His heavy block letters had looked entirely out of place on the notepaper, which had dainty lavender flowers and butterflies in the bottom corner. For all she knew, he'd scoped out the prospects and was back at home—her home—his feet up on the coffee table watching basketball.

She felt her eyes narrow before she forced herself to take a deep breath. *Give it a rest, Tiff.* It was going to be a long three months if she was going to be this negative the whole time. That she knew without a doubt.

"Getting some good shots?" came a male voice behind her, so loud she almost jumped out of her skin.

She turned, forcing a smile that felt tight against her teeth. "Hey, Sheriff."

"How's our favorite town reporter doing? They been feeding you right?" Sheriff Zane thumbed at the station, the other hand giving his belly an exaggerated pat.

"Not hungry quite yet, but don't you worry about me." She gave a little shrug and wiggled the camera.

He laughed and clapped her shoulder. "Well, don't you wait too long. There won't be any left." He peered at her closer, tilted his head. "You doin' all right?"

He knows about James already? Her neck felt warm as a flush crept slowly up her chest to her cheeks. Maybe that was the way it worked with this stuff—the prison called the town, alerted the police, everybody stayed on high alert, watchful in case some ex-con decided to go bat-crazy on some robber rampage.

The sheriff gazed at her, his eyes kindly. "Don't you worry, Miss Tiff. Everyone gets the wedding day jitters at some point. My wife says when it was our turn to walk down the aisle she was so nervous she almost called the whole thing off and forced me to elope!"

Jitters, not James! Her heart stopped its wild flight to nowhere and settled slowly into place.

"And look at you now." She gave him a genuine smile.

"Luckiest man alive, I tell ya." The walkie-talkie on his hip crackled and the sheriff picked it up, muttering some codes and a 10-4 before slipping off into the crowd with a little wave.

She watched him go, her chest still tight.

That was something else she hadn't considered—even if she and

James did their level best to keep things a secret, there was no telling what the sheriff's office had been told. Or who it had been told to.

Bobby's mama, for instance.

And in this town, news traveled fast. She of all people should know that.

After the breakfast, she stowed her camera in her trunk, then jogged across Main Street to Smathers Grocery. Bobby would be there, probably all day.

"Hey, future sis!" Bobby's youngest brother, Ben, called from the bagging station as she walked in, his sandy hair all teenage-tousled as he sliced open a cardboard box with a utility knife.

She couldn't help but smile. "Hey, Ben. Bobby in back?"

"Yeah, he and Dad are restocking." Ben made a face.

Tiff giggled. "Sounds like fun. See ya in a bit."

She could feel herself relax as she walked the aisles, heading toward the back of the store. Being in Smathers Grocery always gave her a good feeling, had done so even before she'd met Bobby. It wasn't a fancy store by any means, which gave it a homey vibe. They still had those cute vintage posters from the sixties with the red-cheeked kids and the moms—moms who probably never touched a drop of alcohol a day in their lives, let alone cussed out their husbands and kids—all wore perfectly white aprons, their pearl earrings and smoothly waved hair just-so as they held pans of freshly baked cookies. "Where We Have It All," was the Smathers Grocery slogan, and signs proclaimed it all over the store. Her boss Rebecca liked to joke that it was like a time warp, and Tiff didn't disagree.

Even Bobby's dad reminded her of one of those old-fashioned store clerks with his stiff green apron and chummy handshakes and grins.

He didn't disappoint now as she slipped through the vinyl divider between the meat section and the back room.

"Why, lookie who we have here!" Mr. Smathers boomed, patting Bobby's arm as they both turned to greet her. His hug lifted her clean off her feet.

Bobby's hug was tender, like he was asking everything and nothing all at once. You okay, his eyes questioned, and she gave a half-shrug, hugged him back.

"You two take some of these boxes out to the trash for me while you catch up. I'll finish up in here." Bobby's dad shooed them off like he knew, and they headed down the hall to the small cluster of trash bins out back.

"How'd it go this morning?" Bobby asked quietly after he made sure no one was in earshot. "Any less awkward?"

Tiff wrinkled her nose. "I didn't even see him. He was gone when I got up."

"Gone, like, forever?"

"I wish. Kidding!" she said to Bobby's shocked expression. "No, gone like job hunting. I guess part of his parole conditions include finding a job and doing community service."

Bobby snagged the two boxes from her hands, tossed them into the bin. "You know, we might be able to use him here . . ."

"No!"

His eyebrows got all puppy-dog. "I mean it."

She turned to face him, taking his hands in hers. "So do I. James can't work here. He just can't. It's bad enough he's here, in my house, in my life again . . ."

She felt her voice catch, and for a moment she was scared she'd lose it right there in the alley behind the grocery.

Bobby just held onto her hands as she squeezed her eyes shut, took some breaths.

When she finally opened her eyes, he was gazing at her.

"You're brave, you know."

She almost laughed. "What?"

"It's hard stuff, the past catching up with you, and you being at the newspaper and all. I'll keep my promise and not tell anyone, and I get why you're upset. You haven't seen him in years, and he's been in jail, and I bet you're crazy-as-all-get-out ticked off at him—"

"It's not just that—"

Bobby held up a hand. "Tiff. He's your brother."

Images of thunderstorms and counting games beneath tattered quilts swarmed her head until she pushed them back. Hard.

"That's the only reason he's under my roof." Her lips were tight.

Bobby's thumbs made slow, gentle circles on the tops of her hands, and he looked like he was going to say more, but then the door to the grocery swung open with a crash.

"Stop all that kissing and get on in, Big Shot." Bobby's middle brother, Zach, stood there, a devilish grin on his face. "Dad needs you. Oh, and hey Tiff."

She gave him a light punch on the arm as she and Bobby jogged up the short flight of steps and back into the store. "Hey, Zach."

As she walked to her car, she realized she felt stronger somehow.

They're a good family. Good for me. In a million years she couldn't picture one of Bobby's little brothers doing the kind of things James had done. Stealing. Fights. Getting involved in a bad crowd that got their kicks from harassing people just because of the color of their skin. Having so many tattoos you couldn't even tell where his skin stopped and T-shirt began.

If Mrs. Smathers thought one of her boys even had one of those tribal tats under his shirtsleeve, Tiff felt sure she'd march him right on back to where he'd gotten it, make them remove it pronto, and give that tattoo artist a what-for till he'd probably want to leave town or change his profession.

The swastika tattoo burned in her mind. She swallowed hard and clicked the button to unlock her car.

Bobby just didn't get it. James might be her blood, but he'd given up the right to be her brother a long time ago.

CHAPTER 9

James

IN ALL HIS LIFE he'd never seen a place like Dahlia, all them nice houses with lights on inside and neat white fences with gardens and flat lawns outside. Two doors down, some kid had left a pink Barbie bike outside like she wasn't even worried someone would come along and steal it.

A bike, now that he could use. Not that he'd take that bike, or any bike for that matter. New creation in Christ settled on his mind, and he could feel himself relax as he walked the pretty sidewalks in the general direction of town. He could almost sense Pastor Chad with him, assuring him that even the worst kinds of men had turned their lives completely on end and gave it all to Jesus. Paul the apostle, for starters. Paul'd done things to the Jews that James and his old crew wouldn't have dreamed of.

But he sure could use a bike, though it felt good to walk, and today at least, he had all the time in the world on his hands. Still, once he had a job he'd have to get there on time, not to mention smell good and not like he'd just walked a few miles to work.

And community service. He had to get started on that, too. A low tightening began in his toes and worked its way up till it was in his belly. *Soon. Just breathe.*

A car passed slowly on his right, and he could feel his back tense up. Somewhere on his left someone started hammering.

He paused a moment, closed his eyes, and settled himself like Pastor Chad had taught him. Seven years in the slammer wasn't a quiet place by any means, but the sounds were all different. Harsh voices and metal clangs and boots. Buzzers and bells that chimed almost like clockwork. Familiar sounds.

Soon enough, he knew, the sounds of this town would become just as familiar. And when he left here, got out of Tiff's business and let her go back to her life, he'd find a new place, a nice place, with new, nice sounds, and he'd adjust again. On his own away from Tiff this time, and maybe that was for the best.

He knew it was hard for Tiff, him being here. She had a right to hate him. Everybody did. She looked all classed up now, clean blue jeans and all that soft long hair. He was glad she hadn't cut it. She looked real good, like she was doing well in life. He'd say happy except for that nameless something behind her eyes. Though maybe that was only 'cause he was here, messing things up for her. She even had tiny pearl earrings in her ears. He'd sneaked a peek at the rock on her left hand, too—whoever the guy was who gave that to her, he must love her a whole lot to save up and buy a diamond that big. He was certain it was a real diamond, too. No fakes for his sister.

"Give it back!" he heard a kid scream from the yard to his left. A girl.

He slowed, saw two boys and some old stuffed thing in one of their hands.

The girl, probably no more than seven or so, had her hands on her hips, two pigtails slashing the air as she stared the boys down.

"Aw, Emmie, we were just teasing you," said the boy who'd taken the stuffed animal—a rabbit, James could see it now—handing it over.

The girl stomped on his foot just like Tiff would've done and ran off toward the house, cradling the rabbit like it was her baby. One of the boys shoved the other, and they both laughed and headed in the opposite direction.

James didn't realize he was smiling till he felt his chapped lips crack.

It wasn't much of a town, he decided when he got to the stoplight. That suited him just fine. There was a laundry and drycleaner just up on the right, and a pizza place. One of those expensive-looking coffee shop places and a ladies clothing store, a couple of gas stations, a sandwich shop and a diner. A couple of guys in overalls walked out of the hardware store on the left, and down another street looked like a whole row of professional-type businesses. No use looking for work there. His parole officer told him to try restaurants first, maybe the factories.

"You're a felon now. Best don't forget that, Steadman," the officer had said, dark eyes all distant like he cared a rat's left ear what happened to James. "Most places won't want you, and the places that'll take you just need you. Stay on their good side, keep your nose clean, and whatever you do make dang sure you show up on time."

James had muttered a yessir.

You're a dirtbag, Steadman, no newsflash there—he'd known that all his life. Now he had the official ex-con status to prove it.

Ahead of him, he saw two ladies in tracksuits and white sneakers coming his way. One had hair straight out of the fifties, all teased up and sprayed so tight it didn't even bounce as she walked.

He tugged the cords on his hoodie and made sure his jacket sleeves were all the way down so none of the tattoos showed.

"Morning." He smiled as they passed, and the one looked startled.

The other one smiled back. "Good morning to you."

James let out a breath he didn't realize he was holding once they were yards away.

You've got this.

And then he ducked into the first open business on his left. Time to find work.

CHAPTER 10

ON SUNDAY MORNING, Tiff dressed for church as quietly as she could, didn't even put on her heels till she got to the front door. There was no sign of James, and his bedroom door was still shut. Sleeping, probably.

Hopefully it'd stay that way.

Peaches knocked against her shins, getting ginger fur all over her black pants, and she sighed, scooped him up, and headed to the kitchen. Cat food went in the bowl, a little fresh water and a swipe of the lint brush across her pants, then she was out the front door and headed to her car.

The steering wheel was a shock of cold against her hands, and too late she remembered her gloves were still inside. But there was no way she was going back in.

The last thing she wanted was James giving her sad eyes about an invitation to church. She knew she should invite him, knew it was the right thing to do. The Christian thing to do.

But she didn't want to. Not today, anyway. And pressing her lips into a line, she shifted the car into gear and backed out of the driveway.

Dahlia Community Bible Church wasn't too far off, and the

night before played and replayed in her mind as she drove. James, all awkward and hunchy on the living room couch, his Bible and an actual book—some tattered guy history-type novel—resting next to him. Didn't even flick on the TV set once. And Tiff herself, all bustling around, fixing dinner and doing laundry and busywork.

They'd talked a little, at least. At dinner, over the lasagna she'd made them—about her job and how he'd meet Bobby the next night and how long she'd lived there and what the townspeople were like.

Well, really, she talked. He just looked mostly miserable. Almost miserable enough to make her feel bad for him till she caught herself.

When she pulled up at the church, Bobby was waiting outside, chatting with Rebecca and Rebecca's boyfriend, Josh.

He held open her door as she got out, and they all walked in together.

"You doing okay?" Rebecca whispered as they stepped into the welcome area and hung up their coats.

Tiff wrinkled her nose. "Not really. It's just . . . weird."

"I bet."

They took their seats and said hi to some of the other people around them. It was a comfortable church, with a bunch of different types of people—some in jeans and sweaters, some in dresses and heels. A couple of the guys had on ties. Marla, the preacher's wife, was all decked out in a gorgeous electric-blue sweater dress with one of those great chunky necklaces she favored, but that was Marla. Between her dark hair and caramel-colored skin, Marla could probably put on a burlap sack and look striking.

That was another thing she liked about the church—the fact that race wasn't a "thing." Bobby's mama's church was nice, a lot like the church Tiff herself had grown up in, but everyone tended to look the same, talk the same, and dress the same. But Rebecca's church was a good blend. If Tiff wasn't mistaken, even some of the homeless people her boss had done stories on last summer attended on occasion.

Rev started by asking if anyone had anything they wanted to lift up in prayer.

Bobby squeezed her hand, and she could feel his eyes on her.

Not a chance, she squeezed in reply.

The sermon was on forgiveness, only it took her awhile to figure out where Rev was going—he used a metaphor about rain washing away the chalk drawings he and his siblings used to make on the driveway outside their childhood home, making it brand-new again.

If only it were that simple.

If only a simple rainstorm could wash right over her and James, erase the past and the pain like nothing had ever happened.

Better yet, wash him far away, right out of her life for good.

In the ladies restroom after the service, she and Rebecca stood at the long mirror over the sinks.

"Maybe next week you can invite him." Rebecca fished in her purse for her hairbrush, started to smooth out her layers.

"Here?" Tiff stared at her. "I don't think that's a good idea."

"It's such a come-as-you-are kind of place." Rebecca frowned.

The swastika tattoo burned in her mind, and the front-page headlines from her town paper all those years ago.

Arrest. Assault.

And worse. Much worse.

She couldn't even bring herself to think it, let alone say it out loud. Even if it wasn't totally his fault, he'd helped. He'd done this. Him and all his friends.

When the words came, her tone was soft, almost numb. "After what he did to that kid, I don't want my brother anywhere near here. It's bad enough he's in my house."

Rebecca looked like she wanted to say more, lots more. Instead, she just reached out and grabbed Tiff's hand, pulled her in for a hug.

Tiff hugged her back. "Thanks."

"I'm here for you. In work and out."

Tiff's throat felt like she'd swallowed a giant lump of mashed potatoes. She cleared her voice, gave a thin smile. "I know."

James was still in his room when she got back home, only now his door was open a crack. She could see him in there, reading something in the chair by the window.

She tapped at his door. "Want some breakfast?"

His expression looked like he was a million miles away. "Ah . . . no, thanks."

"All right. Remember Bobby's coming for lunch around one. To meet you."

"Okay."

"My fiancé."

"I know. Can I help with anything?"

Yeah, by staying out of the way. But she just gave a polite shrug. "Nah, it's nothing. You just relax. See you in a bit."

Before she left the room, she noticed what he was reading. The Bible. If she wasn't mistaken, he'd held it up just a tad so she could see the title, see what he was doing. All for show.

Her palms began to itch. *Calm down, for Pete's sake.*

By the time she changed into comfy jeans and a sweater, brewed some chamomile, and was pulling out the ingredients for lunch, her nerves had settled down enough that she'd started to feel guilty again.

People can change. She knew that. She also knew that scripture well, the one about yanking the log out of your own eye before you worry about the splinter in someone else's.

But Dahlia was her home. These were her people. Not James.

Not anymore.

A shock of cold seared through her thumb, and she looked down to realize she'd nicked it with the paring knife. Quickly, she moved to the sink, rinsed her thumb under icy water, the sensation of cold mixing with cold until she felt nothing at all.

She wrapped it in a paper towel and turned off the tap, hands shaking so bad she wanted to laugh at herself.

Instead, everything just erupted. Big, ugly tears, the kind that made her nose run and her mascara smear all over the knees of her jeans.

Too much! It was all just too much. James, Bobby, all her past—everything crashing in like a mudslide she was powerless to hold back.

Finally, finally, the shaking subsided, and she loosened her fists, felt the sharp indentations left by her fingernails in her palms. Kept her eyes closed, tight at first, then willed herself to relax, to breathe.

"Oh, Jesus." Her voice sounded pitiful even to her own ears.

The floorboards creaked then, and she stiffened.

Opened her eyes.

And saw her brother's bare feet right in front of her.

CHAPTER 11

James

HE DIDN'T KNOW WHAT TO SAY, hadn't seen Tiff cry in who knew how long. Hadn't seen anyone cry. Well, except that one guy in lockdown. But that was just the once.

Are you okay? Can I help?

But the words wouldn't come. He just stared at her, wanting both to comfort her and run clear back up to his own room before she opened her eyes and saw him there.

Now it was too late. He felt it the second she saw his feet, knew there was nothing left to do but stand there.

Let her make the first move.

He shouldn't have come here.

It was selfish, he knew it. Knew it even when he'd asked her, but Pastor Chad and the parole officer had told him it was for the best, and in his heart he knew there was no place else. Nowhere he wanted to go, anyway.

The words tumbled out before he knew what he was saying.

"Look, I can leave." He crouched in front of her, tucked his long legs beneath him on the wood kitchen floor. "This was a mistake, I know it, and first thing tomorrow I'll call my parole officer, there's some prison re-entry program down in Charleston, and—"

"No." Her voice sounded ragged, nothing like the Tiff he knew.

He waited, sensed more than saw her collect herself, steady her breathing.

When she looked him in the eyes, he saw pain. And determination.

"James, listen. It's hard, you being here. I'm not gonna lie. But it's something I have to do."

"Sis, you don't have to . . ."

"I do." She swallowed and took a long breath. "But we need some ground rules."

He nodded. Whatever she wanted, he'd do it. No questions.

She stood then, the sudden movement making him flinch, and stepped to the breakfast table, taking a seat.

He took the other seat, waiting.

"When I came here to Dahlia, I didn't tell anyone about my past—not my upbringing, nothing about Mama and Daddy, nothing about you." Her dark eyes looked like coal in her face. "Not even Bobby. Hear me on this—everybody thinks our mama is dead right along with our daddy, and as far as I'm concerned, she is. You got me?"

Another nod.

"The man I'm getting married to is a good man, from a good, decent family. He loves me, and I'm lucky he does. I'm lucky his family accepts me. This, all this—" She gestured to the kitchen all around them, to the window and the town beyond. "This is my do-over. My second chance."

He of all people knew about second chances.

"I won't say a word, Tiff."

"I mean it." Her cheeks had gained some of their color back, and she smoothed the hair off her face, twisted it into a low ponytail that she secured with an elastic around her wrist.

With her hair like that she looked about fourteen again, only he wouldn't say it.

These last few years he'd learned not to say the majority of the thoughts that tumbled through his mind. Safer that way.

She cleared her throat. "When he comes today, Bobby'll probably offer you a job at his family's grocery store, but I don't want you working there. It's too close."

"Got it."

"If you need help finding something, ask me. I've got a ton of connections."

They were quiet a long moment, so quiet he could hear the tick of the cat-shaped wall clock above them.

"I truly am sorry, Tiff. I don't mean to mess up your life none—"

"I don't want to hear it." Her voice reminded him of their mama's at first. Sharp. An edge toward shrill.

But it's not Mama. It's Tiff. And he could see the tears behind her anger, even if she didn't want him to.

As soon as he could escape back to his room, he cleared out of her way, killing time writing in his journal and trying to nap till lunch. Sleeping in a real bed in a real house made him feel out of sorts still, like he'd checked into somebody else's motel room and put on all their clothes, only the sheets were too stiff and the clothes just a hair too small.

Even the smells were weird. Tiff's house smelled like girl— flowers and cupcakes, all Windex-clean, only without the chemicals to make you sneeze.

Better than back home.

Home. He had to stop saying that. Home wasn't prison, but it also wasn't Walterville, all dusty roads and smoky skies from the cotton mill where everybody's daddy used to work before it all closed down and left more than half the town out of a job. Home certainly wasn't the Steadman place, with the raggedy old mustard-colored couch on the front porch and the barn out back and the fakey-wood-paneled walls in the living room, that ugly single yellow light hanging from the ceiling down over the dining room table 'cause Mama and Daddy liked it dark. Fewer headaches, they said.

And home wasn't here with Tiff, either. Wouldn't ever be.

His throat felt scratchy, like he'd swallowed spicy taco soup with a bunch of crackers inside, the sharp kind that cut the inside of your cheek and the roof of your mouth so fine you don't even know it happened till it burned.

Who needed home, anyway?

James flopped down on the bed, springs creaking loudly, and snagged his Bible off the nightstand. He flipped to his favorite book, Matthew, the part that always caught his breath. Jesus, in the garden before his arrest, begging his buddies to wait up for him, except they let him down, fell sound asleep, and forced him to deal with the sad, lonely night on his own.

Jesus didn't need a home. He didn't need friends. He didn't even need food.

But James sure wasn't Jesus, not by a long stretch. Never could be even the slightest bit close.

CHAPTER 12

Tiff

LATER THAT AFTERNOON, Tiff walked hand-in-hand with Bobby toward town. The wind had let up, which was a good thing. She didn't like to wear gloves holding hands with him.

"He's nicer than I expected, I gotta say." Bobby poked Tiff in the ribs, and she giggled.

"You're saying I painted him out to be an evil villain?"

"Well, let's just say between prison and the scary tattoos I was expecting the cold, silent type. But he's, well. Normal."

Tiff shook her head. "Bobby Smathers, is there a person in this world you don't like?"

"Yeah . . ."

"Name one."

Bobby pulled her closer to him as they walked. "I don't just 'like' you. I looooove you."

She laughed, and then he was chasing her, all the way down the street and past the hardware store to "their" gazebo.

They collapsed on the wooden bench swing, out of breath and giggling like kindergartners. Her cheeks felt hot, as though it was July instead of February, and she wriggled her leg so that her foot lined up right next to Bobby's, two pairs of mismatched shoes, his big laced-up hiking boots and her pink and white sneakers.

Glancing over at him, she saw his eyes were closed, but he wore a big, silly grin. Like the Cheshire cat, without the devious. She'd bet money Bobby didn't have a devious bone in his whole entire body.

She leaned her head on his shoulder and curled up close. "I love you with all my heart."

He opened one eye. "I love you more."

She stuck out her tongue at him. "I love you even."

They sat that way, swinging on the gazebo, until the sky dimmed enough so she could barely see the swing set on the other side of the village green.

"Come on," he stood, tugging her hand so she stood, too. "Let's get you back home. Busy Monday tomorrow."

She huddled against his arm as they walked. "I wish you didn't have to go home."

"Just a few more months. Then we'll be good-and-proper married."

She did the math in her head—James would be long gone by then. Life would be back to normal.

"I can't wait."

He kissed her hair and squeezed her closer. "Me either, baby."

When she got back to the house and Bobby'd driven off, she nestled on the couch with Peaches for a long while, the TV volume on low, lamps dim and cozy all around her. There was no sign of James, but his bedroom door was shut, and she could see the glow of light beneath. Reading probably.

James—reading. In all their life she didn't think she'd ever seen him pick up a book. If he wasn't out with friends he was doing pushups, or tossing a ball from one hand to the other.

She guessed years behind bars would change a person. It was probably read or, well, go nutso.

People change, Tiff. She knew it was possible—for some people.

And giving Peaches one last scratch under his chin, she turned off the lamp and climbed the steps to bed.

Three days later, Tiff sat in the newsroom as Millie, the receptionist, and Dinah, the ad representative, did their mother hen routine. Rebecca was out, Rotary Club breakfast or something, and the wind was so cold that morning that a single customer hadn't walked in. Even the wind blowing at the cracks in the door felt frigid. She read over the paper, which had just come out that morning. Rebecca had put her piece on a string of car break-ins on the top right—not the lead, but close to it, and she'd been fielding calls all morning. Everyone had questions. The calls were almost welcome—at least they gave her something to think about. Something besides James. Maybe it wasn't too late for him to get reassigned someplace else. He'd mentioned that home down in Charleston . . .

"What's wrong, sugar?" Millie pressed her lips into a thin line, staring hard.

Tiff shifted in her desk chair and cradled her coffee cup in her hands. "Nothing . . ."

Dinah eyed Millie, then leaned in. "Love spat?" she said in a stage whisper.

"No! Really, nothing's wr—"

Millie sniffed. "Bobby's mama."

"No, no . . ."

"You coming down with something?" Dinah's eyes flicked to the Lysol spray in the corner.

A bubble of laughter tickled Tiff deep in her belly, but she swallowed it down, kept a straight face. "Y'all, please. I'm just tired."

"Reallllly."

"Really!" Tiff crossed the room to the coffeemaker, busied her-self pouring a cup. James had been gone before she'd gotten down-stairs this morning. *Maybe he'd found a job. Unless . . .*

When she turned around, they were still looking at her.

She couldn't help it—she laughed. "What!"

Millie sighed. "Honey. We've worked with you three years now, day in and day out. We can tell when something's up."

"Oh, my word." Tiff gazed at one and then the other. "I'm tired. I've got wedding plans, I've been staying up too late, and maybe I am coming down with something, who knows?"

"All right, all right." Millie pursed her lips, wiggled a bit in her chair. "Go easy."

Dinah gave her a sassy wink. "Stayin' up too late, huh? Bobby doesn't have some other man he's got to worry about, now?"

Tiff's cheeks flushed. "Watch your tongue!"

"Don't be teasing our girl. She's way too sensitive as it is," Millie said in a low voice to Dinah.

"I am not," Tiff barked as the door swung open with a bang, icy air whipping through the newsroom as Rebecca sailed in, slam-ming the door shut.

"Mm-hm."

"Am not what?" Rebecca gave a wave as she thumped her leather bag down on her desk.

"These two busybodies think there's something the matter with me and they don't believe me when I say I'm just tired." Tiff eyed Rebecca.

Rebecca's lips twisted. "Well, I have been working you overtime lately."

"And they say I'm way too sensitive."

Now her boss bit back a laugh. "Ah, now, that . . ."

They were all still laughing minutes later when the phone rang.

"Tiff, line two!" Millie sang out.

Tiff wiped laugh-tears from her eyes and tried to answer in her professional editor's voice. "This is Tiff, may I help you?"

"This is Sheriff Zane calling. Got a minute?"

Instantly, Tiff's heart coiled tight, like a snake. *He knows about James.*

"Ah, sure thing. What's going on?"

Her knees felt shaky as she sank into her swivel desk chair and turned toward the computer.

"Wanted to ask you a couple questions. That is, if you don't mind." His voice sounded casual. Almost too casual.

CHAPTER 13

Was I supposed to let him know about James? Am I in trouble? She swallowed thickly, pressed her damp palms against her corduroy trousers.

Or worse—is James in trouble again? Did he do something illegal?

Did he hurt someone?

Belatedly, she realized she hadn't responded. "Oh, no problem at all! It's good to hear from you!" *Tone it down, Tiff.* "Ask away."

The sheriff sighed. "Remember a few months ago, that bank robbery over in Aberville?"

What did that have to do with James? "Yeah . . . I covered the story. You caught the guys, if I remember right. Two brothers?"

"That's the one. Do you remember if Bobby ever mentioned anything about them?"

Bobby? She considered. "Well, I know one of the guys worked at Smathers Grocery a month or two. Got fired for mouthing off to Bobby's daddy."

A low chuckle came from the other end of the line. "Sounds like our character. Say, Bobby work with him much?"

What does any of this have to do with James?

"I mean, a little. Said he was a bit of a jerk, one of those guys with a chip on his shoulder bigger than his left foot."

Maybe this didn't have anything to do with James at all. Maybe it was just her jumping to conclusions again, being all paranoid because—

"He at the store today? I'm gonna swing by, see if I can ask him some questions."

"As far as I know." Tiff frowned, considering. "Wait, ah—is Bobby in trouble?"

"No, no! Not at all. Just a few routine questions is all. Don't you worry about a thing." The sheriff's voice was so smooth Tiff wanted to scream.

"I mean, he didn't know the guy well or anything. Sheriff, what's going on?"

"Off the record?"

Tiff bit her lip and eyed her boss, who was on a phone call of her own and didn't seem to be paying much attention to Tiff's call. She knew Rebecca positively hated it when anyone offered stuff off the record.

"Yes, sir," she muttered.

Sheriff Zane lowered his voice all confidential-like. "He's been talking a bit in jail waiting for his trial. Think he might know something about the car break-ins."

"Oh!" Her palms weren't slick anymore, and the lump in her throat started to dissolve. *Nothing to do with James after all. Or Bobby.* She felt her heartbeat begin to return to normal.

"Just sit tight on this for now. I'll let you know if anything pans out."

They hung up, and Tiff slipped to the restroom, locking the door with shaky fingers. If she went all paranoid every time the sheriff called or she had a lead on a crime-related story, she'd be a basket case by the time April rolled around.

She ran the water on warm a few minutes, letting her now-chilly hands thaw out. A dab of lemon-scented lotion and a quick shake of her hair, and she felt like herself again.

And suddenly starving.

"Who wants pizza for lunch?" she asked as she stepped back into the newsroom. "I'll make the run!"

She decided to walk instead of drive to the pizza place, a decision she regretted five steps out the door. Zipping up her coat against the wind, she tugged her hat down snugly over her ears.

Almost no one was out walking in the chilly gray, though plenty of cars were on the road. One of the things Tiff liked best about Dahlia was that it always felt like life—like people had something to do and someplace to go and were actively going about their lives doing just that. Nothing like Walterville, with its dusty streets and old-looking buildings that seemed to say tired, drawn, on the downswing.

Not that Dahlia was some big happening place, either. But it was her place. She liked it.

After three years there, she liked popping into the hardware store or the diner and being greeted by name, like she was somebody's daughter or friend or something. And now that she was engaged to Bobby, it was even better—like she'd gained a whole new status. *I fit.* Even before she'd met Bobby, it had felt like that, but now. Now was a whole new ballgame.

Pushing open the doors to Village Pizza, Tiff took a breath, inhaling deeply.

"Smells good, don't it?" The dark-haired, heavyset lady behind the register cracked her gum and leaned heavily on the counter.

"Sure does. How's it going, Alana?"

"It's going. Let's see—a mushroom slice and a side salad?" Alana's fingers bent over the cash register, ready to ring her up.

"Better make it a whole pie. The whole office is hungry today."

Alana called out the order to her husband, who was roaming around somewhere in the back, and punched at the register.

"How's that new boss of yours settling in?" Alana eyed her. "Things still going okay?"

Tiff bit her lip. When Rebecca'd moved here from New York last spring, it had been really rocky at first. She could tell Rebecca didn't like her much, didn't like any of them, really. Alana had picked up on it—she had a nose for drama—and started referring to Rebecca as the Witch of the North till Tiff finally had to tell her to stop. Well, tell her in as polite a way as Tiff knew how. She'd started talking about how much Rebecca had changed, warmed up, promoted her, come to Jesus. Alana got the picture fast. And now that her boss was dating Josh Jamison, and had done that big newspaper spread on the pizza place last month, she'd risen more than a few notches in Alana Beckwater's eyes.

Still, Alana was Alana. She liked the dirt.

"Great!" Tiff paid, then took a seat at one of the small tables to wait for her order.

Village Pizza was tiny, dingy, and had such bad fluorescent lighting Millie'd stopped going, even if she was distant kin to Alana's husband. Said the glare gave her headaches. But Tiff appreciated it. It was one of the few places that seemed determined to keep its decidedly low-key, no-frills vibe even after most of the downtown shops and restaurants teamed up and started the whole small-town cutesy décor thing.

Alana slipped to the back, and Tiff busied herself on her phone, making her to-do list and checking her email. Her stomach was just starting to growl when she heard footsteps and stood, ready for the big Village Pizza box Alana was surely holding.

Only it wasn't Alana who'd stepped behind the counter.
Her breath caught at the same time as his, and they locked eyes.
It was James.

CHAPTER 14

James

HE AIMED FOR A CASUAL SMILE, only his lips twisted up wrong. "Hey."

The trays he was carrying went all slippery in his hands, and he tightened his grip so he didn't drop them.

But before Tiff could reply, the pizza lady was coming up behind him with her boomy, no-nonsense march.

"Here ya go, Miss Tiff," the lady said and cracked her gum. It almost sounded like one of those Fourth of July popper things you toss on the ground to make the kids jump and squeal.

The lady—Alayna, Alanna? He still didn't have a clue if he was saying it right—held out the pizza box over the counter, waited for Tiff to step up and take it.

Tiff kept her gaze on the lady, smiled like it was no big thing. "Thanks, Alana. Smells like heaven."

"Don't it?" Alana's smile was wide, and she cast a glance his way, thumb out. "Got us a new hire, too."

Tiff's smile was tight. "Good for you. Gotta hurry back," she said without meeting his eyes. "See you soon! Stay warm."

She was gone like lightning, so fast James blinked a moment, shaking his head to be sure it had actually taken place. That was the

good and bad thing about so much alone time in the slammer—
his imagination would take off like crazy, and he'd find himself
inventing entire conversations, entire scenarios, entire days in his
head like they were real. He'd probably rehearsed seeing Tiff, talking with Tiff, and even bickering with Tiff so many times he wasn't
even sure at this point which of them had actually happened.

James kept his head down, setting the trays beneath the counter
like Alana had showed him, then hurried to the back to help Lou,
her husband. Lou owned the place, or at least that's what they'd
said, though it was pretty clear who called the shots.

"When you're done back there with Big Lou, come on up front
and help me restock," Alana hollered as he rounded the corner and
slipped the black dishwasher's apron back on so he could finish
what he'd started. "About time for our lunch crowd."

"Yes, ma'am." He bit back a sigh.

Seven years. He might be a new person in Christ, but standing
there at the metal two-tub sink, soapsuds sloshing over his worn
Nikes and the steam rising up in his eyes, it felt like he'd never
even left Walterville.

All the dreams he'd had—going to the city, making it big, going
into business for himself, something in the car trade. All the stuff
he thought he'd maybe accomplish one day, just to show his good-
for-nothing parents he was worth a darn and not some lowlife
afterthought like they'd always treated him. All down the tubes
thanks to one stupid, stupid night now seared on his soul for eternity.

His closed his eyes a moment, heard the guy's yells. No, not a
guy—a boy. Just a kid, if he were honest. Felt the panic just like
that night, as he'd tried to stop it all, turn the whole blasted thing
around. If it weren't for Mike and Dex, DJ, Tommy, and that
whacked out girl in the miniskirt egging them on . . .

No.

He scrubbed harder at the pan, scrubbed so hard his knuckles scraped against the steel wool. It was nobody's fault but his. Pastor Chad had taught him that—he needed to take Personal Responsibility for his actions. He'd done that thing. Hurt that boy. Others had, too, but it didn't change the fact.

Didn't change what he'd done.

"You're gonna scrape that thing raw," came a loud male voice from behind him, and James jumped, almost dropped the pan with a clatter into the sink.

Lou.

"Sorry—overkill." James tried to laugh, but the smile felt like a grimace.

"Overkill's better than underkill." Lou clapped him on the shoulder, heading toward the back office. He called over his shoulder, "When you're done with that, take the trash out back, then see what Alana needs."

The cold was a shock against his damp arms as he hauled the heavy black trash bags out the back door and down the steps to the dumpster. Still, it felt good. Woke him up a bit.

No sense drowning in the past, Steadman. Three months here, maybe patch things up with Tiff and get his community service and job skills done, then he'd head on. Maybe over to Myrtle Beach, or down to Charleston. When that got too much he could always head inland, toward the center of the state. Vic from inside had a family hog farm, someplace outside Orangeburg a ways, and he said his daddy always needed help, didn't care one bit if you'd been locked up or for what.

"Aren't you cold?"

The voice came from the far side of the alley, over toward one of the businesses whose back doors opened up into the shared space. James looked up to see a dark-skinned man in a navy peacoat watching him. A collar shirt and tie poked out of the coat, and

James figured him for a shopkeeper.

James looked down, realized the gray hoodie wasn't really warm enough. He needed to get a decent coat. Well, that and a lot of things.

James tossed one bag and then the other into the trash. "Now that you mention it, heck yeah. It's freezing out here."

The man whistled, peered up at the sky. "Only gonna get colder. Weather's calling for snow tomorrow, maybe."

Great. "I hope not."

The man smiled. "Sick of being cooped up?"

James gave a little smile-nod, trying not to wince. If he only knew. The last snow day he'd seen had been a month ago. The white flakes had looked almost pretty coming down on the fence in the prison yard, the gray sky beyond all hazy and soft-looking. It would've been perfect except they made them stay inside all day, and Sanger and a few of the guys from the third block got itchy and started puffing up their chests till the guards blew their whistles and made everybody go on mandatory silent mode back in their cells. That part he didn't mind so much, but for not being able to see the snow anymore.

Back in Walterville, it never snowed much, but he'd loved it when it had. For just a little while, everything looked clean and right, just how Old General Walter must have planned it back in the day when he'd founded the town, those days when ladies wore those big hoop skirts and the men all sported big crazy moustaches and carried sidearms bigger than their boots. He'd have liked those days.

"Stay warm," the man in the navy coat gave a small wave and ducked back inside whatever shop he'd come from.

James blinked, then hurried back in himself. It was cold, and besides, he had work to do.

Work was good. Especially hard work—then he didn't have to think.

They let him out at three, gave him all the paperwork to take home and fill out. He folded it in a thick square and stuffed it deep in the back pocket of his jeans, then decided to go for a walk.

Payday was Friday, Lou'd told him, and they'd give him a small advance if he wanted since he was new in town. The man had winked like he knew what that was like.

"You got a place to stay?" he'd asked him.

"Yeah, I'm good." He said it like it was no biggie. But it felt good that he'd been asked. Almost like Lou cared.

Two more days. Then he could get some gloves, maybe a coat or something. Start saving up for a bike.

The sun had come out, so he took the wide loop back home, which took him past a thrift store, plus more churches on one street than he thought possible. The thrift shop had a few winter items in the window, and James made a mental note to go back Friday after work. He knew if things got real bad he could ask Tiff for money, but he didn't want to ask his sister for anything else. It was bad enough he'd had to ask to come in the first place.

Besides, it was good to be uncomfortable. A little cold wouldn't kill him.

He walked on, keeping his pace up. Fast walking kept the cold at bay. Not to mention kept him from thinking.

At the corner he glanced up, noticed the sign. Church Street. It sure fit.

The churches looked so big and nice, the kind of places where you had to dress up real good to go to. Nothing like the worship space in prison, all folding chairs and harsh lights and a bunch of guys gathered knee-to-knee. He barely remembered what real church was like, thought he'd been once, maybe twice as a kid.

That time when Miz Rice, the principal, promised them all a bag of Halloween candy if they'd show up at her church that one Sunday. And the day Tiff had dragged him along with her, though he'd snuck out early for a cigarette, pretended he'd had a bellyache. Church wasn't his sort of place.

Still wasn't, he had to admit. He'd take Jesus any day of the week, but church people? That was a whole different ballgame. The last thing he wanted was to feel even more out of place, have even more people give him the side-eye or look down their noses at him. He could read their thoughts, almost like they were all in some comic book with big balloon bubbles over their heads. Scumbag. Loser. Worthless.

Passing one of the churches, he noticed a sign on the door advertising a community outreach thing that weekend. A thought struck—a church might be the perfect place to do his community service hours. Though maybe not that church. He eyed the massive stained glass windows, the gleaming wood double doors, the fancy arches. They'd probably take one look at his tattoos and decide they could handle the work themselves, thank you very much.

Maybe a smaller church, one that looked a little shabbier on the outside. One that didn't look like you needed to be wearing a suit and tie just to walk in the door.

Show me the right place, God. James slowed, then came to a full stop. Closing his eyes, he forced his breathing to steady, forced himself to hear the trees around him, the faint sounds of cars a few blocks away.

Guide me.

He felt calmer when he opened his eyes. He didn't have a solution, but that was all right.

He would.

CHAPTER 15

Tiff

TIFF COULD FEEL Mrs. Smathers watching her as she took the big bowl of mashed potatoes from Bobby and spooned some onto her plate. Not too little, not too much. She passed the bowl to Bobby's brother Ben, who scooped out a giant dollop of white like it was his last meal ever. It was Thursday night, and they were all gathered around the Smathers' big dining table—her, Bobby's parents and brothers, Bobby himself, all as comfortable as can be. *Right.*

Bobby squeezed her hand beneath the table. "Did you tell Mama about the article?"

Mrs. Smathers leaned forward, smiled her encouraging smile.

Tiff took a small sip of ice water. "Tomorrow I'm going to interview your friend, Janie Harris, about the coat ministry she does." She gestured to the window, where pellets of sleet pattered against the pane. "With all this cold weather, there's a real demand for warm clothes."

Mrs. Smathers nodded all big. "Oh, good! Ben, don't you have a coat from last year in the back of your closet?"

"Prob'ly," Ben said behind a mouthful of potatoes and peas, chewed and swallowed at his mother's pointed look.

"Well, if you get it tonight after supper, Tiff can haul it over to

Miz Janie when she does her article." Mrs. Smathers turned to Zach, beamed. "How about that coat of yours? The one with all those . . . patches."

"Nuh-uh!" Zach wiped his mouth, reached for the platter of beef. "That jacket's part of my legacy. I'll wear it to my own funeral!"

"Zachary Marvin!" Bobby's mama gasped.

Tiff swallowed back a grin, and Ben jostled her with his elbow, snorted out a laugh.

"Now, boys." Mr. Smathers said from the head of the table. "You know your mama can't stomach that sort of talk."

"Sorry, Mama," Zach said like he meant it, but Tiff caught the smirk as he slid a few pieces of meat onto his plate.

"I've got one I can donate," Bobby said. "Gloves, too."

The rest of the dinner was spent talking about which sort of flowers Tiff and Bobby should and shouldn't have at their wedding, and the shower Bobby's mama wanted to throw for her in the fellowship hall at church, "since you don't have family 'n all."

"You don't have to," Tiff said, touched at the gesture.

"Oh, sweetheart. It's the least I can do for you. My—my almost-daughter."

Mrs. Smathers said it like she meant it, and Tiff could feel Bobby shift in his seat next to her, lean closer. She knew it made him feel good, her and his mama getting along. She needed to try harder in that area, she knew. Try like she meant it.

"Thank you." Tiff said into the quiet. "That, well, it really means a lot."

She and Bobby loaded up the dishwasher after supper, her rinsing, him stacking the plates inside all neat, like a puzzle. Ben and Zach were off collecting coats and doing homework, and she could hear the TV blaring in the living room, where she knew Bobby's parents were curled up on the sofa, watching.

"You know, James and I are about the same size," Bobby said, taking the soapy-wet glass she held out and sliding it into the top rack. "Why don't you take one of my coats and pass it on to him?"

She frowned. "I don't know. Won't he feel . . . like, pitied?"

"I imagine he'll just be flat-out happy. I bet he doesn't even have a coat. You seen him in one since he got here?"

She thought a minute, realized he'd been wearing that same gray hoodie every day. Some sister she was.

"You're right." She bit her lip, immersed her hands in the soapy dishwater. The heat felt good. "I honestly didn't even think about it."

"Hey, you've got a lot on your mind. No big thing," Bobby said lightly, then jutted his chin at the dishwater. "Any more left in there?"

They finished loading up, and Bobby helped her pile all the coats and gloves and a couple scarves in the trunk of her sedan.

His goodnight kiss was soft, and she buried her head in his arms a long moment, wished she didn't have to go home. Or at least, go off without him. Wished they were already good-and-proper married, when she could change her name and leave the last remnants of her life as a Steadman behind forever.

"I'm glad Mama wants to throw you a shower. I was hoping she would." Bobby opened her car door, and she slid behind the wheel, starting the engine.

"It's really sweet of her," Tiff said, and meant it.

"I just hate that you don't have your own mom here, helping you. Why, I bet your mama's looking down from heaven, smiling to know her baby girl's got a new family surrounding her with love."

That, or drunk and holed up in some seedy bar. The dinner she'd just eaten suddenly felt like a boulder in her belly. She wished for a moment she'd never implied her parents were dead. Better yet, wished James himself would just disappear and she could go back to pretending she had no past at all. A fresh start. Clean and new.

"If you don't mind, I think I'm not gonna mention the coat's from you," Tiff said. "Don't want him feeling all poor relation and what-for."

"Good idea." He blew her a kiss and shut the door, waving as she backed out of the driveway.

A fresh start, she thought again, then said it aloud for good measure.

But try as she might, she couldn't get the image out of her mind. Mama, all bone-skinny doing shots at the kitchen table. Daddy dropping the stew, potatoes and carrots and little chunks of meat all over the scratched up linoleum, slurring his words while he cursed at his wife, threatening to leave for good this time. That was the night he'd gone all crazy drinking, whipped too fast around the bend in his car, and wound up dead.

Guess he did get to leave, after all.

Months later, everything she owned in that stupid blue suitcase, Tiff had left, too, vowing never, never to return.

That was the last time she'd laid eyes on her mama. Hopefully forever.

At home she set the coat by the back door, where James couldn't miss it. Stuck a pair of gloves and a hat on top.

Climbing the stairs to her room, she saw the light under James's door, knew he was home. Reading probably.

You could knock. Say goodnight. But the thought flitted away almost as soon as it crossed her mind. Nope.

He might be staying in her house, but it didn't mean they were still family. Like a past-due bill, he was an obligation she had to meet, just for a while longer. And then he'd be gone.

And she'd be free to be Tiff Smathers, every ounce of Steadman erased forever.

Dreams woke her twice in the night, and the circles under her eyes were dark the next morning. In the bathroom mirror, she dabbed on extra concealer and swiped a brush through her hair. For a moment, she could see her mama in the reflection, and a surprising burst of anger sliced through her. Straightening her shoulders, she glared above the sink, met her own gaze. *Not on your life.*

She grabbed her pearls from the jewelry box. Bobby's granny had given them to her right before she passed away—just after they'd announced their engagement, in fact. They'd made her feel worthy, accepted. Even if she didn't completely believe it. She gave a tug on the clasp to be sure they were fastened, spritzed on a touch of perfume, then gave her appearance the once-over.

James was awake, she could hear him fiddling around in his room, and she hurried past his door, jogging down the stairs to pour a travel mug of coffee and a quick bowl of cereal. Then she slipped on her coat to face the cold.

"Morning, Mrs. Crenshaw." She waved at the old lady next door, the woman's stern face set in what Tiff was sure was a permanent scowl.

Mrs. Crenshaw's little white dog yapped from her neighbor's porch, and Tiff giggled, wiggled her fingers his way. "Morning to you, too, Choppers."

Mrs. Crenshaw sniffed but raised her hand in a curt wave.

Tiff stuck her purse and workbag in the backseat, then realized she'd forgotten her coffee. She dashed back into the house, snagged the cheerful yellow "Rise and Shine" mug, and relocked the door.

"Wedding still on?" Mrs. Crenshaw's scowl twisted a little. Tiff thought maybe it was trying to be a smile.

"Yes, ma'am. Last Saturday in September."

"Good. Not proper for a young lady to be living alone."

Tiff bit her tongue.

"They catch that car thief yet?" Mrs. Crenshaw muttered.

"Not yet. Hopefully soon."

Tiff started to slide in the car—but not before she saw her brother slip from around the back of the house, headed toward the sidewalk.

He didn't look her way, gave no sign whatsoever that he even knew her.

Still, she could sense Mrs. Crenshaw's back straighten, feel her gaze narrow. Almost hear the thoughts racing through her head. That Steadman girl. No good.

Trash.

Tiff's heart fluttered. Jamming the car into reverse, she backed the car out and was gone.

CHAPTER 16

James

COLD AIR HIT HIM like a smack as he pushed open the door to Village Pizza and stepped out into the afternoon sun. But James didn't mind. Today was payday, and he had a new coat, not to mention two full hours to make it to the thrift shop before they closed. Hopefully, they'd have a bike in decent enough condition, and then he'd really be set.

Two teenaged girls passed him, their zigzag-patterned backpacks bouncing almost in sync with the sway of their ponytails. One gave him a cute little smile, but he kept his eyes down and pretended like he didn't notice. Ladykiller, Tiff used to call him back when. Now, he'd prefer just to be invisible.

The coat was a good one, only a tiny bit big, and it made the wind much more bearable. He made it to the thrift shop in no time and pulled open the door.

The place smelled like cough drops and those dried flowers Tiff kept in the basket in the hall bathroom, and the fluorescent lights flickered just enough that he could tell the place was probably pretty old. Maybe as old as the skinny gray-haired lady who sat behind the counter, perched in one of those swivel chairs with a high back, a paperback in her hands and her glasses slipping low on her nose.

"Hi, there, sugar. You just let me know if you need any help." Her smile was warm, and she gave a little wave.

He let himself relax. "Thank you, ma'am."

In the back, he hit the jackpot—two bikes, both a bit scratched up but with good tires. Not too bad on the price, either. He rolled one out, the black one, and hopped on. The size worked, too.

He browsed the racks a few minutes, finding a sweatshirt and two pairs of jeans in his size. As he shopped, he found himself watching the other customers—an older kid with his mom who looked like he'd rather be anywhere but there, and a couple ladies carrying big bags like they were hunting for treasure and chatting ninety miles an hour. There was another guy, too, a tall dark-skinned man with his son, talking with the skinny worker-lady behind the counter.

James approached the counter tentatively, the clothes draped across one arm and pushing the bike with the other.

"Ready to check out?" the lady asked James, her eyes kind. "Oh, good, another bike sale!"

The boy by the counter spun around, looked at the bike like it was a pile of French fries and he was ready to dig in. His hand snaked out like he wanted to touch it, and James couldn't help but chuckle.

"I take it you're a bike fan," James said.

"Yeah," the kid said, eyes still on the bike. He was cute, all eager and fresh and young.

The dad laughed, and James saw he was the man he'd seen behind the restaurant the other day, when he'd been taking out the trash.

"Pizza Guy!" the man said, his voice a rich boom in the small store. He shook James's hand like they were old friends.

"Shop Guy," James said back, all chummy-like, surprised at how easy it felt. He cocked his head. "Are you at the hardware place? Or the shoe place?"

The man waved a hand. "Nah, that's my buddy's shop. Hardware. I just visit there a bit."

"More like every day," the kid said, elbowing his dad. "Rev here, he's a pastor."

That explained it, why it felt so easy to talk with him. James felt his shoulders relax just an inch. "Nice."

The lady brought an air pump from around the counter then, and made sure the tires were good and filled.

"We might have one a'these, too, if you need one," she said, gesturing to the pump.

James wandered back to where she'd pointed, found one that wasn't in bad shape. By the time he got back up front, the kid was on his knees checking out the books down the aisle, and the pastor and the shop lady were laughing about something.

She rang up James's purchases and stuck the clothes and pump in a bag. "Need any help loading?"

James shook his head. "Nah, I'm biking home. Thanks."

The pastor guy grinned. "If you're new in town, come on by Dahlia Community Bible Church on Sunday. Devon and I, we'd love to have you."

Church. An actual church, not a prison-cell church. He thought about it on the bike ride home, the wind not so bad with the coat and gloves, but still bad enough to make him wish for spring. He'd run it by Tiff, see what she thought.

Half of him hoped she'd be there when he got to the house, but the other half hoped he'd have it to himself. He'd gotten used to alone time the last few years to the point that he craved it now, not to mention it was flat-out hard to be around his sister right now. He didn't know what he'd expected coming here—hadn't thought it through much beyond just feeling plain bad about what he was putting her through.

But he hadn't expected so much quiet. Like they were tiptoeing over some dead mouse in the center of the floor and nobody wanted to pick it up.

What would Jesus do in his shoes? That was a joke. Jesus wouldn't have messed up his life like James had, thrown everything away for stupid kid games and anger and pride and rage and hate and all the other bad dark shadowy junk that used to churn up inside him all those years like a washing machine kicked into overdrive. No, James couldn't even come close to "Son of God," not even close enough to imagine what Jesus might do if he were as dirtbag-rotten-dumb-as-nails as James Steadman.

A gust of wind shot through him, yanked the pity right out. He glanced up at the gray sky, saw a patch of clouds part just enough so he could see beyond. Not blue sky, exactly, but a lighter gray, a bluish-gray. Like hope.

It hit him then that a better way to think on it might be what Paul might do. Paul'd been rotten like him, but he'd turned his life around, turned the rotten into good.

Dinner. The thought popped into his head as he cycled up to the house, rolled the bike around back. He'd seen some spaghetti noodles and sauce in the pantry when he'd been rummaging around this morning. He'd cook her dinner.

Of course, she'd been out the last three nights. Avoiding him, he was sure. He'd avoid him, too, truth be told. But dinner he could do.

If she actually came home.

She didn't come home. Texted him some line about needing to volunteer at a church thing with her boss. He'd left her plate covered in plastic wrap in the fridge, scribbled out a note and stuck it on top, "In case you're hungry." He tried not to be bitter. But dang, it hurt.

He tried to think about it and not to think about it as he took his new bike for a spin around town the next morning. The icy wind stung his bare knuckles, and he let it make him good and mad a moment. He'd probably forgotten the gloves on purpose, if he were really honest with himself.

He biked so far out the white picket fences and porch swings and yard-gardens started to give way to chain-link fences and a few doublewides, then a couple of gas stations and a ratty-looking corner store.

Up ahead, he saw the pastor guy and his kid from yesterday, right outside a brick church building. James slowed the bike, watched as what he assumed was the kid's mom come out with a pocketbook on one arm and a basketball cradled in the other. He saw then the boy was wearing what looked like a basketball uniform.

The pastor guy hauled an overstuffed trash bag from the back of an SUV parked on the street, then stopped to give his wife and boy a kiss and watch as they climbed into the SUV and drove off.

"Need a hand?" James cycled up.

"Pizza Guy." The pastor laughed, mopping at his face with a handkerchief. "You've got perfect timing."

The bag was heavier than it looked, and James brought it up the steps and inside the church, setting it down in the corner where the pastor pointed.

James looked around the dim room and saw the tables all set up, with chairs neatly tucked beneath.

"Y'all having a party in here?"

"Nah, that's just from giveaway night. We do it every Friday—dinner and free clothes and stuff. That's what's in the bag, in fact. Donations for next week."

The man flicked on a light, and fluorescents wobbled overhead, then cut on. One gave a pop and went dark, and the man shook his head, headed for what James assumed was a utility closet.

"Want me to do that for you, Reverend, ah . . .?" James offered as the man pulled a low stool and a box of bulbs from the closet.

"Just call me Rev. And I got it, thanks. I'm not old yet." The pastor made a face and James laughed.

"I bet with a kid your son's age, it probably feels like you're his age again."

Rev shrugged. "Devon? He's our foster son. Hopefully adoptive, soon. Maybe this summer, Lord willing. But yeah, he keeps us on our toes."

James had known a few foster kids. None of them like Devon, who didn't give off even a whiff of anger.

Rev hopped down from the stool, then surprised James by chucking the burned-out light bulb across the room into the big open trash can in the corner—a perfect shot.

"Still got it!" Rev did a score-dance, and James laughed for real, realized he liked the guy.

They walked back out front, and James picked up his bike from the grass, straddling it.

"Thanks for the help. And I mean it about tomorrow—come on by." Rev pointed to the church sign. "Worship's at eleven, and we usually do a big potluck after."

James gazed at the sign, then at the building, his heart thudding. *Just ask.* He swallowed hard and tried to make his voice sound casual.

"Ah, do you ever have need for help around here?" He rushed on before he could lose his nerve, blurted, "I just got, well. Released. And I've gotta do community service hours. I mean, if you need it."

Rev didn't even bat an eye, acted like he got asked that every hour of the given day. "Absolutely yes!" He even looked a bit relieved, and James wondered if that were for show or real.

"Really?"

"Yeah! I used to have a couple'a high school guys help me with stuff, but they're all in basketball the next two months. In fact, my wife and I were talking this very morning about needing someone. Pizza Guy, you're an answered prayer."

James coughed back the zip of joy, made himself go all cool and natural. "Well, great, then."

Rev mopped at his face again and tucked the handkerchief in the back pocket of his jeans. "Tell you what. If you've got time today, see if you can bring me the paperwork. Or Monday's okay, too. Or even tomorrow, if you come to worship."

"Will do. I'll try to bring it later this afternoon. I don't have to work till four."

"Most excellent, my friend."

Rev's handshake was extra-vigorous, and James grinned, calling goodbye as he pedaled off down the street.

Then his stomach flipped as he realized.

He'd have to tell the pastor what he'd done. To that boy.

CHAPTER 17

Tiff

TIFF WAS SURE EVERY PHONE that could possibly ring at the *Dahlia Weekly* was doing so. It was Monday morning, and she sat at her desk rubbing her forehead, eyes closed. The other hand cradled the phone to her ear.

"Sure thing, Mr. Carpenter. Just send it by Friday at two and we'll get it in," she said, trying to smile like she'd been taught so the caller could hear friendliness in her tone. Even if she wasn't exactly feeling it. "No, no. No arrests on the car break-ins yet. They're working on it."

She hung up the phone and caught her boss's eye.

"You okay?" Rebecca mouthed from her own phone call.

Tiff nodded, then crossed the room to the coffeemaker for another cup. A tall one. It had been a weekend of headaches and hiding out, and she'd half-hoped for a peaceful Monday—but only half. Her rational side reminded her Monday in the newsroom was prep day and the second-busiest day of the week and to buck up, buttercup.

She added a liberal dose of coffee cream and sat back down, ready to put the finishing touches on her article.

Later, when the phones had settled down enough for actual

thinking and Millie had gone off on an errand, her boss leaned across the desk wearing her let's-talk expression.

"You look like you're about to explode." Rebecca's voice was kind. "What's going on?"

"Just a headache."

"Tiff—"

"A bad one."

Rebecca sighed and propped her elbows on the table, all big-sistery. "I know you, Tiff." Her voice was quiet, even though they were the only ones in the newsroom. "And I know you're a lot like me, keeping all your stuff all bottled up inside."

"I'm trying not to. I really am." Tiff kneaded the muscles in her neck, which were extra tight today. Her stomach twisted, and she swallowed back her inclination to keep her everything's-fine mask on.

Finally, she turned in her chair, faced her boss. "It's just, well, James. Wanting him to disappear, feeling guilty for wanting him to disappear, going batty cause he's there living in my house, cooking me dinners I don't want and trying to mend fences and—"

"He cooked you dinner?"

Tiff knitted her fingers in her lap, let out a big sigh. "Yeah, Friday. Only I wasn't there, missed the whole thing 'cause you and I had giveaway night and I never told him. I found his sad little note in the fridge. With the leftovers."

Rebecca's eyes went all puppy-dog. "Oh, Tiff!"

"Tell me about it! So I guilt-cooked for him Saturday to make up for it, only he worked till ten. Between that, and dinner with the Perfect-as-Pie Smathers family on Thursday, and Bobby's inability to talk about anything but the wedding, I've got a headache so big I want to burst."

She'd even skipped church Sunday, spent the whole day in bed reading magazines and binge-watching shows she'd loved in college.

"You've got to relax."

"I don't think I know how." Her chest crawled. *How am I going to make it till Easter, when James finally leaves?*

Rebecca rummaged through her top desk drawer, then passed over a folded notecard. "I'm giving this to you."

Tiff opened the card to find a thank-you scrawled to her boss along with a little printed "one free chair massage" business card in the local coffee shop's new upstairs studio, good anytime.

Even a massage sounded exhausting.

"I never have time for this stuff anymore, but it does help." Rebecca gave her a small smile. "Went quite a bit when I was trying to get my depression under control last summer. Please—go today if you can. Or sometime this week. At the very least your muscles will be looser."

Tiff realized she was rubbing her neck again and tucked her hand back in her lap. "I'll try."

"Do it. Trust me on this." Rebecca leaned over, fished in her purse for her wallet. "Also, food helps. The paper is buying today—production treat. Want some pizza?"

James in his Village Pizza apron flashed in her mind. "Not pizza. But how about subs?"

Tiff did the lunch run instead of her boss, grabbing four sandwiches for the office on the newspaper's tab from that cute new bistro that had just opened on Main.

While she waited for the guy behind the counter to make her order, she grabbed a seat at one of the iron tables and leafed through the newspaper from the next town over. There was a story about another car break-in, and she made a mental note to tell her boss, maybe even call the sheriff.

The bell over the door tinkled. Tiff looked up to see a young woman breeze in, all decked out in booties and a sweater dress, every strand of hair in place like she was a cover girl.

"Well, look who's back in town!" The sandwich guy grinned at the woman.

Sweater-woman's smile lit her face as she unwound a chunky, expensive-looking scarf from her neck. "Adam Markette. It's been a long time."

Her drawl was so heavy it had to have been an affectation.

The guy leaned against the counter, Tiff's sandwiches forgotten. "Here for lunch?"

No, dummy, she's here to play basketball. She stole a quick glance at her watch.

"Sure am!" The woman smiled again.

"Wait, let me guess—turkey on wheat, hold the mayo. Right?"

Sweater-woman sucked in a breath like she was either genuinely amazed or the best actress this side of the Appalachians. "How did you remember?"

"I think you came into my daddy's shop every Saturday for my entire senior year of high school," the guy said, his cheeks now decidedly pink above the collar of his yellow Dahlia Bistro shirt.

The woman laughed, her hair swishing just so. "I forgot about that! And now you're here?"

"My sister and I own it, together. Opened just two months ago." The guy looked proud.

"Oh, how is Chrissy? Is she still dating Nathan Carlisle?"

Tiff cleared her throat.

Sandwich guy blinked and looked down at Tiff's unfinished subs, his hands moving quickly to add the remaining condiments and then wrap up the four. He tucked them all neatly into a bistro bag.

"Here you go, miss. Sorry about the delay!"

"No problem," Tiff said sweetly, rising to take the bag.

"I didn't mean to cut in front of you," sweater-woman said, cocking her head to smile at Tiff, her eyes warm. "Just got back in town and, well. It's been a while!"

"Oh, you didn't cut! Welcome home." Tiff gave a little wave, headed toward the door.

The walk back to the office felt good. A cool breeze made the day smell like early spring, and in front of Mr. Lolligan's, she thought she could see the maple tree starting to bud. Just barely, but still—a hint was better than nothing.

Maybe I will try that massage tonight. She pictured herself there, peaceful and happy—a regular young woman with a promising career, a ring on her finger, and a wedding date set. She shouldn't have a care in the world. James would be gone in a couple months, and she and Bobby would be setting up house all fresh and brand-new like she'd never even been a Steadman.

Far away from Walterville and that trashy farmhouse she'd grown up in, stinking of liquor and unwashed clothes and dirty dishes and Mama's cheap perfume.

She was gritting her teeth so hard, clutching the bag so tight, utterly lost in her thoughts—and almost ran smack into someone.

"Good thing I wasn't a pickup truck!" she heard, looking up to realize she'd run straight into Bobby.

"I am so sorry!"

He grinned down at her, snagged the bag of sandwiches. "Mm, you brought me lunch!"

"Ah . . ."

"I know, I know. I stopped by the paper to bring you lunch, only because I'm trying my hardest to win the Best Almost-Husband in the World prize. Rebecca told me where you'd gone."

Tiff smiled up at him, stomach tumbling in that still-scary roller-coaster rush she got when he looked at her just like that—dimples and wild hair and safety all wrapped into one handsome package.

"You brought me lunch?"

"And chocolate." He winked.

She laughed and hugged him again. Holding hands, they walked back down the street to the newspaper office, him still holding the bag of subs and her feeling every inch the old-fashioned girl with her courting-fellow carrying her books. Even if she did feel slightly guilty she hadn't even thought to get him lunch, or think to ask if he wanted any.

"I love you, Bobby Smathers," she said.

But the words got lost in the wind.

CHAPTER 18

James

HIS HANDS FELT like they'd been coated in cooking oil instead of sweat as he pedaled toward the church Monday afternoon. He'd wipe them on his jeans, and a minute later they'd be slick again. It was like trying to hide fear from God—it always came back to bite you.

Coward. He'd run all weekend from what he knew in his heart he had to do. He'd known Saturday, known the second he'd gotten that cannonball-sized pit in his belly.

The last thing he wanted to do—tell Rev what he'd done, why he'd been locked up, why he needed to do community service—was the very thing he had to do.

He'd wrestled with it all weekend like he was trying to bargain with God. He'd pulled out that sheet the probation officer gave him, with the list of suggested service locations. He'd even pulled out the Chamber of Commerce directory and gone down the list of churches and agencies and other places, determined he'd do anything but go fess up to Rev. Turn him into an enemy.

But God kept steering him back. Pointing him toward the exact thing he wanted to escape.

Now, pedaling toward the church, he figured out why—it was

part of his punishment. He'd done that thing, hurt that boy, and there was no getting out of it. It was seared on his soul forever, no matter how hard he prayed or cried or ran from it.

That night came back to him so suddenly he slowed the bike and finally came to a full stop, closing his eyes against the memory. It didn't matter that he hadn't been the one who'd thrown the final punch that landed the kid in the hospital, almost paralyzed for life. Only by the grace of God had the kid—Marcus—made a full recovery. *Marcus.* He made himself think it, picture his face, the way his eyes had gone from little Os of surprise to full-on terror. The kid had a name. And a family.

And they'd all almost taken it from him. They all—James, DJ, Big John, Tommy, Mike, Dex—played a part. It went from a sick game, picking on the kid just 'cause they couldn't stand the sight of him, 'cause they felt he'd disrespected them, to something far worse.

He felt the world slowly narrow and spin around him till he had to just close his eyes, focus on his breath, his heartbeat thudding all thick like a hammer in his chest. They'd beaten him, stood around him laughing and throwing punches till finally someone realized the kid had stopped moving, that maybe they should stop. DJ'd started it, he always did, all riled up because his girlfriend had said the boy had given her the eye. Didn't matter that she was a flirt who gave everyone the eye, James himself included. They hadn't even thought, just reacted—jumped in and started whaling till the kid was a bloody mess on the street. DJ'd done most of the beating, Big John, too. But James hadn't stood back like some innocent party, like his public defender had tried to argue. He'd thrown his share, not to mention all the hate he tossed out, egging them on.

Get him.

Teach him a lesson.

After, Big John, Mike, and Dex, they'd had the sense to run. But no, not him. He and DJ and Tommy and that stupid girl had gone on like they hadn't a care in the world. Gone to that bar, even. Robbed that convenience store. Taken that gun. Gotten so mind-blowingly wasted nothing even mattered anymore. He barely remembered being arrested. Him, the only one they caught.

All that time, the kid was bleeding on the street. They didn't even care.

Eyes closed, he whispered it again. He'd whispered it a thousand times, but it'd never be enough.

"Forgive me."

Standing there, straddling the bike in this weirdly peaceful town his sister had chosen to call home, he felt the tears build. He tried to rehearse what he'd say to Rev, how he'd try to explain that once he'd hated people for the color of their skin, their accent, their difference. Hated them so much that he'd spent seven years in the slammer and now was going to spend the rest of his life making up for that one screwed-up night. Now he understood. Now he saw the truth—we were all the same deep down, all God's kids. But that didn't excuse the past. If anything, it made it hurt worse.

James swiped at his face, the tears all but gone by the time he'd recovered enough, gathered enough resolve to just get it done.

Go there. Fess up to Rev. Watch the man's face change as he realized what a dirtbag James was.

Then head home—head to Tiff's—and spend another sleepless night beating himself up for all he'd done wrong.

If only he could just avoid the whole thing. Skip right to the going home part. He knew what was going to happen, knew there was no way Rev would let him do community service there now, given what he'd done.

But for whatever reason, God wanted him to do this thing. Face it.

And so he would.

Just get it out of the way.

Putting his foot on the pedal, he stepped off, pedaling hard and fast now. Straight to the church.

He found Rev in that same room with all the furniture, talking to a young Spanish-looking couple, two ragamuffin-looking children pulling at their hands and the hem of their mama's oversized coat.

"See you Sunday," Rev was saying as they turned, smiling, two big bags of what looked like winter clothes in their arms.

The littlest kid, a girl with big black eyes, gazed up at him. She reminded him of a friendly Enrique, his old cellmate.

But James just waited, hands in pockets, for them to go.

He felt Rev's eyes on him, but he wouldn't meet the look. Just needed to get it done and get gone. Fess up and go.

"You look like you've got the world on your shoulders, my friend." Rev's voice, when he finally spoke, was quiet in the big room. "Here. Come on back."

James looked up to see the preacher headed toward the open doorway, followed him back and through a maze of kitchen stuff and a huge closet filled with food and clothes and whatnot. Back to a room with a desk and a couple of chairs.

Rev sat behind the desk and motioned to the chair.

"You okay?" he asked when James sat.

But the words wouldn't come. He'd rehearsed them over and over, all weekend long. Now it all felt wrong.

"I—I'm not sure I can do community service here after all." The words fell out of his mouth in a tumble, and he sat there, let them sink in between them, fill the room.

Rev didn't say anything for a long time. "Why?"

James couldn't read his tone. He looked down at his hands, the lick of the one tattoo, that one, poking out. Just enough. His heart was pounding, and his hands had gone from wet to bone dry.

"I've been in prison, and I . . . ah . . ." James heard the words come out, in his own voice even, but somehow it felt like he hadn't said them. In fact, it felt like he'd somehow stepped out of the scene and was watching the whole conversation unfold, a movie he was watching. A movie starring him.

"You don't have to tell me." Rev's voice was gentle.

"I hurt someone. Bad." Again, that sensation of watching. Almost like a dream.

Rev was quiet, and James could tell he was thinking. Then, slowly, Rev reached out, toward the big black leather Bible on the edge of his desk, and set the Bible between them.

"Do you know Jesus?"

"Yes!" The dream-like sensation disappeared, and James could feel himself front-and-center again. He looked at the pastor, looked him deep in his eyes. "Yes. I do."

"Know him, the real way. Know he's your savior. Know everything we could ever be or do is nothing without him. Know everything we ever did before in our past—the bad stuff, even the worst stuff—is erased." Rev cocked his head, all humor gone. A flicker of sorrow glimmered in his eyes for an instant, then disappeared. "Do you know him like that?"

James nodded. The way Rev said it, it felt like Jesus himself was in the room with them.

"Rev, I do. I didn't . . . before. Before I went in. But I got saved in there, really and truly saved. I'm still working on getting over the past. That's the hardest, for me. But I'm working on it."

Rev raised his hands, almost like a blessing. "Then it doesn't matter what you did."

James looked at him like he was crazy. "How can it not matter?"

Rev looked sad. "My friend, we all have darkness in our past. Myself included. I'm here to help if you need to talk. But you don't have to. It really doesn't matter. What matters is that you're right with Jesus, that you and Jesus have it worked out. I'm . . . well. I'm just a man."

Here goes nothing. Before he could lose his nerve, James pulled his hand from his lap, the right one, slid up the sleeve.

And turned his wrist so the tattoo was there between them.

They stared at it a moment, the ugly black swastika blaring like a siren. James felt the tears rise up, but he pushed them back, gritted his teeth. No tears today. No sympathy. Time to own up.

He hated that tattoo. Hated it so much he'd cut off his right arm if it came to it. For now, though, the idea of working, of saving up enough money to get the ink removed, that's what kept him going.

"My friend, that doesn't matter." Rev's voice was low.

James met his gaze. "How can it not matter?" His voice shook.

"You served your time. You've repented, asked for forgiveness. Right?"

"Yeah, but you don't know who I was—"

"I think I can guess. Let me ask you a question. Is that still who you are today?"

No! James shook his head hard. "No, sir."

"Do you mean to harm me? My wife? Little Devon? Any of the people in this church?"

"No! Never!" James blinked, horror washing over him. "I promise!"

Rev gave a sad smile. "I believe you."

The tears did come then, rising up and spilling out, silent. James sat a time, his head in his hands. After a minute, Rev pushed a box of Kleenex across the table, and James took one, mopped at his face.

"There's only one catch, though," Rev met his eyes again.

James's stomach tumbled. *Here it comes.*

"If you're gonna do your community service here, I want you to come worship here, too." Rev's mouth twisted in a grin. "Think you can handle that?"

CHAPTER 19

Tiff

On Wednesday after work, Tiff sat at one of the metal café tables at Joe Mama's coffee shop, pretending not to stare too hard at the trio of young girls next to her. They looked like they didn't have a care in the world—and probably didn't. Her hands cradled the round white mug and let the heat work its way through until her palms and fingertips stung. She could almost smell the coffee before her—dark and nutty with a hint of sweet wafting up, both prickly and way too syrupy at once.

She rubbed at her nose and forced a smile as Rebecca slid into the chair across from her, some whipped-cream-and-caramel-drizzled concoction in her hands.

"Mm, yours looks like dessert," Tiff said.

"That's the hope." Rebecca gave a wicked grin and scooched her chair in close.

Her boss looked pretty today. Prettier than normal, her blonde waves all tousled over her shoulders. Relaxed—that was it, and happy. Far different from the tightly wound big-city version of Rebecca, who'd moved here last spring. Tiff suspected her new romance with cute widowed dad Josh was part of the reason.

"I'm glad we could do this." Rebecca took a sip and leaned back, like she was surveying the coffee shop for the first time.

Behind her, the late afternoon sun was fading to a cool blue twilight. A rush of wind on the street outside sent some lady's papers tumbling, and Tiff watched as she scrambled to pick them up. It looked chilly, and Tiff was grateful they were inside, all cozy and warm. Joe Mama's was a fun place, with books, high-end lotions, and artsy collectibles stacked neatly on the shelves. A few metal tables were scattered around the room, most of them filled with friends like them, chatting after a long day.

A yawn slipped out as she turned her attention back to Rebecca.

"You've done a lot of that today—yawning. Not sleeping well?" Rebecca asked.

Tiff made a face. "Dreams. I fall asleep just fine, but last night I think I woke up three separate times."

"Bad dreams?"

More like full-on nightmares. "Somewhat." Tiff shrugged. "I guess, well, James being here brings back some . . . icky memories."

Not to mention suspicions. It didn't help that the start of the car thefts almost perfectly coincided with James moving to Dahlia. He better not have anything to do with it . . .

Rebecca's eyes softened. "Memories. I can imagine!"

The dreams had been a blur, mostly—her a kid again, back in Walterville, hiding out in the barn, or in her narrow twin bed, covers over her head as Mama and Daddy went at it again, hollering, glass shattering in the background, curses thrown at each other like knives at a target. Last night's dream had been the worst. She'd woken up convinced she was still back there, only this time she was trapped in the barn as flames began to slowly lick at the walls around her. She must've awakened James, because she could hear him tapping at her door in the early hours of dawn.

"You okay?" he'd called through the crack.

"Fine." She'd choked out the word, raspy, then cleared her throat.

"I'm fine."

Fine, of course. Fine as in an "in my own bed, safe in Dahlia, bright future ahead" kind of fine.

But the deep-down kind of fine, like when the choir at church sang "It is Well with My Soul" fine? Far from it.

Now, Rebecca before her, Tiff waved a hand like the dreams were smoke drifting away on the wind. "Just dreams. And probably wedding jitters."

"Is, well, James going? To the wedding."

"No way!" Tiff reigned in her emotions, smoothing her long dark hair behind her shoulders. She took a sip of her latte, imagining James far away from Dahlia on the day she and Bobby took their vows. A girl could hope. "I mean, he'll be off somewhere, some other part of the state by then, I imagine. Probably couldn't even get time off work."

"Probably," Rebecca said, but Tiff could almost feel Rebecca's thoughts, her questions. Her worries.

"Seriously, the dreams are nothing. Really."

"I'm just worried about you, Tiff. The county council story yesterday . . ."

Heat rose in her cheeks. "Sorry about that. I should have checked the spelling on that guy's last name. And I know the lead should have been a lot stronger."

"I'm not worried about that—more just worried if you're okay." Rebecca eyed her hard. "You know I'm here for you. And if you need a few days off or anything, a week . . ."

"No!" The coffee sloshed into the saucer a little, and Tiff bit her lip.

"Hey." Rebecca reached across the table and took her hand. "I might be your boss, but I care. You're my friend now—the younger sister I never had. If anyone, I probably know the most about keeping all my secrets under such tight wrap that I almost imploded from the pressure."

Rebecca had a good point. Last summer, Tiff remembered what it looked like from the outside—her boss got more and more tense with each passing day, like she was drowning and she was struggling just to keep her head above water and the paper afloat. Much later, around the holidays, her boss had told her about the troubles she hadn't wanted anyone to know about way back then: how just before she'd moved to Dahlia she'd been so depressed she'd almost taken her life. Rebecca was almost like a new person now—she was going to church, she had a super-sweet boyfriend who was truly one of the nicest guys Tiff knew in town, and as far as bosses went, she was pretty much perfect—encouraging, understanding, jumping in when her employees needed her but steering clear for the most part. Oh, yeah, and she was also now part owner of the newspaper, which was making a huge difference on a whole bunch of levels.

"Have you tried talking to Rev at all?"

Tiff shook her head. She liked her pastor a ton, but he was a man, and she could only say so much. "Nah, but I did think about chatting with Marla."

"She's a good listener," Rebecca nodded. "I know from experience."

Rebecca's phone buzzed, and she glanced at it, a little smile lighting her face.

"Josh?" Tiff asked.

"Yep! Dinner at his house tonight. Apparently JJ wants to make us pancakes."

JJ? Tiff didn't even know Josh's son could cook yet.

"I'm not sure he can," Rebecca replied when Tiff said as much, and they laughed and gathered their things to go.

Walking to her car, Tiff glanced over at Smathers Grocery. Bobby's car was still parked on the side. She decided to wander in, maybe grab a frozen pizza and say hi. Other than their surprise lunch on Monday, it had been days since she'd spent time with Bobby. They were doing inventory tonight, so she knew he'd be working late.

Bobby was nowhere in sight when she walked in, so she made a beeline for the candy section and snagged a bag of Jolly Ranchers, his favorite.

"Shh," she told the clerk, who rang up her sale and pointed to the back, where Bobby was working with his dad.

She passed a pretty woman in booties and tights poring over the canned goods like she was searching for the Lost Ark among the green beans. Tiff could tell by the perfect wave and the hairband matching her tights that it was that sweater-dress girl from the sandwich shop the other day. Tiff hurried past, on toward the back office, the candy hidden behind her back.

"Well, if it isn't the future Mrs. Bobby Smathers," a cheerful voice boomed, and she looked over to see Bobby's dad coming around the bend. He kissed her loudly on the cheek. "Hey Tiff. Looking for my oldest?"

"Yessir." She let the Jolly Ranchers bag peek out just a bit, and he laughed.

"You got yourself a good woman here, son," Mr. Smathers called out as Bobby walked up, clipboard in hand and a grin on his face.

"Got that right, Pop." His arms were around her now, and she melted right in for a hug—but not before she snuck the candy into the grocer's bag he wore at his waist.

He winked and looked down, pulling out the bag. "You do know the way to my heart . . ."

"And you know the way to mine." She giggled.

"Why don't you take five, Bobby, spend a bit of time with your lady," Mr. Smathers said, tossing a goodbye wave over his head as he rounded the corner and headed up front.

They walked out back, the evening just starting to fade to full-on night. Tiff took a seat on the stoop as Bobby opened the bag and popped a piece of candy in his mouth.

"You've been busy this week." It was more of a question than a statement, and as the words came out, she tried to soften them with a sweet smile.

"Yeah. Sorry—kept thinking I could call today, but the day just got the best of me."

"It's fine! It's not like we're joined at the hip or anything . . ."

Bobby gave her a funny look. "That's not what I meant."

"I know!"

They were quiet a moment, the chilly twilight settling over them like a thin blanket. In the distance, Tiff could see the first few stars begin to dance on the horizon, like fairies in the forest, someone had told her once. James, more than likely, though maybe she'd made it up herself or gotten it from a book. She preferred that. Thinking all her happy thoughts from childhood stemmed from her brother only made her feel even more guilty than she did about where they were now.

"You look like you got the world on your shoulders, Mischief."

Tiff stuck her tongue out at the nickname, but she smiled. "Nah, everything's good."

"Mm-hm. Not supposed to lie to your husband."

"Almost-husband." Tiff held up her engagement ring finger, wiggling it around just so.

He reached out, tugged on her ponytail. "Close enough."

She grabbed his hand and pulled so he got the message and sat down heavily on the stoop next to her.

"Any better at home?" he asked.

"With James? I guess." She shrugged. Between Bobby and Rebecca, she imagined she was bound and determined to master the no-sweat, no-biggie act like nobody's business. "Hey, you want to go out tomorrow, maybe grab dinner at that Italian place in Ab-erville?"

"Tomorrow? It's Friday. You know Fridays."

"I know. But—"

"And then Saturday, remember, my Mama's cooking for us and the Millers . . ."

Argh. That she'd totally forgotten. Dinner with the Smathers family and their crotchety next-door neighbors sounded like the farthest thing from fun and relaxing she could imagine.

"Maybe Sunday?" he asked.

"They're closed." She pushed back the disappointment and mentally scoured her closet, wondering if she had anything clean and proper enough for a Smathers dinner or if she had to spend Saturday doing laundry.

A thought struck. "Bobby, ah . . . does your mom or dad know yet about James?"

"Your br—? No way!" Bobby looked horrified.

His reaction felt like a slap. "Oh."

He frowned. "I thought you didn't want me to say anything . . ."

"No, I don't. Well, I think I don't. It's just—"

A clang sounded behind them, and Tiff whirled to see Bobby's younger brother Zach in the doorway.

"Say anything about what?"

"Nothing!" They said it at the same time.

Zach looked from one to the other. "You two aren't planning to elope or nothin', are you?"

"No!" Tiff said.

"Dude, really. It's nothing." Bobby's eyes were serious, and Tiff watched his face. "We're not eloping. It's—it's just wedding stuff. That's all."

Zach held up his hands and laughed like he thought he was hilarious. "Okay, okay, don't shoot. Or, well, if you do, at least tell me the big secret first."

Bobby's stare didn't waver, and his voice sounded odd. Almost cold. "Drop it, Zach."

"Bobby, it's really okay." She made her voice sweet, but inside, her chest began to prickle. Why was he acting this way, like some big shot jerk? Zach was a pain, but the kid was seventeen. He was supposed to be a pain.

Bobby stood up. "I mean it."

Zach looked about as surprised as Tiff felt—his eyes like dimes, perfectly round, and his mouth open like he was going to say more. Finally, he turned on his heel and shrugged like the whole thing was water slipping down a playground slide.

"Whatever," Zach muttered as the door slammed shut behind him.

Tiff tucked her hands between her knees. When she finally spoke, her voice was low, but she knew Bobby could hear her. "What was that about?"

"Just forget it."

"I don't want to forget it. That wasn't you just then, or at least not the you I know. Did something happen between you tw—"

"Tiff, it doesn't concern you."

"What?" His words were a shove. "What do you mean it doesn't 'concern' me?"

Bobby sighed, his jaw tight. In the twilight, he didn't even look like himself. He looked like Some Guy. Some cocky, reckless guy. "It's just a dumb brother thing. A family thing."

She blinked. Her chest began to itch. "I thought I was your family, too." *Now the truth comes out.* It felt like a line was being drawn between them: her and him. Her and The Smathers Family.

A line she couldn't ever cross.

"Tiff." He said her name like he was talking to a child. "You are. You know what I mean . . ."

"Maybe I don't." She stood, knees weak and heart pounding. Rage bubbled up and threatened to spill, like lava spewing from a volcano, and she knew she couldn't contain it. The door—now. "I—I've gotta go . . ."

Bobby's hands went up. "What in the world . . ."

Everything she wanted to say, everything she knew she couldn't measure up to, felt millimeters from her lips. She pressed them down, hard, like she could keep them in.

Not here.

Not now.

The anger started to melt and unshed tears threatened, pricking the back of her eyelids, pooling like a tidal wave. *Go.*

"It's . . . been a hard day." Her voice cracked on the last word, and she reached out, brushed the front of his apron with her fingertips. "I'll call you later."

He stood like he was frozen, mouth open, eyes like his brother's had been minutes before. Little round Os.

She fled, the door banging shut behind her, rushing past Zach like she didn't see him, down the canned good aisle and toward the door. Rushing past sweater-dress girl, who was checking out, chit-chatting with the clerk without a care in the world.

The tears came when she reached her car, still parked in front of the *Dahlia Weekly*. Stupid. It was stupid to be mad at Bobby. She wasn't a Smathers, she knew that. And truth be told, she never would be. She'd always be Tiff—not a Steadman, even if that was technically her legal name. But not a Smathers, either. Just Tiff, like a nomad or a gypsy, nameless and rootless.

And very much alone.

CHAPTER 20

James

FRIDAY MORNING FELT almost like spring as James stood on the ladder outside the church, sliding the letters on the welcome sign just so.

"Got grace?" the letters spelled out, with the service time and invitation below.

James had to admit, the sign looked good. Rev had him do a fresh coat of paint the other day, and while it still looked old, now it looked good-old. Well tended.

Grace was something he and Pastor Chad had spent a long time talking about over the last few months before his release. He still didn't understand it, how God would forgive someone like him for all the bad stuff he'd done, not just to that boy but all the stuff. Every day he felt like he remembered something new—stealing candy from that ice cream truck and hiding it in his top dresser drawer. Skipping high school science so many times he would've flunked it had he not batted his eyes at that young fresh-from-college teacher and tugged at her compassion strings so she'd let him squeak by with a low C. Jumping those Mexican guys in the bathroom at the gas station for a measly five bucks and a quarter. Pretty much every carjacking ever.

Thinking about it all now made him feel like a total dirt bag—worse, as if someone had taken the nastiest can of black oil and filled him with it, all the way up to the top. He remembered details, even, that he'd long forgotten, like the look on the younger Mexican guy's face, the way the guy had squeezed up all tense and James had just laughed at him, taunted him about his size. There was no way some skinny five-foot-nothing kid could take him on, especially not with DJ beside him. The guy's brother or friend kept muttering something to the kid in Spanish, talking him down. At the time it all meant nothing, just another joke. Just another score. Now was different. He couldn't stop thinking about the look in the guy's eye, that raw frustration.

Or the ice cream truck guy, babbling on about his mortgage and his kids even as he threatened to call the cops. James hadn't cared a whit, just grabbed the stuff and fled. He knew the guy wasn't gonna do anything.

Now their faces ran before him like some weird old-fashioned cartoon book, the kind you open and flip to make Mickey Mouse do his somersault. The Mexican and the ice cream truck guy. The teacher and her soft blue eyes, all droopy and sad like a cow's as he recited his calculated sob story. That dorky girl on the school bus with the flute case. The kid with the stutter, the one who'd been Tiff's friend awhile till James scared him away.

Every one of them—his "victims." Every one of them he'd wronged in some way or another.

And now, in spite of it all, God forgave him. It didn't seem fair or right.

That must've been how Jonah felt—a good guy, called by God to do something crazy-scary, eaten alive for running from his fate, finally sucking it up and doing what God told him to . . . and then the big bad Ninevites got grace instead of destruction. No wonder Jonah was ticked. Just 'cause they'd turned their lives around didn't seem like a good enough reason for a Get Out of Jail Free card. Some things James would never understand. He guessed he was lucky God was God and not a regular old human like him. If the tables were turned and he were God, James sure wouldn't let himself off scot-free.

"Nice work!" James heard behind him.

He turned to see Rev, all muscly and relaxed looking in basketball shorts and a black hoodie.

"Thank you." He surveyed the sign and the painted brick, nodded at the pastor. "Gotta say, your message makes me want to come worship Sunday."

"You should! Isn't Village Pizza closed Sunday mornings?"

No sense lying even if he wanted to. "Yessir, it is."

"Alrighty, then." Rev clapped his hands like it was settled. "So, how much longer before you gotta head in today? An hour?"

"Just about."

"Wanna give me a hand with the tables inside?"

Every Friday, Rev said, they held that giveaway thing where people could come have supper and get whatever free stuff they wanted, like clothes or shampoo.

"Usually Devon and Marla help me set all this up Thursdays, but now he's started basketball and, well, you know how that goes," Rev said, sliding one of the long rectangular tables from the closet and nodding to James to grab the other end.

James nodded back like he knew. Basketball? Please. After school James was either hiding out with Tiff or messing around with his friends, at least till he was old enough to get a job and earn a bit of cash. Who had time for sports?

Still, he kinda envied the preacher's kid. Maybe he'd have turned out different if he'd done stuff like that in his free time.

Then again, he was a Steadman. He knew the score.

They made quick work of the setup, then James helped Rev cart some boxes to the trash bins, and before he knew it, the pastor was signing off on that week's community service hours.

"Come on by tonight." Rev lifted a brow as he passed the papers over. "There's music, usually, and the food's outta this world."

"Nah, can't. I gotta close tonight. Besides, I've got most of the things I need already." And Giveaway Night sounded like the kind of thing he'd want to escape the second he walked in. That many people in one small place? No thanks.

"Maybe next time. We can always use the help. And you can add it to your hours, too."

"Maybe." His hands felt hot and sticky as he clutched the sheet with his hours.

The moment he could, he fled the church, riding as hard and fast as he could down Main Street and toward the house. Tiff's house.

What was it about the pastor that made him itch? James guessed it was all that kindness. He wasn't used to it, that was for sure. And it made him feel . . . funny. Like, he wanted to be kind back, only maybe he was afraid the pastor might ask way too much in return.

Tiff's car was parked out front when he rode up, not something he normally saw on a weekday. Immediately, his mind filled with reasons—she was sick, or something bad happened, or . . .

"Tiff, you okay?" he called, walking in.

Wherever she was, she didn't answer. Climbing the stairs to his guest room, he grabbed a clean pair of jeans and his long-sleeved pizza T-shirt, then hopped in the shower to rinse off before work. When he came out, she was just opening her bedroom door, looking startled to see him.

He eyed her—messy hair, no makeup, still in pajamas. "You're sick."

"I'm fine."

"Well, you look sick."

"Thanks."

"Don't mention it." He stuck out his tongue, wanting to laugh like the old days, like they used to.

Only, there were no old days. Not anymore.

"Seriously, want some cold medicine or somethin'?" James motioned to his room. "I know I've got some pain relievers—"

"No, I'm actually not sick." She sighed, twisted her hair into a low ponytail. "Just tired."

"Oh." That he could see. The dark circles popped against her pale skin. He frowned, searched for the words. "Everything okay at work? With Bobby?"

"Yeah, yeah, all fine. Working too hard is all. I needed a rest day." She snorted and rolled her eyes. "My boss 'made' me."

"Nice boss."

"She sure is."

They stared at each other a moment, then James finally cleared his throat and scooted toward the stairs. "Headed to work. Let me know if you want me to bring you home a pizza."

"It's okay."

"Really, I can. It's no trouble . . ."

"James." Her voice sounded all huffy, like she was talking to a kid. "I'm good. Really, Now go to work."

It wouldn't have bothered him much after that, only when he ran into Bobby at the gas station, he looked about the same way she did.

"You and Tiff must either be working crazy hours or you're both coming down with the same sickness," James said, giving the guy a smile as they stood in front of the energy drinks.

Bobby blinked and stared at him with a blank expression until James could all but see his eyes settle on the hoodie, the tattoos. Saw the recognition flash.

"Sorry, man. I was out of it." Bobby shook his hand, then snagged a lemon-lime flavored drink from the gas station fridge.

"Tiff is sick?"

"She says she's not, but I'm not so sure she's right. Looks like a frizzy-haired cat in PJs, you ask me."

Bobby frowned.

"What, she didn't mention anything?" James cocked his head as he reached for a blue half-liter.

Bobby started to say something then shrugged, headed for the counter. "I'll check on her in a bit. Thanks, man."

He paid for his drink, slapped James on the shoulder, and was gone, James staring after him.

CHAPTER 21

TIFF SHIFTED ON HER PILLOWS and tried to get comfortable, but it was no use. Two days moping, two days pretending Bobby and their stupid, no-good, aggravating-as-all-get-out fight wasn't front and center in her mind—it was downright exhausting.

Peaches meowed at her bedroom door but she ignored him. He just wanted food, which was all he ever wanted. That and petting, only she'd nudged him off the bed after he kept sitting on the book she'd been trying to read—also to no avail.

"Twenty minutes," she growled in the cat's direction.

Peaches blinked expectantly. "Of course, human," she imagined him saying in his snooty cat voice.

She bit her lip. She knew she was being mean. And unfair. Poor Peaches didn't do anything to deserve this. It wasn't his fault her stomach was in knots over Bobby and the nearly forty-eight hours they'd gone without talking.

Well, he'd texted her. All of six times, all trite little "hey, what's up, miss you" messages like nothing at all had happened between them. All of which she'd promptly ignored.

Or tried to.

The last one, this morning, just read, "You busy?"

It was like he was taunting her, waiting for her to make the first move, waiting for her to play the let's-make-up game.

It was all such a game. And she was tired of games.

Peaches gave a throaty meow as if in agreement, and Tiff let out a sigh, then flung the covers back and stomped out before she could change her mind.

"Come on, you crazy cat," she said, but she scooped him up and petted him gently as they slowly walked toward the stairs, Peaches purring loudly with every step.

She caught a glimpse of herself in the hall mirror, rubbed a hand over her still sleep-crusted eyes.

James. He'd thought she was sick.

In a way, she was sick—sick and tired. Tired of it all.

Tired of James being here, tired of faking it, tired of having to work to be good enough for the Smathers family, as if they were the perfect example of all things good and right in the world.

Compared to her family, they were just about perfect, but then again, you could say that about most every family. That wasn't even the point.

She was just plain tired.

Peaches dug at her with his back legs, and she set him down, then paused, her eyes flicking toward James's room, his closed door.

Even Bobby. Bobby, who she thought was her person, her future and hope, didn't really think she was good enough. He just wanted her to play the game still.

That's not fair, Tiff. She knew it in her heart.

Their spat echoed through her mind. "I thought you didn't want me to say anything," he'd said, the look in his eyes raw. It stung, like she'd just run a cheese grater across his knuckles.

Deep down, he was right. Of course he was right. She's the one who'd told him not to tell.

He was playing her game, not the other way around.

Except.

I wish he'd just see the game needs to stop.

The thought ran an electric shock through her. Head still on her knees, she squeezed her eyes shut and let the truth course through her. She wanted him to take the lead, knock some sense into her, yet she was fighting the very thing she wanted. Why? Pride, maybe. Pain. That was for sure.

And maybe, just maybe, she'd been stuck in the bottom of the bucket so long she plain liked it there. It felt . . . familiar.

She eyed James's door, thought about the story she was working on for next week. Four more car break-ins. He'd be at work all afternoon. All evening, too.

Before she could change her mind, she was at the door to the guest room, turning the handle.

His room was surprisingly neat. The bed was made—something she didn't think he'd ever done when they were growing up—and his books were stacked neatly on the nightstand, his Bible right on top.

Show-off. Of course he'd put the Bible on top. She wondered what he was really doing in there each night.

Quickly, she crept to the mattress, felt beneath. Nothing hidden there. The drawers to the dresser next—also nothing.

She checked the pockets of his two extra shirts, hanging in the closet, and in his jeans from the night before, tossed in a ball near the trashcan.

If he was hiding anything, he must know better than to bring it into her house. She wasn't sure if she was relieved or disappointed.

Her stomach felt all queasy and rumbly then, and she realized she hadn't eaten all day.

A plaintive cry came from around the corner. Peaches. He hadn't eaten, either.

She looked around the room once more, making sure there was

no sign she'd set foot in there. Then she turned and shut the door behind her.

Padding downstairs to the kitchen, she fed herself and the cat, then stacked her plate in the dishwasher and headed back upstairs to the shower.

Twenty minutes later, her hair wrapped in a towel, she lay damp and thoughtful on her bed. Above, the fan did its slow spin, and she watched one of the blades till her eyes couldn't keep up anymore.

Her phone buzzed on the nightstand, and she wiggled until she could close her hand around it, pulled it over to her. It was a text.

From Bobby.

Her heart pounded as she clicked on the message.

James said you're sick?

James. Of all the . . .

She caught herself. Maybe he was right. Maybe she was sick.

And being sick as a reason for avoiding Bobby's texts was far more understandable than being stuck in the bottom of her own bucket.

Her fingers pecked out the reply before her mind could catch up.

I'm better now.

His message came right away.

I've missed you.

Tears pricked, and she closed her eyes, swallowing past the thick lump that had suddenly formed in her throat. A moment passed, then another.

Swiping a hand across her wet cheeks, she typed back:

I've missed you, too.

His knock, later that afternoon, sounded tentative.

She stepped to the door, dressed in a simple cotton shirt and loose shorts, her hair top-knotted and just a slick of balm on her lips.

Bobby stood on her doorstep, a bouquet of pale pink roses in one hand and a white paper bag clutched in the other.

"Up for dinner?" His eyes twinkled, and she pulled him in for a hug, wrapping her arms around his waist tightly.

Breathing him in.

At her kitchen table, sandwiches finished and just a few fries left to share between them, she leaned over in her chair, resting her head on his shoulder.

Her words, when they came, were soft.

"I'm sorry."

He pulled back so he could look at her, and her at him, and ran a hand gently over her cheek.

"Tiff. I'm sorry, too."

She hugged him again, closing her eyes, listening to his heart beat steady somewhere beneath his green Smathers Grocery sweatshirt. She could still smell the day on him, a mix of chilly air and the scent she'd come to associate with the grocery store, something between spices and cleaning supplies and Bobby himself.

"I shouldn't have gotten all mad at you." Her words were a mumble against his shirt. "It wasn't your fault."

"Hey." He patted her softly like she was a baby or a dog, all tender and sweet, fiddling with the bun on top of her head till she unburied her head from his shirt. "I'm fine with telling my parents about your brother. I was only trying to respect your wishes, is all."

Respect. Of course he's that good. That decent. Her face flushed with embarrassment.

"I get that. But honestly, Bobby, do you think we should? Tell them."

He was quiet a long moment. "Really it's up to you. It's your decision."

"But what do you think?"

He cut his eyes at her. "We don't do secrets well in my family. I mean, look at my mama . . ."

A giggle escaped her lips. Bobby's mama was about the most loose-lipped person she'd met, and the most outspoken. Even more than Millie, at the newspaper. She remembered the time Bobby's dad had that cancer scare. They'd talked about little else at the dinner table for weeks till the tests revealed it was all negative, to the point that Tiff knew so much about Mr. Smathers's bathroom habits she was mortified for him. You could say one thing about the Smathers family—they certainly were an open book.

"I see your point."

"Seriously, though, Tiff. Just because we Smathers don't keep much to our chests doesn't mean that's best, or best for you. And remember, telling my mama also means telling half the town."

She grabbed a fry, considering. She wasn't sure she wanted everyone to know she had a brother like James.

She wasn't sure James wanted that, either.

"You know what, Bobby, let's keep it to ourselves. I'm not sure I'm ready for all of Dahlia to know my business."

Bobby squeezed her hand. "It's totally your call. I'm willing if you are."

Of course he was. She gave him a sweet smile.

"I'm sure."

Bobby's eyes flashed. "Oh! Not to change the subject, but I have good news. The Millers canceled for dinner tomorrow. Some stomach bug. So if you're still interested, let's do that Italian place you like in Aberville."

She poked him in the ribs lightly. "Are you asking me out on a date, Bobby Smathers?"

He pulled back to gaze at her, loosening the elastic from her bun so her dark hair tumbled over her shoulders "Why, yes. I am."

She fed him the last fry, then settled back in his arms again, thinking.

"How about this. Let's save date night for next weekend. Tomorrow night, let's you and me have supper at your place. Maybe I can pick up some tips from your Mama on living life open and secret-free."

A girl could try.

The next night, Tiff helped Mrs. Smathers bring the covered dishes to the long oval dinner table. She lit the ivory candles carefully, cutting the tips first with the kitchen scissors just like she'd been taught by Bobby's mama so the wax didn't drip all over the tablecloth. Tiff wasn't sure cutting them made any difference, but she certainly was no expert. Besides, it was easier to go along with Bobby's mama, who had long-held opinions about pretty much everything.

"You feeling better, hon?" Mr. Smathers asked, taking his seat at the head of the table. "It's been going around."

She flushed. "Yeah, it wasn't as bad as Bobby probably said."

Mr. Smathers lowered his voice, hammed a wink. "Does a man good to fuss over his lady. Don't you stop him from doing that."

She giggled as the rest of the family took a seat. Zach was out with friends, but Bobby's youngest brother, Ben, was there.

"So, Tiff." Ben turned to her the moment the blessing was done. "They catch 'im yet?"

"Catch who?" Bobby said behind a bite of food.

"The car break-in thief. Or thieves. It's usually a ring, right?" Ben scooched his chair closer to hers, leaned in.

"Nothing yet." Tiff shook her head. She'd been looking into the story Wednesday, but then Thursday she was a wreck, and by the end of the day Rebecca'd told her to take the next day off. Forced vacation, her boss had said with a smirk, though Tiff had seen the concern, too.

"I heard a lady had her purse stolen right outta her backseat yesterday. She'd just gone to the bank, had a bunch of cash in there, too. Stole her purse clean gone, and her fancy sunglasses, too."

"Why'd she leave her purse in her car with all that cash in the first place?" Mrs. Smathers tsked. "Sounds fishy to me."

"I do it all the time." Mr. Smathers shrugged.

"Chu-uuu-uck." Mrs. Smathers dragged out the name like it had three syllables.

"Just being honest." Mr. Smathers smiled in Tiff's direction.

"Fred at the grocery said it was his sister." Bobby stabbed at a piece of chicken.

Tiff shook her head. "I don't think they know anything yet. Or if they do, the sheriff's not saying."

"That's just like Don Zane. All some big show." Mrs. Smathers sighed dramatically and took a sip of her ice water.

"Now, Arlene."

"Don't you 'now Arlene' me, Chuck. You know the sheriff as well as I do."

"We went to high school with him," Mr. Smathers told Tiff. Of course they did. The Smathers family knew everybody.

Bobby's mama shivered. "Well, I sure do hope they catch him

soon."

"Or catch them," Ben said, eying Tiff.

"Me, too." She smiled at Ben, and Bobby squeezed her hand. She squeezed back.

"Are y'all going to the church festival later?" Ben asked Bobby.

Bobby shrugged. "Nah, I don't think so."

Bobby's mama blinked at Tiff. "You're not covering it for the paper?"

"Nope, my boss wanted to go. She and Josh are taking his son."

Mrs. Smathers sniffed. "That poor child. Wonder how he feels about a Yankee stepmama."

Mr. Smathers stuck his tongue out at his wife. "I'm sure he'll like it just fine, Arlene. When they get to that point."

She swatted back at him. "Oh, hush. And yes, Ben, you can borrow the car. You still picking up Nick and that Bowser boy?"

"Yeah. Them and . . . ah, Hayley Motts and her friend." Ben's neck started to pink. "If that's all right, ma'am."

"Motts?" Bobby's mama sat up a little straighter. "Natalie's kid sister?"

Ben's neck went from pink to red. "Ah, yes, ma'am. She needed a ride."

Bobby's mama took a small bite of rice, nodding approvingly. Next to her, Tiff could feel Bobby sigh.

"That's a good family." Mrs. Smathers dabbed her mouth with her napkin and tossed her husband a significant look. "Don't you think so, Chuck?"

"Don't see why it matters, but sure, they are."

"Have you seen Natalie since she's been back in town, Bobby?"

Tiff caught the look Mrs. Smathers cast in Bobby's direction.

"I heard she was back, that's about it." Bobby helped himself to another serving of rice and a big ladle of string beans. "Natalie and I, we used to hang around a bit back in high school," he told Tiff.

Mrs. Smathers hooted. "Hang around? Why, they went to the junior prom, the senior prom, and they were Homecoming King and Queen one year, to boot."

Tiff swallowed and tried to smile like it was no big deal. *That kind of friend.*

"She moved away for college, got herself some big swanky job, and was just about to get married to some man from Tennessee. Something happened between them, I don't know what, and now she's back. Her mama says she's looking for work, too."

Bobby smirked at Tiff and scooped another mouthful of dinner. "I swear, Mama, you should work for the paper. You know all the town's news."

"Oh, hush. Anyway, she's cute as a button. Ben, by all means you give that sweet little Motts girl a ride. If she's anything like her sister, she's a catch and a half."

"We're just friends, Mama." Ben looked like he wanted to crawl under the table.

"Mmm-hmmm," Mrs. Smathers said, batting her eyes toward her husband.

Mr. Smathers just rolled his. "Arlene, would you quit with the matchmaking?"

They all laughed. But inside, Tiff couldn't help herself from wondering about this Natalie girl. Cute as a button and a good family? Something about the way Mrs. Smathers said it made her feel . . .

"You wanna take a walk with me?" Bobby squeezed her knee.

Tiff looked up to see Ben halfway up the stairs and Mrs. Smathers gathering a few of the platters to take to the kitchen.

"You two go on," Mrs. Smathers shooed them toward the door. "Your daddy'll help me clean up. Go talk about that wedding of yours."

She winked at Tiff, but behind the wink, Tiff felt sure she saw something else. Something like a smile, only not quite.

The night was cold and crisp, so crisp they could hear every footstep. Tiff curled her arm through Bobby's as they walked down the path and out toward the pretty sidewalk. Before them, it felt like there were miles and miles of trees, though she knew it all ended at the stoplight. The Smathers family had lived in that house thirty years or so, but it had been Mr. Smathers's childhood home before that, passed down to him after his own daddy had died and his mama had moved in with Bobby's aunt. Same with the grocery, come to think of it.

"Whatcha thinkin'?" Bobby's tone was light.

"History!" She shook her head, her breath making little puffs in the cold night as they walked. "Your family's just steeped in history. This house, the grocery, your whole family, it all goes back ages and ages. And your mama, she must know every single person in this town!"

She meant it to come out giggly and cute, but to her ears it edged on whiny. She leaned her head on his shoulder to soften her tone, snuggling in a bit tighter as they walked.

"Sometimes it's a huge pain," he said.

She laughed, but he shook his head.

"No, really! Sometimes I envy you, not being from here. Nobody knows your entire life story. You could have invented an entire history for all anyone knew and no one would be any wiser."

If you only knew.

He huffed, but not unkindly. "Me, they know the good and the bad. The time I wet my pants tagging along at the blood drive when I was six, that year I won the school spelling bee, the time I got my foot stuck in Mr. Barber's wood fence and they had to call the rescue squad. Every wrong step, every achievement. Sometimes both in one."

"You wet your pants? At the blood drive?" The thought of a

young bladder-challenged Bobby caught her heart, and she smiled to imagine it.

"Yup."

"But." She gave him a sidelong look pinching back the grin. "Surely no one's thought of that in years."

He covered his mouth. "Yolanda Lewis from the pharmacy? Reminded me of it just two days ago. 'Oh, it's Bobby Smaaaaathers,'" he said, mimicking her high-pitched voice. "'I remember that time when you were just up to here on your Mama's hip and made that pee-pee mess all over the church fellowship hall. We could smell it for daaaaays even though we mopped it three times!'"

"You are kidding!" She burst into laughter.

"Nope!" His eyes were wet he was laughing so hard. "Ah, and Homecoming! If I knew then the ribbing I'd still get all these years later just for that one silly night . . ."

"I'm getting married to the Homecoming King." Tiff stuck her nose in the air and pranced a little, hand fanned out at her ears. "Lucky, lucky me."

Bobby slung his arm over her shoulders and she snuggled back in, hugging him.

"I'm the lucky one." He smiled down at her.

The words played at her lips as they walked, and she couldn't keep it in any longer. "That was with Natalie?" She didn't look at him, just kept her eyes on the starry, crisp sky like she didn't have a care in the world.

Bobby sighed, still smiling. "Yep, Natalie Motts. Cutest girl in school."

"And your girlfriend?" Her words were light, gentle, but her heart began to thud.

"Oh, yeah, a few years at least." Bobby shrugged as they walked along. "She was sweet. You'd have liked her."

"Maybe I'll get the chance to, now that she's moved back and all."Tiff couldn't keep the edge out of her voice this time, but Bobby didn't seem to notice.

"Maybe so." He kissed her cheek, but she kept her eyes fixed on the sky. "You okay?"

"Of course!" They reached the end of the street, stalled. From here they could cross to the square or head back. Only, if Tiff had her way, they'd keep walking. Clear on out of town.

He started to nudge them across the street toward the square, but she tugged on his hand. *Don't do this, Tiff.* But she couldn't stop. It was like an itch, a burning bubble, that started deep down inside her and just had to work its way up. All the way to the top.

"Why'd you two break up?"

"Who? Me and Nat?" Bobby stopped, his brows all bunched together so they almost reminded her of a furry caterpillar. "I don't know. Kid stuff. Who even remembers?"

"So it's 'Nat' now." Her voice sounded cold to her ears. *What are you doing? Stop this nonsense.*

"Yeah, that's what everyone calls her. Nat Motts. Tiff, what's going on?" Even his voice sounded hurt now.

"Oh, nothing." Tiff gave a wave like she was shooing a fly. "It's just you think you'd have told your fiancée about this girl you dated for years who's suddenly moved back home. A girl so serious your mama brings her up at dinner."

"Tiff Steadman, you know it's not like that! You know how Mama is. She's . . . she's got no filter! You know that. She didn't mean nothin' by it. Why, she had us go out walking so we could plan more wedding stuff, for goodness' sake!"

"Sure she meant nothing," Tiff muttered.

Bobby stopped as if she'd slapped him. "I think we'd better go back."

Tiff pulled back, lifted her chin. A long moment passed between them.

Finally, voice low, she nodded. "I think we'd better."

When she got to the house, she dug in her coat pocket, feeling for her keys. *Thank you, God.*

She clicked her locks. "I'm not feeling well. Please tell your parents I said goodnight."

He didn't say a word, just watched her climb in her car, back out of the drive, and rumble down the road toward home.

CHAPTER 22

Tiff

SHE AWOKE THE NEXT MORNING groggy and sniffly, like she really did have a cold. Her neck felt achy, and for a moment she couldn't feel her feet. Then she realized Peaches was sound asleep right smack on top of them. She moved her legs and he meowed softly, snuggled deeper into the soft down comforter.

Nine-oh-five, the clock said when she peered at it. On this of all mornings, she was tempted to skip church. But she knew she needed to go. Besides, Bobby always picked her up and they went together. In spite of last night, they hadn't canceled or anything. And she could use the preaching this morning, that was for sure.

Last night. She groaned and grabbed her pillow, burying her face in it. What in the world had come over her? She'd acted like a child. Worse than a child—a toddler. Petulant, stupid, jealous, and all for what? For some girl Bobby'd dated so long ago he couldn't even remember why they'd broken up.

Or could he?

Stop. She forced herself to breathe, to count down in her head. Anger had never been a problem—that was James's thing. Back when she was young, she was too worried about getting cornered, whipped, or screamed at to ever let anger bubble up in her. Survival

128

mode, she called it. She even kept an old coffee can in her room just to avoid running into Mama and Daddy if she had to go to the bathroom in the middle of the night. Not that she ever needed it, but it was there just in case. No, she was much more a fear girl than an anger girl. So where was this coming from?

Nerves. Between James and this wedding coming up ... well, no wonder she was a wreck, right?

She grabbed her phone from the nightstand, scrolled to his name.

Hey. I'm sorry.

It took Bobby six long minutes to reply.

Hey ... It's okay. I know you have a lot going on.

She bit her lip, typed: *It's no excuse.*

Less than a minute passed, then: *I forgive you.*

The breath she didn't realize she was holding tickled up and out. *Thank you, God.*

She took a quick shower, slipped on a pretty sweater dress and those cute high boots with the chunky heels Bobby liked, and dabbed perfume behind her ears. A couple of swipes of mascara, blush, and lip gloss, and she was ready.

James's bike was gone when she stepped outside to wait for Bobby's car, and she realized she hadn't seen her brother in two days.

Suits me. Truth be told, she was counting the weeks till he was gone.

Then she could finally put it all behind her—all the bad, all the Steadman—and walk down the aisle with her head held high.

Tiff Lacey Smathers. A Steadman no more. Never to return.

She zipped her coat tight against the chilly morning, and then Bobby was there, and she was in his truck and holding his hand and all was right in the world once again.

When they got to the church she sat a moment, seatbelt still unbuckled.

"Bobby . . ."

He gave her a sidelong glance. "Are you gonna ream me again?"

Then she realized he was joking. Her laugh bubbled out, just this side of loopy.

"That's just it. I'm really sorry. First Wednesday night, and now last night. I—I guess I'm far more stressed out than I think I am." A breathless giggle escaped, and then a tear threatened. *Not today.* She forced herself to grin past it. "Happy tears," she pointed. "Anyway, I think the pressure of all this business with my brother is just wearing on me, you know?"

Bobby just looked at her, a small smile on his lips. "I know."

"It . . . it's just hard."

"I understand."

She wished he really did understand, truly understand. But how could he? How could anyone who grew up normal even imagine? Still, she smiled up at him, forced herself to lose herself in the moment—in all she wanted him to be and then some.

"You always get me, Bobby Smathers."

They walked into church and hung up their coats near the front. Someone called Tiff's name, and then there was chitchat and all the churchy small talk and Rebecca was hugging on her neck and asking how she was, and then they were all walking into the sanctuary.

The music had started, and it was overly warm. So warm she wished she'd chosen anything but the sweater dress this morning.

She was faced the other way, talking to Bobby about something silly when they reached the third row, started to slide in.

And then he turned. The guy on the end.

James. It was James.

She didn't even think. Didn't have time to think. The churning in her stomach started, raced like a hot poker up her throat.

And she was running—walk-running as fast as she could.

Out of the sanctuary. Out the front door.

She'd forgotten her coat, but it was too late. She barreled down the road in her chunky high-heeled boots, running so fast she could barely breathe.

CHAPTER 23

James

WHY HADN'T HE WARNED HER? It was the least he could have done.

The look of horror on his sister's face when she'd started to slide into the pew, hair all soft and pretty against that dress, like some girl in a shampoo commercial, only to see him. Him, her brother, surely from her reaction her worst nightmare—that wasn't something he'd likely forget. Not for a long, long while.

He dug his fingernails into his palms as he sat under the big droopy tree, leaves fat and slippery, somehow both at once.

It was how he felt. Fat—not physically, but fat with sin. Fat, thick with the weight of it all. But slippery, too. Cause the weight was just too much.

Here, in the silence of this forest, far from anyone's eyes, James could cry. And so he let himself. The tears came like a waterfall, like he'd been holding them back so long they didn't roll like regular tears but gushed out in a smooth, watery line, wetting his face and soaking the neck of his sweater.

Crying was something you didn't do behind bars. Not that he was a stranger to it, but for the most part he'd had to hold it all in, keep it all in check. Shut his emotions down and go all robotic, like he was some walking, talking machine and not flesh and blood. It was the same thing he'd done most of his life. A body could only get beaten so often, screamed at so often, before you either believe it or you shut it off, fight it.

At least, he thought he was fighting it. *Not so sure anymore, are you, tough guy?* He and Pastor Chad had talked about it a bunch. How fighting back isn't turning off the hurt but just not letting it happen any more. Or if it's gotta happen, at least knowing deep down in your belly it's just not right.

He'd cried a bit with Pastor Chad. The other guys, the other Christians, did, too. But back in the cell he shut it off like a big ol' chunky light switch.

His neck felt cold now, and he wiped his face, realized the tears had stopped. Good.

His sister's face flashed before him again, her eyes—dark like coal against her pale skin, all round and scared-looking.

Stupid. Stupid of him to just walk into church like he could, like it was nobody's business. It hadn't even crossed his thick skull this might be Tiff's church, too. There were, what—twenty churches in town? Not twenty, but a gob for such a small place. He'd figured she'd be at one of those big and proper ones, not Rev's little brick regular-looking church.

And it felt good, too, at first. Being there, like he wasn't a scumbag, like he was one of them. He'd wandered in all shy, not really sure he'd stay the whole time, but then that white-haired lady'd grabbed him all nice like she meant it, and helped him find a seat up front next to that family. He'd seen Rev once or twice, walking back and forth, getting all ready to do whatever pastors do, and Rev had smiled all toothy and happy at him. Happy to see him. James.

After Tiff ran out, Bobby'd run after her, but the song started in full just then, and the people next to him were standing and clapping, and he felt his body rise, too.

Going with the flow. Tucking it all down like he always did. He'd toughed it out the whole service like it was nothing, like he hadn't just wrecked his sister even more just by being there.

Stupid. Least he could have done was write her a note or something. The worst part was he thought she'd be happy. He'd gotten up early, fixed breakfast, made extra eggs, too, in case she wanted some. Normally she was up early on Sundays too, singing her songs and talking to that cat and doing all those lady things. But he hadn't heard a peep from her that morning, not the second or even third times he'd walked back upstairs to grab something from his room. The guest room. And finally it was time to go or he'd be late—riding a bike took longer, not that he was complaining.

Funny how a person could always see exactly what to do right after the wrong's already happened. If he could do it over again, he'd have tapped at her door, told her he was going to church and he'd see her later, not slunk around like some coward. Then at least she'd have known.

The tears built again, but this time he rubbed at his face. *No more.* As Pastor Chad always said, there was a fine line between owning your wrong and feeling sorry for yourself.

He stood then, his back sore from where he was leaning against the tree, brushed cold twigs and other woodsy stuff off his jeans, and looked around. He'd seen this forest the first night, when Tiff had driven them both back from the bus station. And he'd biked by it once or twice, on his days off.

In the distance, he thought he could hear what sounded like a river, decided to wander down and check it out.

Even in just a sweater, it didn't feel so cold, especially now that he was walking. There was a path, and he took it, walked all the way down till he saw the river, kept on going till he got to the end and some tunnel thing, keep-out signs everywhere. The sort of place where he and his friends would have been up to all sorts of no good, back in the day.

Then he walked back, slow and lazy-like, and he rounded a curve where the river looked so pretty it took his breath away. It was a God place if he ever saw one, that was for sure—the sun had come out in full force now, shining so bright it made the water look like it was dancing with sparkles, and as he watched, a couple of squirrels rustled up in the trees and must've knocked some leaf or hole, 'cause now the sun had made its own sun-path, a beam like a spotlight all soft and hazy.

"Hey mister!" The voice from behind made him jump.

He turned and saw a guy and two kids coming up the path. The guy had a bucket and a fishing box, and the boys carried poles. One of the kids, the one who must have called out to him, was waving at him now. He had freckles all over his face and a big grin with a hole where a tooth had been on one side.

The other kid was a skinny little black boy, and the guy must have been Freckles' dad. They set their stuff down by a tree, the freckled kid still grinning.

"You wanna fish with us?" the kid asked.

He wished. "I don't have a pole." He raised both hands with a shrug. "But thank you for askin'."

"You can share mine!"

James couldn't help but laugh. Most of the time, chatty people gave him the crazy bug, but this kid he didn't mind so much.

The guy, a freckly version of the boy, gave him a wave. "I'm Josh Jamison. This chatterbox here's my son, JJ, and—"

"I'm Devon!" The other kid passed him a pole.

James peered closer. Rev's son!

"I know your daddy," James told him, then his stomach tumbled and he wished he could bite back his words. He was just a kid, but who knows, maybe Rev had told his son some of James's story, about the community service and the jail time. Maybe the kid knew things. Would say things.

But either Rev hadn't or the kid didn't care, 'cause the boy smiled in a way that lit up his eyes like a sunbeam.

"Rev? He's not actually my real daddy, but he's gonna be. I saw you. At the place with the bikes."

The freckled kid—JJ?—nodded fast. "Yeah, he's gettin' adopted."

"Nice. That's real nice."

"Sure is!" Devon said. "My mama died, and then my granny had to go in the old folks home, so now I get to live with Rev and Marla and we're getting a dog, maybe two, and next year we might even go on an actual vacation. To see Marla's mama and daddy up in Cincinnati. He's a pastor, too, just like Rev!"

He talked so fast it made James's head spin, but it was cute, all kiddish and natural-like.

"My mama died, too. That's why we got to be such good friends, me and Dev here." JJ slung his arm around Devon's neck. "We go fishing every Sunday, mostly. This here's our favorite spot!"

James eyed the dad, who was bent over the tackle box pulling out lures and stuff, but he didn't even bat an eye. The kids probably yammered on like this all day long and he was used to it.

"Fish bite the best here." The dad winked at him. "You're welcome to join, us, really. Way more fun to fish with four, and Becks can't come today."

JJ whispered loud. "Becks is his girlfriend. She's super pretty."

"And super nice," the dad whispered back just as loud, and everybody laughed.

Fishing did sound fun, but not today. Not after . . .

His belly flip-flopped again as Tiff's face flashed through his head, her round eyes so gigantic in her head they looked like they'd pop out if she opened them any wider. Not just round eyes—scared eyes. Scared like some startled doe. Like all those kids he and his buddies would run up on back in the day, back home, picking at 'em or stealing their lunch money or whatever trouble they were raising.

He needed to get back to Tiff's, apologize. Maybe talk it out. *How could I have been so blasted dumb?*

"Nah, thanks, but I gotta get back. Got some plans this afternoon."

The boys looked bummed out, like they'd really wanted him to join. The dad just nodded.

"I get that. Well, rain check. Like Devon said, we're usually here most every Sunday after church."

"Thanks." James looked around for his bike and remembered it was a ways back. "See ya."

They said their goodbyes and he walked off, back the way he'd come, almost wishing he'd stayed. He tossed a glance over his shoulder when he got halfway down the path, and they were all bent over, getting their poles ready, laughing and all. Happy.

Free. In a way he'd never be.

A cloud settled over him as he walked on, and the air felt cooler suddenly beneath the trees now that his body wasn't all heart-thumpy from his walk and that mess of crying he'd done.

Dinner. He could cook her a dinner, like he'd done that once. Maybe scoop the cat litter, by far his least favorite thing to do under the risen sun.

And a letter. A letter for sure.

He wished he had some paper with him now, but it was all back in his room. The guest room, he reminded himself, shaking his head. *Don't get comfortable.* He was leaving soon, he'd promised Tiff.

Maybe sooner than soon.

His throat burned a moment, and he swallowed. Maybe Tiff would want him to go now. Maybe that was the best thing anyway.

But he had a job now, and community service. Pastor Chad said whatever he did he needed to try to keep the same job, the same stuff going for the next few months to show he was "stable" and "on the right track." Maybe Rev could let him stay at the church, if worse came to worst. Just till it warmed up a bit more. He'd heard some guys talking about a shelter, too, over in the next town, but truth be told that was the very last thing he wanted.

He might not have a choice.

His bike was where he'd left it, behind some bushes at the edge of the forest, and he hopped on, pedaling till he got to Main Street. Most of the stores were closed on Sunday, which was a bit of a pain even if nice, old-fashioned, but the gas station was open.

Parking his bike outside, he wandered in, holding the door for a lady who gave him a cute smile at first, then kinda shivered, like he was bad news or something. *You are bad news.* He dropped his eyes, slunk to the cooler for a Gatorade, then peeked down the extras aisle, where he found what he was looking for.

A blue spiral notebook and a pack of cheapy ballpoint pens.

He pedaled down Main till he found a quiet corner where he could settle beneath a tree. Then he opened the notebook and began to write his sister.

CHAPTER 24

SHE'D RUN. Faster than fast, as if her muscles had transformed into those of horses, those racers Mr. Adams had back home. She'd run so hard and long she couldn't even feel her legs, not worrying about her breath or the scream in her chest or the burn that coursed through her like she'd somehow caught fire and only running would put it out.

Behind her, she'd heard Bobby, calling her name, but it didn't matter. None of it mattered. *Go!* She'd had to, had no choice. Her body had taken over—no time to think.

Through the woods, past the river, pounding through brush.

She hadn't even known where she was headed till she saw it up past the turn. The storm drain, the very place where Devon had almost gotten himself killed last summer, though of course through no fault of his own. That business with the rotten-awful uncle, all the stuff that led up to Devon moving in with the pastor and his wife.

The keep-out signs there now were fresh, and she could see some police tape still remained from where they'd cordoned it off after the flood and the search. "Caution," blared one in traffic-orange. Danger, read another. Keep Out. Trespassers subject to fine.

She'd slipped past, still breathing hard from her run, grabbing the grate for balance as she'd slid through and inside. As she did, she'd noticed the big rip on her sweater-dress, tugged back her sleeve to see a four-inch slice where the branches had snagged her. It didn't hurt, not really. In a way, she was grateful for it—she could focus on it and not the tumble going on inside her own chest.

That's where she was, still. Didn't know if it'd been fifteen minutes or five hours. For all she cared, she could stay there all night.

The tunnel was cool and dark, much cooler than the day outside, but it felt good to sit there alone in the hazy black. Her dress was already ruined, so she didn't have to worry about the mud and damp seeping through beneath her thighs.

She scooted back, wriggling up so her back could rest against the wall of the tunnel, wrapped her arms tight around her knees.

From here, she could see the river, but no one could see her.

James. In her own church of all places! Was he trying to mess with her? Or was he just that stupid? Not that she'd told him it was "her" church. But still . . .

She butted her head against her knees, ready for the tears to come, but instead, there were no tears. There was just rage, hot rage. Burning rage.

She pressed her palms against the floor of the tunnel, felt the jagged concrete of the storm drain jab against her flesh. It hurt but a good hurt, the kind she craved. She pressed harder, the heel of her hand against the concrete. Again and again.

The slice on her arm stung now. Good. She focused on the pain, on the throbbing in her hands, on the dank, fishy odor of the tunnel and the river beyond.

Why? Why-why-why-why-why?

It was too much, all just too much. Squeezing her eyes shut, she let her head bump back against the tunnel wall, but that was a hurt she didn't want.

She'd never asked for any of this. Not a single bit. It wasn't fair.

Wasn't it enough she'd grown up the way she had, clawed her way out the only way she knew how, moved all these miles away, only for it all to catch up with her again?

For a moment, Mama's face flashed before her. Eyes that never quite saw her, unless they were focused on whatever Tiff had done wrong. Stringy brown hair, skinny arms, thin lips that seemed pressed in a forever-frown, like she'd tasted the sourest of sour and wouldn't open up again for nothing.

That or she was laughing, that crazed high-pitched shriek at whatever Tiff's daddy was saying. Fighting or laughing—no in-between.

"Tiff, bring us a cold one!" she'd holler, nubby cigarette dangling from her fingers, curled up on his lap like she was some teenager. Her daddy'd just laugh and laugh, until the laughs would turn and Tiff would be holed up in her room, desk chair jammed beneath the handle as the crash of glass or cursing would change to yelling and one or the other of them would stomp out to the car and roar into the night.

Once, they were gone almost three days straight before one of them came home again. Some other kid might've been worried, not known what to do. Her, she wasn't worried one bit. Relieved, truth be told. She'd get up, pour some cereal and milk, sit at the kitchen table like the house was hers, dream of how it'd be one day when she was all grown up and on her own. Everything she'd become.

Not a single ounce like them.

And it was working, too! She'd escaped, hadn't she? Made it through college on a full ride, kept her grades up even working nights at Macabee's, landed herself a real job in a place where not a single soul knew anything about her. Everything erased, just like she'd wanted it. A fresh start. A new life.

Now James. Coming back into her life and wrecking it all.

She screwed up her face remembering Bobby calling after her. *Tiff, wait up! Tiff, let me help!*

But not even Bobby could help. The only thing that could help is if James crawled back into the hole from where he'd come, taking every last memory of Mama and Daddy and Walterville and all the pain and fights and nonsense back with him.

The tears came then, ugly blubbery tears, soaking her tights, soaking the hem of her torn-up sweater-dress. *Please, God, make him go away. Make it all just go away.*

Finally, spent and shivering, she curled up in a ball there at the base of that storm drain and fell fast asleep.

She couldn't see the time when she woke up, but the sun had moved clear on the other side of the sky. *Ouch.* Her hip ached, and her left leg had fallen asleep. She shook it, pins and needles dancing wildly.

Scooting up to the opening of the tunnel, she peered at her watch. After three. She fumbled for her cell phone, remembered it was still back in the church, tucked deep in the pocket of her coat.

Bobby was bound to be good and mad. And worried. What kind of a girlfriend—what kind of a future wife—tore out of a place like a crazy woman? Like she had? And Rebecca. Rebecca'd been two steps behind him, she remembered now. Her boss had to know by now she had a screw loose. Had even forced her to stay home Friday for just that very reason. "Mental health day," Rebecca had called it, and they'd both laughed at the time.

Tiff's heart did a roller-coaster flip in her chest. *I've got to set this right, or else I'll be out of a job* and *a husband.*

Back where she started.

With nothing.

Cars whizzed past as she walked the mile or so back to the church. She tried the door, but it was locked.

"Hey, there, Tiff. You doin' okay?" A woman's voice. It was Rev's wife, Marla, at the parsonage next door, loading some boxes in the back of their SUV.

Tiff jumped and forced herself to give an embarrassed smile. "Had to run out of church earlier." She patted her belly, the perfect excuse suddenly coming to her. "I haven't been feeling so good, was afraid . . . you know."

The lie worked—Marla gave a sympathetic smile. "It's going around! Rev had it a couple weeks ago. Bobby was looking for you."

Tiff scrunched up her nose. "I bet he is. I feel so bad—didn't even have my cell phone to call him. It's still in my coat."

"Oh, gracious." Marla fumbled in her pocket, held up a finger. "Wait one second, I'll let you in to get it."

"Thank you," Tiff said gratefully a few minutes later when Marla held open the church door and ushered her in. "I sure hope you don't go getting this, now."

"Same here!" Marla took a step back but laughed good-naturedly.

Tiff slipped on her coat and pulled out the phone. Four missed calls and seven text messages.

They stepped back out to the street, and Tiff gave a wave. "See you in a few days."

"Need a ride?" Marla looked concerned.

Tiff just waved her off. "Nah, walking is good for this, I think. Least it makes me feel better."

"All right now, sugar. If you're sure."

"I'm sure." Tiff waved and walked off, back in the direction of her house.

She called Bobby, but it went to voicemail.

"Hey," she said, not even trying to force the humble. Even to her own ears, she sounded pitiful. "I'm sorry I ran out on you. I just got my phone back. Seeing James and all, and then not feeling good, I just had myself a good talk and a good cry with God. Headed home now, so call me when you can."

She disconnected, then texted Rebecca: *Sorry I worried you. All good now.*

The phone wasn't even all the way tucked into her pocket when it began to buzz.

"I'm so sorry," she said again, expecting Bobby.

But it was Rebecca. "Where are you?" her boss sounded worried.

"Walking back home from church."

"In this cold? I'll be right there."

The line went dead, and five minutes later Rebecca's sleek gray car was pulling up to the sidewalk. "Hop in," she said, rolling down the window.

Tiff's cheeks flushed, and she climbed in.

"I feel like such an idiot."

"It's okay . . ."

"It's really not." Tiff shot her a look out of the corner of her eye. "I'm sure Bobby's hopping mad."

Rebecca wrinkled her nose. "He was pretty worried about you. But I told him you probably needed some space to sort it all out."

"My stomach was all messed up this morning—"

"Mm-hm." Rebecca flicked her eyes back to the road as she drove but didn't push it.

"I feel better now. Much better."

"Good."

They pulled up at her house. James's bike wasn't there, and she breathed a sigh of relief. Maybe he'd steer clear all day. She could see Mrs. Crenshaw next door on her knees in the garden, her dog bounding up and down the fence line in a blur of white.

Tiff put her hand on the door. "I promise you, I'll get my head straight."

"Tiff . . ." Her boss had that big-sistery concerned look on her face still.

"No, wait." Tiff put up a hand, swallowed. "I know I've been wacky lately, and I don't mean to be. It's just . . . anyway, I'm getting it together, and it's not going to impact my work. I mean that."

Rebecca's eyes softened. "I know that, Tiff. I'm not worried about that. I'm just worried about you."

"I'm fine. Or, at least I will be. Promise."

Rebecca nodded, though her eyes still looked worried.

"You know, after everything I went through last year, I was in weekly therapy a long, long time," Rebecca said. "I still see my counselor, too, though now we just check in once a month."

Therapy. The idea of unburdening herself on some expert's couch sounded anything but appealing.

"It really helped, Tiff. Helped me get my head together. Between that and Jesus and, well, time—it was a real godsend. Here."

Rebecca rummaged through her wallet and pulled out a business card, passing it over. The card listed a counselor's name and contact information.

"She's great. And she's a Christian, too."

"Thanks, Rebecca."

Tiff climbed the steps to her front door and found Bobby's note taped to the handle. "Please call me," it read.

Next door, Choppers was yapping at her like she was some criminal.

"Hey there, Choppers." She waved, pocketing the note. She tossed an overly friendly smile Mrs. Crenshaw's way. "Garden's gonna look real nice come spring, Mrs. Crenshaw."

The woman glared at her beneath her floppy shade hat, but she held up a hand in greeting.

Inside, Tiff sagged against the closed front door and pulled out her phone again to text Bobby:

> *I left you a voicemail. Home finally. I am so so sorry. Call when free.*

Peaches meowed at her feet, and she followed him into the kitchen, poured extra crunchies in his dish, and filled a bowl for herself with cereal and milk.

She ate it upstairs in her bed, her ruined sweater dress tossed in the trash. Then she slept again, slept for what felt like hours.

She wasn't sure when he finally came back, but she woke to clomping up the stairs and then a soft tap-tap against her bedroom door.

"Sis?"

She stayed quiet.

"You okay in there?"

He tapped again, wiggling the handle, but she'd locked it. Thankfully.

What sounded like paper slid beneath her door, and then his footsteps were clomping away again, back to his room, then back downstairs.

She heard the front door open and then close again, and only then did she sit up, tiptoe to the door, and grab what he'd slid under.

It was a folded-up note with her name scrawled across the top.

"Tiff, I made a mistake coming here," it began.

She flopped belly-down on the bed and gritted her teeth. Whatever he had to say wouldn't change anything, but she couldn't resist reading it.

> I'm sorry. I should have told you I'm doing community service at the church, should have told you I was going to worship this morning. I just didn't think. I didn't figure on

that being your church, didn't think in a million years I'd run into you.

Community service? There? Tiff blinked. Between Rev's skin color and it being a house of the Lord, it was the last place on God's earth she expected her brother to volunteer. Probably doing it for the looks, she sniffed. Impressing some parole board with his racial healing and his newfound "faith." As if. She sure hoped Rev knew what he was getting into. And Devon. Her heart lurched.

She gripped the letter, kept reading till the end.

If you want me to move out, I will. Just give me a few days to get my stuff together and find someplace else. I never meant for any of this to cause you pain. I'm sorry for all the wrongs I've done.

Your brother always, James.

She wanted to punch someone. Instead, she settled for balling up the note and zinging it toward the trash can, where it landed right next to her ruined dress.

Get it together, Tiff. She swallowed back the bile and stood on shaky legs. No, she wasn't going to make him move out. She wouldn't give him the satisfaction of knowing he'd gotten to her. She was a survivor, always had been and always would be.

She caught a glimpse of her reflection in the mirror, lifted her chin, and stared herself down.

She'd handled far, far worse than this in her twenty-four years. She wasn't about to let her brother or her past wreck any of it now.

CHAPTER 25

Tiff

THE LONGER TIFF SAT THERE in that bed, palms itchy and heart all wiggly thumpy, the madder she got. Restless.

And hungry. The burning in her belly was more than anger. She looked at the time, realized she hadn't eaten anything all day but that small bowl of cereal.

James. She wondered where he'd gone at this hour. Probably out breaking into cars or hustling some other nice soul. *Changed, my foot.* She should probably search his room again.

Forget him.

Peaches was scratching at the door, and she sighed, stuck her feet in her slippers and padded to the door.

He looked up at her all pitiful, green eyes blinking mournfully in his ginger face.

"Guess you're hungry too, huh." She bent to scratch his neck, then scooped him up, cradling him all the way downstairs.

In the kitchen, he wriggled till she set him down, and he made a beeline for his empty food dish.

"Okay, okay."

She dumped crunchies in his bowl, then opened a can of wet food for him. He devoured it like he'd won the Kitty Lottery.

Hungry in earnest now, she bent into the refrigerator to see what she might fix.

Right smack front-and-center was a plate of scrambled eggs, bacon, and a few potatoes, all covered in plastic wrap. Her tummy rumbled. *Not on your life.*

She grabbed the plate, walked directly to the trash can, and dumped the contents in before she could change her mind. *The nerve.* No way was she taking charity from James Steadman of all people.

But the thought of eggs did make her mouth water. She found a clean frying pan and cracked fresh eggs in a bowl, added some salt and pepper and a dollop of milk. She ate them standing at the counter, barely tasting a thing.

It had been a long time since she'd been this good and mad. A flash came then, the day she'd stared across at her brother in that visiting room at the state prison and decided he was no longer fit to call family.

"You're gonna be okay, Lil Sis," he'd said then, like she was the one needing soothing, like she was the one locked up for who knew how long, her whole future blown to bits.

She'd stared back at him, wanting so bad to shove him, smack that blasted puppy-dog poor-baby-sister-what-have-I-done look right out of his eyes. Smack him so hard there'd be no coming back.

But of course she couldn't. Wouldn't. She'd settled for a glare.

"We're done, James. You and me—done." The fury in her voice had surprised even her. "No more brother-sister nothing, you hear me? Don't write me. Don't try to call me. You dug this hole, did this thing. I'm done with you, done with Mama and Daddy, done with it all. I mean it."

Her palms had stung, and she remembered looking down at where her fingernails were digging into her flesh. One had just about drawn blood. Good, she'd thought—tangible pain felt better than carrying it all in her heart.

She'd walked out that day and never looked back. Buried it all in one big mass grave of the past for good, just like it deserved. Set her sights on the future, on school, on her fresh start.

There, standing at the kitchen counter, empty plate still gripped tightly in her hands, she let the fury snake its way back. It wasn't her fault they were back to haunt her. None of it was her fault. It was all on them.

The pocket of her pajama pants buzzed, and she remembered she'd stuck her cell phone there.

Bobby. His name flashed across the screen. A text. Her heart tumbled. At least he was okay. In the back of her mind she'd been worried something had happened to him, some actual, dire reason he hadn't called back. Her logical mind told her it was a small enough town that if something had happened, she'd be one of the first to know, but still.

Her hands trembled as she pressed the button, read his words.

> *Sorry I didn't call. I do love you and I'm glad you're okay. But if I'm being honest, I am upset. Going to bed early tonight. Let's talk tomorrow.*

She swallowed. I love you, too, she typed, then pocketed the phone again.

She rinsed her plate, eyes blurring as she squeezed back angry tears, and set it in the dishwasher.

Even Bobby. Mad at her because she'd broken down and run out of church. Couldn't he tell she was hurting and desperate? Couldn't he understand her whole world, everything she'd worked for, was crashing in?

No. Bobby was a guy, a normal guy, just like the rest of them.

No one got it. No one understood the sheer force of will it took to stuff a mountain of pain and fear and rage back into a tiny crayon box and shut the lid tight. Didn't even answer her text, didn't call her back, because he was "upset."

It wasn't like she'd yelled at him, was mad at him. All she'd done was run out of there. Now she was to blame.

She thought of the business card Rebecca had slipped her—therapy—and gritted her teeth.

Then again, Bobby had a right to be upset, or at least worried. She leaned with both arms against the sink, trying to steady her breathing. He didn't understand, hadn't grown up like she had. No one had. His family was picture-perfect, Mama Smathers all proper and right, taking her boys to church and fixing Sunday dinners and raising them up to know things, like how to tie a tie or say "please" and "thank you" or hold the door open for a lady even if you don't want to. Mr. Smathers all quiet and hard-working, running that grocery store day after day, coming home to his family and reading the paper and mowing the lawn.

Those Smathers boys didn't know one single thing about fending for themselves, having to cook supper when you're seven years old or how to jam a chair just right under your door handle so your stupid-drunk parents couldn't get in and beat on you because you left your cereal bowl in the sink.

Tiff closed her eyes and felt the world shift. *No more.* Pictured all the crazy—all the mess with her brother, all the anger, all the memories—balled up like that note James had written her. Balled it all up into one giant, crinkly, smushed mass and stuffed down deep in the bottom of the wastebasket. Better yet, the garbage disposal.

Gone for good.

James might be here, but Tiff wasn't giving him any more power over her life. Tomorrow she'd wake up nice and early, get all pretty, get her head straight, and get into work like a normal person. She'd finish both her articles first thing. At lunch she'd go see Bobby at the grocery, set things right again. She'd talk with James, get an ironclad plan set for how long he had left and where he was going next.

She'd get on with life, tuck it all away. Handle it.

Show life who was boss—her. Tiff Almost-Smathers. Newspaper editor, responsible adult, fiancée. Survivor.

Who needs therapy?

She set the coffee for the next day, flicked off all the downstairs lights, and resolutely climbed the stairs back to her room. She picked out her clothes for the morning, down to the jewelry and shoes, and got her work bag all ready. Washed her face, flossed, and even remembered to put on lotion.

She climbed into bed and was asleep in minutes. She was ready.

The next morning she woke up before the alarm and lay still a moment, eyes closed. The house was quiet all around her. Was Bobby still mad? Her eyes flew open and she stared at the ceiling, peering for the cracks she knew were there but couldn't quite see in the pre-dawn light. She hoped he wasn't mad still, prayed he wasn't. But in her heart, she knew it'd be okay.

Today, she'd set everything straight. For good. With Bobby, and with James.

Had her brother even come home?

She shouldn't care, didn't really care, but curiosity had her in the bathroom, face washed and clothes on, and putting finishing touches on her makeup in ten minutes flat. She cracked the door and saw his own bedroom door across from hers was closed. It had been shut yesterday, too, which didn't mean anything.

Peaches, asleep on the living room sofa, barely budged when she ran a hand over his soft fur on the way to the kitchen.

An energy bar and a quick fill of her coffee travel mug and she was out the door, the morning sky still dark with just a hint of glow on the horizon. Her breath puffed out as she clicked the locks on her car door, set her work bag in the backseat.

She could see James's bike parked in front of the house as she slowly backed her car out of the driveway. Mystery solved. *Not like I was worried or anything.* It was just good to know where he was. Keeping tabs. Like the old days, except not.

At the newspaper office, she had her first story knocked out well before official business hours and was halfway through the second when a key turned in the lock.

"Mornin', sunshine!" Millie, the receptionist, hurried in, her bag clunking around her legs as she walked to her desk. "You beat us."

Rebecca followed close behind, turning the closed sign to open and shutting the door.

"I'm pretty sure New York was never this cold," her boss said, shivering as she crossed the room to her own desk.

Tiff laughed, kept her eyes on her computer screen. "That I somehow don't believe."

Rebecca peered over her shoulder. "How's the county council rewrite going?"

"Just about done," Tiff said, typing. "I emailed you the other one, on the school zoning. Oh, you still want me to call that lady about the grand opening?"

"Nah, I took care of that Friday when you were out. And the latest on the car thefts, too."

Tiff swallowed. If it were James, she'd kill him with her own bare hands. Well, not really, but at least chase him so far out of town he'd lose her number and never come back. "Great."

Fifteen minutes later, Tiff hit "send" and swiveled her chair toward her boss. "Just emailed it."

Rebecca eyed Millie, who was on the phone talking like the call would go on a while.

"You doing any better?" Rebecca mouthed.

Tiff nodded extra hard. "Completely. Back on track."

Rebecca gave her that come-on-now look.

Tiff shrugged and kept her voice low. "Really. I had a lot of time to think yesterday. I'm sick and tired of playing this weepy little victim all the time. You-know-who and I are sitting down tonight, working out his exit plan, and bam." She pantomimed wiping her hands clean. "Done."

Rebecca looked impressed. "Yay for you."

Tiff grinned, tipping her head toward her boss. "I learned from the best."

"Now you're talkin'."

They both laughed, and then the phone was ringing again and deadline day was in full swing.

The morning passed in a flurry of phone calls and typing news copy. It was after one by the time Tiff looked at the clock. She'd almost worked through lunch! Not today—today she had a mission to complete.

In the car outside the grocery store, Tiff grabbed the notebook she kept in her console and scrawled out her apology, just in case Bobby was too busy for an actual talk. She raked her hands through her hair, added a touch of color to her lips, and dug in her purse for the mini perfume spray, which she spritzed on her wrists. Then she pulled down the visor, checked her reflection. Not bad. She spritzed a little extra scent on her apology letter just for effect.

Bobby's truck was parked in his usual spot, just like she'd expected. All she had to do was go in, track him down, and be her sweetest, kindest self. Her real self—not this half-crazed, roller-coaster emotional wreck she'd been lately. No wonder he was upset.

Bobby wasn't up at the front when she walked in, or behind the counter at customer service, his normal spot on Mondays.

"Hi, Mr. Smathers," she waved at Bobby's daddy, who was carrying a box taller than himself toward the cereal aisle.

"Hey, Tiff," Mr. Smathers said but kept walking, hurrying wherever he was headed.

Bobby wasn't in the back either, or in produce. She grabbed a salad from the bin to bring back to the office, kept searching.

Finally she rounded the last corner, by the meats, and saw him. He was at the end, over by the open-air coolers.

But he wasn't alone.

There was a woman with him—a girl. A pretty girl. That girl in the booties and dress from the sandwich shop that day, with the perfect hair and teeth.

Bobby's ex, Natalie Motts.

Tiff's feet felt like they were stuck to the grocery store linoleum with superglue. She stared, watched him smile and laugh.

Watched the girl put her hand on Bobby's arm like they were old friends, point at something on her cell phone, something they were peering at. *No.* Her heart began to hammer.

"Nat, I do remember that! It was so long ago!" Bobby laughed, his whole full-body laugh. The laugh he used with her.

The salad Tiff was holding tumbled to the ground then, lettuce and tomatoes and croutons in a messy heap at her feet, and they both looked up, saw her. The girl—Nat—curved her lips in a friendly smile, but Bobby's eyes locked on hers, round.

Something flashed across his face. Surprise? Anger? Dread?

It couldn't be. Not Bobby. Not him!

Tiff felt her shoulders straighten, almost regally, and her chin jut high. *This isn't happening.*

Slowly, she turned and strode toward the front doors, leaving the mess of salad right where it lay.

CHAPTER 26

No KEYS. Tiff rubbed her palms at the thought, cursed her own foolishness. No note, either. She'd left them both in a pile of salad, silent witnesses to her humiliation.

She stood there at the car, no way in, staring at her purse on the front seat, the cell phone tucked inside, and waited for the tears.

But her cheeks were dry.

She glanced back at the entrance to the grocery, at the lady and her baby walking in through the sliding doors, at the old couple walking out. Then she turned, glanced across toward the newspaper office.

Oh, Jesus. She closed her eyes, the chilly breeze gently lifting her hair. Like a caress.

This time, there was no Bobby running after her, shouting her name, calling out for her to stop. This time, she didn't run.

She just started walking.

At the corner she kept going. It felt good to walk. She let herself feel the rhythm, the wind flitting through her long hair.

Every step shed a tear she didn't have to cry.

She walked on, walked all the way past the center of Dahlia, past their gazebo and their swing. Past her house and on, left at the gas station and past Rebecca's Granny's house, which was Rebecca's house, too.

She walked past Mr. McMasters's garden, where come summer there'd be blueberry bushes out front, past the school where she'd been four mornings ago, remembered the happy laugh-shrieks of the kids as they showed her the project they'd made, smiles wide and innocent as they lined up for the camera.

Her body knew where she was going even if her mind didn't. And when she got to the small brick church, looked up at the simple cross up top and the familiar wooden front doors, and sank like a ragdoll on the first step, she closed her eyes again. *Thank you.*

But instead of going into the church, she found herself standing up on shaky legs, walking next door to the parsonage.

To Marla.

The pastor's wife answered Tiff's knock like she knew she was coming. Took one look at her and wrapped her in her arms.

"Oh, baby girl," Marla whispered into her hair, patting her like she was four instead of twenty-four, and all the tears Tiff had been holding back just poured out like a busted carton of milk.

Marla led her inside, and they sat in the living room a long, long time, Marla patting her, Tiff sobbing it all out not in words but in wails and moans. Her head was on Marla's lap, and it didn't feel weird at all like it should but how Tiff imagined heaven would feel, like Marla was some angel, some mother-angel.

Words didn't matter. What could she say?

Finally, the tears subsided. Tiff rubbed at her eyes, pulled up so she could look at Marla.

"He—he was with her."

Marla didn't ask who, just let the words fall between them, settle like dust. Her brown eyes were liquid pools of sadness, and she cupped Tiff's face in her hands.

"Are you sure, Tiff? Sometimes what a body sees and what's real aren't always the same thing."

Tiff let her eyes fall shut. The way the girl, the way Nat, had rested her hand on Bobby's arm, so familiar. The way they'd laughed.

The look in Bobby's eyes when he'd looked up, seen Tiff standing there. Frozen.

It was the look of someone who'd been caught, someone whose secret had just dumped out and now sat like a puddle of dirty washwater in the middle of the kitchen floor.

Someone exposed.

I'm sure, she wanted to say. Except she wasn't, not really. She couldn't even trust her own brain anymore. Her own instincts.

Marla reached out then, grabbed both her hands. Squeezed.

Tiff squeezed back, held on tight.

"There's more."

"Your brother?"

Tiff swallowed. "I didn't know he was doing community service here. Had no idea."

Marla pressed her lips together. "Rev told me last night. Felt real bad he hadn't put your last names together, hadn't thought you might be kin."

"It's not his fault. James and I look nothing alike. Besides, I'm still new here. Haven't even officially joined."

They sat, quiet in the still room. Tiff could hear the faint tick of the wall clock, looked up to see it was after four.

"Come." Marla stood. "Let's have some hot chocolate."

Marla made it the old-fashioned way, standing at the stove, stirring, the repetitive clank of the metal spoon against the saucepan oddly comforting. Something good-smelling was simmering on the back of the stove, a soup or stew, and Tiff felt her body relax, let it all just pour out. Marla let her, the words rolling out soft and raw between them.

"You've been keeping this all bottled up inside you," Marla said just once, eyes full of understanding like somehow she knew. Like she'd been there, too. By now, she was seated with Tiff at the kitchen table, mugs between them as if they did this every day of the week. "You were bound to break."

Looking at it now, Tiff wondered why she'd hadn't seen it that way before.

"I think you're right, Marla." A chuckle spilled from Tiff's lips as she gazed across at the pastor's wife, all strong and put together from the chunky amethyst necklace to her dark-wash jeans to how she seemed to know exactly what to say. "It's funny. The more I try to get it all together, the more of a train wreck I become."

"One of these days, I'll tell you my story." Marla took a sip of hot chocolate, eyed Tiff over the top of the mug as if she knew what she was getting at. "It's too long for today, but come back and talk to me again. You and I have a lot more in common than you might think. Only God . . ."

Marla pointed skyward and let the words sink in.

As if on cue, the kitchen door banged open and little Devon bounded in, bright orange basketball in his hands and Rev trailing not far behind.

"Well, hey there, Miss Tiff!" Rev boomed like he saw her there in their kitchen every day of the week. Maybe that's what regular people did, go baring their souls instead of keeping everything locked up tight inside. "You staying for dinner?"

Tiff blinked, remembered her car parked back at the store. Realized she'd never even gone back to work.

"I—I can't." She tried to smile at the pastor, but the expression felt more like a grimace.

"You're missing out. Marla's the best cook this side of Mississippi." Rev clapped her shoulder kindly as he moved through the kitchen, gave Marla a kiss on the cheek on his way toward the stairs.

Devon gave Marla a hug and Tiff a little wave, then raced

through like he had places to be and things to do. Tiff could hear his kid-feet bounding up the stairs.

"Take your high-tops off in the house!" Marla shouted after the boy, then smiled back at Tiff.

"Sure you don't want to stay? There's plenty."

Tiff shook her head, pushed in her chair. "I never told Rebecca where I was going. I've got to get back." She bit her lip, debated, then blurted, "And I left my car back there, too."

Marla stood with her, grabbing her car keys and her pocketbook from the hook by the door.

"Well, that I can help with." She smiled at Tiff and held open the door.

Marla dropped her at the newspaper office.

Tiff could see Rebecca's car still parked outside, and a rush of relief spilled over her. She looked again, saw her own blue car parked there, too. *What in the world . . . ?*

Rebecca burst from her chair when the door banged open and Tiff walked in.

"Tiff!" Her boss wrapped her in a hug so tight Tiff could barely breathe. Rebecca pulled back, looked into her face like she was going to say more, then pressed her mouth in a quivery line and hugged her again.

"I'm sorry I worried you," Tiff mumbled into Rebecca's hair.

"It's okay, I knew—"

"How?" *Bobby*. Tiff felt like someone had stabbed her in the chest with an ice pick. "He came here?"

Rebecca nodded, eyes shiny, and Tiff could see her boss's face was all blotchy like she'd been crying.

"He was here the better part of the afternoon. Brought your keys by."

"I guess he told you."

"Tiff, it wasn't what you think."

Oh, no. Tiff knew exactly what she'd seen. Or did she? She pulled away from Rebecca, afraid to say a word for fear she'd lash out at her. Say something she'd regret.

She sat heavily in her desk chair. Her purse and car keys rested on the edge of the desk, and she stared hard at the keys—the monogrammed key chain Bobby'd given her, with her initials, back before he'd officially proposed. A cursive T on one side, an L on the other, and a big swoopy S in the center. No one knew but them it stood for what he told her he'd intended: for the S to represent not Steadman but Smathers.

A wave of dizziness washed over her, and she sank her head into her hands. This couldn't be happening. Not to them.

Tiff could hear her boss roll her desk chair around so it was right up next to her own, heard the hiss as Rebecca sat down heavily.

"Look at me, Tiff." Rebecca's voice was firm.

Tiff swiveled her way but kept her eyes trained on her hands, now clutched in Rebecca's own.

"That girl he was talking to? There was absolutely nothing going on between them. She was some old girlfriend who'd just moved back in town—"

"Nat," Tiff whispered.

"Yes, Nat. Not five minutes before you walked up they'd run into each other, and she was showing him some pictures on her phone. It was completely innocent."

Tiff set her jaw. "I don't know about that, Rebecca."

"Tiff, he swore up and down . . ."

"You didn't see the way she had her hand on his arm, all 'Oh, Bobby this and Bobby that' and all that nonsense! You didn't see the way he looked at her. The way he laughed with her. Rebecca, they were out-and-out flirting." Pain seared through her temples, and she rubbed at her head.

Rebecca put a hand on her shoulder. "Tiff Steadman, that boy loves you! I mean, he L-O-V-E loooovvvveeees you." She drew out the word in a way that normally would have made Tiff laugh, but not today. "Do you hear what I'm saying?"

Tiff said nothing, just breathed. In and out. In and out. The room was starting to spin.

"Tiff. I don't know what you saw or think you saw, but I know what's true. He is your fiancé, he's one-hundred percent in love with you, and he is flat-out, straight-up worried about you."

"I hear you." Tiff's voice was small.

Rebecca wrapped her in another hug.

Finally, she pulled back and squeezed Tiff's hands.

"I promised Bobby I'd text him when you got here."

"Rebecca . . ."

"I promised. And you know it's only right."

Tiff knew it. Only she didn't much like it.

Rebecca stood and went to her own desk. Tiff could hear her tapping out something on her cell phone, presumably some message to Bobby.

Tiff wondered how many messages her own phone held. She glanced at her purse, where she knew her phone was tucked. Pondered pulling it out, seeing what he had to say, only she didn't want to hear any excuses. Any lies.

Her eyes stung, only the tears wouldn't come.

Bobby must have been waiting for Rebecca's text. She could hear the thrum of his truck as he pulled up outside, heard the door open and then close with a bang. Heard his footsteps walk slowly to the door, twist the handle.

She couldn't look at him.

"I'll drive Tiff's car." Rebecca's words seemed to echo in the tension. "Granny will pick me up at your house. She's on her way home from volunteering anyhow."

Tiff and Bobby said nothing to each other on the drive to her house. Tiff just curled up in the passenger seat, leaned her head against the window, and watched the town pass by.

A couple times he cleared his throat, and she squeezed her eyes shut. Don't talk, she pleaded, as though her thoughts could will him silent. Don't say a word.

And then they were at her house, and he was ushering her inside, twisting her own key in her own door lock like she was some incapable child.

"I know you're upset." His voice was soft.

At his words, she went from numb to full-on rage in an instant. *Upset? You have no idea.*

CHAPTER 27

Tiff

Upset? "What did you say?"

Her voice was quiet, controlled, but she couldn't contain the shake.

He didn't look at her, just led her to the couch and flipped on a lamp like he owned the place.

Sat down.

Instead of sitting next to him, she perched cross-legged on the other end of the couch and trained her eyes on his until he raised his gaze to hers.

"Upset?" she repeated. The vein in her temple throbbed thick and hot.

She wanted to scream, tear her hair out. Tear his. *No.* This time she wasn't going to get hysterical, wasn't going to run or stomp out. This time she was going to face this like a woman.

"Tiff, you're blowing this out of proportion—"

"Bobby Samuel Smathers, don't you even for a second shut me down like I'm the one who's crazy, like I'm the one who . . ."

His hands shot out, grabbed hers, but she yanked them away, glared at him.

"I saw you." Her words were a hiss.

Bobby's jaw tightened. "You saw me with an old friend who just came back in town showing me pictures on her cell phone. Tiff, that's what you saw. Don't make this out to be more than it was."

The look on his face in the grocery store zinged through her mind. Shocked. Caught.

"She was awfully familiar."

"That's just Nat!"

"Well, that's not okay." She scooched back even farther, crossed her legs tighter so she was seated upright and jammed against the sofa pillow so she could look at him better. About as far away from him as she could be. Every muscle in her body felt like a tight cord.

"Tiff, look. Clearly, this is a really hard time for you. Harder than I can imagine. I want to be there for you as you walk through this, but it's like you're bent on walking through alone."

Born alone, die alone. The words came unbidden, and she shoved them back.

"If you're talking about my brother, which I imagine you are, you don't have to worry about that anymore." Her words sounded cold to her own ears. Almost professional. "I counted up the days today. Sixty-eight days till he's gone—that's just shy of ten weeks."

Bobby shook his head. "And then what?"

"What's that supposed to mean?"

"I mean, he's gone as in gone forever? Tiff, he's your blood. He's family. He'll be at the wedding, he'll . . ."

"He will not be at my wedding."

"Our wedding." Bobby sounded hurt.

She raised her eyes to the ceiling and forced herself to breathe. "Of course 'our' wedding. That's not what I meant. And I have no intention whatsoever of letting any inch of my past have a part in my future. Once he's gone, he's gone."

She could hear the shrill in the last word. If she had a mirror, she knew exactly who she'd look like. Mama. She shook her head at the image, forced it away.

"Look, Bobby, you don't know what I went through growing up. You don't know all the details of what he did to wind up in prison. I went through great pains burying it all away, thought I'd done it for good."

"I know what he did, Tiff." His voice was gentle. "But I also know he served his time and he's trying to move on. I mean, he was at church yesterday, for gracious' sake!"

"Come on, Bobby. It's just an act. Who do you think's the one doing all those car thefts in town?" The words slipped out, but once her suspicions were out, she felt bolder. Angrier. "Don't even tell me you haven't thought about it."

"Tiff, listen to yourself." Bobby pulled back and stared at her. His eyes got all big, and she peered closer, realized she wasn't seeing things.

Bobby had tears in his eyes.

It stunned her into silence.

"I love you." His voice cracked. "Love you with all my heart. But I see now you've got a lot of healing to do. We can't be walking down the aisle till you get straight inside, let go of some of that pain. I get that you grew up hard . . ."

She stopped listening. *Can't be walking down the aisle . . .* Her heart felt like it might freeze inside her chest.

"Wait a minute. Are you calling off our wedding?" Her words sounded like shattered glass. Tears stung the back of her eyelids, tears she wouldn't release. *No. No no no.*

"That's not what I'm saying!" He reared back like she'd slapped him.

She was afraid to speak. Afraid to say a word.

"I just want you to let me in, Tiff. I want to know what you went through. The past isn't all bad if it made you who you are. It made you Tiff. The woman I love."

"I am who I am in spite of my past, not because of it. Hear me? You didn't grow up with a mama and daddy who drank into oblivion, beat each other senseless, sometimes beat you too just 'cause they could." She squeezed her eyes shut as the words tumbled out. "You didn't grow up scared to go to sleep without your door jammed shut, a chair beneath the handle just in case. Didn't spend school nights sleeping in the barn with your brother for fear your parents were gonna burn the house down. I left it all behind the day I left home, Bobby Smathers. Left every bit of it. That woman wasn't my mama. She just birthed me and then plumb forgot about me for the booze. I left her without a backwards look. For all I care she can burn in h—"

"I thought your mama was dead." Bobby's words were quiet.

Her eyes stayed shut, like if she forced them to stay shut she wouldn't have to face what she'd just done.

Or just undone.

A minute passed, then another. She could feel his eyes on hers.

She opened her eyes, started to speak, but Bobby reached out gently. Tenderly.

Cupped her face.

"You ask me, this past you left behind? I'm not sure you left it at all. Sounds to me like it's eating you up inside. Sounds like it's something you're gonna have to face up to, like it or not."

His hand on her face felt warm, sweet. She wanted to melt into it. Forget the past!

But his hand pulled away, and he sat across from her, a sad smile on his lips.

"I don't think it's any accident your brother got released from prison when he did. I think God wants you to sort this mess out before it gets the best of you."

"It's not going to get the best of me."

"I know."

Bobby stood and picked up his keys from the end table.

"Where are you going?"

"Home."

"You're . . . leaving me?" The words came from her lips, but to her ears they were coming from a stranger's.

"I'm not leaving you. But I am going home. You take your time. Focus on your brother. Sort stuff out in your head."

She looked up at him, eyes glassy with tears and pain. *You think I'm crazy. Crazy like Mama.*

"When am I going to see you again?"

"I don't know. But you don't need to worry about that. You just need to focus on you. Get Tiff sorted out."

"Are we still engaged?"

"Tiff." He held up a hand. "You don't need to be thinking about that right now."

"Bobby!"

"Tiff. Stop."

Her heart felt like it was going to break as she watched him walk to the door. Turn the handle and twist the front door to lock behind him. Step through and close it softly behind.

She sat frozen on the couch, her cheek still slightly warm from where his hand had cupped her face not minutes before. Heard his truck fire up, then jam into reverse and back out, onto the street.

Away.

Gone.

She wrapped her arms around her legs, let the tears fall hard and fast. *You're all alone.*

CHAPTER 28

James

IN HIS BEDROOM James had tried not to listen to what was going on downstairs, but the walls were thin, and he could hear most everything.

His fault. It was all his fault.

If he could have escaped through the window without them hearing, he would have, but of course they'd have heard him.

When she'd gotten to the part about the car thefts, and church all being an act, his chest seized up and his stomach went all rumbly like he was about to be sick.

It was one thing to think he wasn't wanted, to think she was just putting up with him till enough time had passed. But it was a whole different thing to know it was truth.

She didn't even want him at her wedding.

Not that he'd have gone. By then he'd maybe be down in Orangeburg, working the farm with Vic or doing something else. Something to get his own life back on track.

But knowing she didn't want him there, that hurt. Bad.

He heard Bobby leave, heard his sister wailing on the couch. Sounding like a little lost puppy, all pitiful. Worse almost than she'd sounded when they were kids. Then, she'd just been scared.

Now, he was hearing the sound of flat-out shattered loneliness, the sound of no more hope. Gone.

His heart broke for her, and he wanted to go to her, like when they were young.

But she didn't want him comforting her anymore. Not ever.

That was it. Tomorrow he'd talk to Rev, see if he could stay at the church, or maybe Rev knew somebody he could bunk with awhile. Just ten more weeks, just like Tiff said.

If worse came to worst, he could call his parole officer, tell him things weren't so good at his sister's and see if he could get him into one of those in-between places.

James sat heavily on the bed, his weight making the springs creak. His Bible was where he'd left it this morning, right on the edge of the nightstand, and he picked it up, stared at the cover, the words "Holy Bible" stamped in gold on top. His sleeves were pushed up at the elbows, every tattoo blaring loud and clear and nasty.

He remembered each one, each story. The chisel after his Daddy'd beaten him so hard behind the shed he broke his nose. It wasn't the first time his nose had been broken, but it hurt like blazes. After, James had been working with some hand tools, picked up a chisel. He'd held it there in his hands, rage flaring hot like he'd just injected fiery fuel into his veins and it was racing like mad to get to the finish line. If his daddy laid a hand on him again, James knew exactly what he'd do with that chisel, daddy or no daddy.

Lucky for him, James's daddy steered clear.

The pair of dice, six and five on their faces—his numbers. Gotten those after he'd jacked his fifth and sixth cars for Bone Willem, earned himself a nice stash of emergency cash. All gone now, of course.

The skull and crossbones on his forearm, that had been his first ink. Took three times to get it just right. He'd wanted it authentic

Pirate style, all kill-or-be-killed, take-what-you-want, everything he thought he stood for in those days.

The hammer, for his old gang. Everyone in the crew had one.

And the last one he could see on that arm. He wasn't even sure Tiff knew about that one, even though he'd gotten it for her. A small black mangy cat, fierce but tender. Just like his sister.

Back then, back when he'd gotten all those tats, he'd thought they'd really, truly meant something. They represented who he was, who he wanted to be. Now they all just looked stupid, like some little kid's coloring book all up and down his arm.

He could barely remember that guy. His life before the slammer was just one hazy chunk of climbing trees and watching out for his sister and stealing cars. Like he wanted to become the very thing he hated—a dirtbag just like his old man, all his cares resting solely on Numero Uno. Forget everybody else.

Looking down at the Bible, James debated opening it, but he didn't think he could handle it tonight. He'd always known he was worthless, but reading all that stuff from Paul made him feel lower than low. New creation was one thing, but what was he reading this morning, all that stuff about holiness? There was no way under the sun he could get that good. Not someone like him.

"It's times like this, when you don't wanna read your Bible, that you've gotta pick it up right quick," Pastor Chad had told him more than once.

James gritted his teeth. Downstairs, Tiff's crying had faded to silence.

Maybe she'd fallen fast asleep on the sofa. Or maybe she'd already put herself to bed and he was too caught up in his own memories to notice.

He sat there, Bible in hand, not sure where to start. Then he found himself setting the book down, climbing to his feet, and tiptoeing downstairs.

Before he could lose his nerve, he stepped off the bottom stair. Peeking over the couch, he saw her there, legs drawn up and fists all tight like she used to sleep when she was a kid.

A wave of tenderness washed over him as he watched his sister breathe in and out, in and out. Funny, he hadn't let himself really look at her till now, like he'd been afraid to meet her eyes full on.

It was dumb, he knew it. Not like he'd done anything to her when he'd done all that bad stuff. Not like he'd hurt her when he'd helped put that guy—that boy—in the hospital.

But right now, staring down at her, it felt like he had—like he'd wronged his own Lil Sis.

He rubbed at his face as the thoughts settled in and was surprised to find his cheeks were wet.

That was the thing about sin. The realization hit him without warning. Doing bad, doing evil, wasn't just hurting himself. It was hurting the people he loved.

It was hurting Jesus, too. Like one more nail he, James, was nailing into his own savior's flesh there on the cross.

The ache in his chest spread, and he sank to his knees, the tears flowing down his cheeks till he could see a few drop on the floor, run together in a tiny pool.

A pool of pain.

James had gone and turned into his own daddy, the very thing he'd run from. Worse than Daddy, for as far as James knew, his daddy hadn't ever gone to prison for aggravated assault.

You're bigger than your sin, James Steadman. Pastor Chad's voice whispered through the room as James sat there on his knees, the tears drying on his cheeks. *Christ died for you so you could have new life. All you've got to do is grab hold of it and turn toward the good, let the bad drift away.*

Not let the bad chase him down and eat him up daily like he'd been letting it.

James rose on shaky legs and crept to the armchair, where the soft blue blanket was folded neatly.

He tucked it around his sister there on the sofa.

She stirred, eyes hazy with sleep. "James." She murmured it, and his heart soared. Then her eyes fell shut again and she was off in dreamland.

He'd set things right with her one way or the other. He wasn't sure how, but he would.

He didn't know how he did it, tired as he was, but he didn't let sleep come that night. Instead, he read the Bible all night—the "good book," Pastor Chad called it. Read into the prophets, a lot of which he didn't understand, but they made him sit up straighter. They sure weren't lying when they said the Christ was foretold.

At dawn he slept an hour or so, then woke up again when he heard the front door slam shut and Tiff's car start in the driveway.

After eight, the clock told him.

He showered and dressed, fixed some eggs and sat at the kitchen table all proper, even poured himself a tall glass of water with his coffee.

When the sun was good and high, he set out on his bike toward the church.

The wind had settled down, and the day was far warmer than it'd been yesterday. He looked around as he pedaled, at the twiggy ghosts of trees outside of businesses, imagined them all fluffy with leaves come summertime.

Not that he'd be here when summer came, but he bet it'd be pretty.

When he got to the church, he parked his bike on the side, knocking loud on the fellowship hall door as he twisted the handle and let himself in.

"Rev?"

"Back here. That you, James?"

James didn't know why, but the words warmed his heart. "Yessir."

He wandered through the empty room. He could still smell whatever'd been cooking the day prior, some mixture of spices and meat and sugary sweet. Dessert.

He found Rev in his office finishing the last bite of a doughnut. Rev gestured to the open box, and James took one, rubbing the doughnut powder on the thighs of his jeans as he sat in the chair across from Rev.

"Don't you go telling my wife you caught me with sweets, now." Rev winked, and James could tell he was kidding. Rev and his wife seemed bent on this cat-and-mouse over healthy eating, him breaking the rules and her setting them.

"Your secret stops with me, Rev."

Rev burst out laughing, then took another, smaller, doughnut bite. "Woman's prob'ly got my office bugged with some hidden camera, knowing her, but at least she's keeping tabs on me."

"She probably planted those doughnuts for you to find."

Rev laughed again. "You might be right. So." Rev finished the doughnut, chewed thoughtfully. "I don't know why I didn't put two and two together, but I'm a bit thick sometimes. You're Tiff Steadman's brother?"

Shame bubbled over. "Yessir. That's why I'm here—"

"I'm not saying you should've told me or anything." Rev held up his hands. "That's your business. But it does explain why she looked at you like you were some ghost in worship on Sunday and ran out before the music even got started. I take it things aren't so good between you—and that she didn't know she'd be seeing you here."

James winced and looked at his hands, laced together in his lap.

"I didn't think."

"Humans aren't wired to be perfect in how we do things, my friend." Rev peered at him. "How'd she take it?"

James met his eyes. "We haven't seen each other."

"Ah."

Rev took another doughnut, offered the box again to James. They ate in silence. James couldn't remember the last time he'd had a powdered doughnut. High school, maybe.

"I try to stay out of her way." James shrugged. "We're both always coming and going, and I worked a long shift yesterday."

"Ever hear that story about the man who wanted to buy his dream house?" Rev finished the second doughnut, closed the box, and pushed it out of reach. James guessed even preachers had temptations. "Kept waiting and waiting for the owners to put it on the market, then kept waiting for the price to drop. Finally it sold out from under his nose for lower than market value, far less than he'd have paid. He waited so long he waited himself out of an opportunity."

"Like me and Tiff," James said.

"Could be."

"Rev." James swirled the words around in his mind like he was taste-testing them. "I've got to get out of her hair. It's gonna get ugly, I just know it. You think I might be able to stay here? At the church?"

Rev sighed, a long whooshy kind of sigh, like air being let out of a saggy balloon. "I know it'd be easiest if I said yes. But you know it's not the right thing."

I know. The silence settled between them.

Then James asked in a small voice, "Think you might be able to talk to her for me? To Tiff." He waited, but the preacher still didn't say anything. "You're her pastor and all. Maybe you can tell her some of the stuff I can't."

Rev turned sad eyes on him again. "I can try, but truth is, I don't think that's the best thing, either."

"Well, what is, then?" James huffed out a breath he immediately regretted. "Sorry. I'm . . . frustrated. She—she thinks it's all a con."

"A con?"

"Thinks I'm not really a Christian, thinks it's all a big act, thinks I'm the one who's been going around breaking into cars."

Rev blinked. "Are you?"

"No!" James sat up straight. "I mean, no to the car stuff. I see why she thinks it—I used to do some real bad stuff, stuff like that, when I was a kid. But yes to the Christian part." A dry laugh escaped his lips. "That's the only thing keeping me hanging on, if I'm tellin' the truth."

"You and me both." Rev held up a fist and James met it for a knuckle-bump, but not before James saw the sliver of the swastika from beneath his own sleeve.

James pulled his hand back, tugged his sleeve down, and tucked his hands in his lap again.

"I did some real bad stuff, Rev. Stuff that makes me sick inside to think about." James's voice was so soft he could barely hear himself.

Rev scooted the chair so he could lean back, crossed his arms behind his head all casual. "Did I ever tell you why I became a pastor?"

James considered. He'd never wondered why any pastor decided to become a pastor.

"I don't know. I guess I just figured you were really into church, like all the music and the preaching and such. Like, born that way." James tried to picture Rev as a kid, imagined him dancing to the organ music and helping light candles and doing all that religion stuff.

Rev bent over he was laughing so hard. "Not in the least. Fact is,

I couldn't stand church for the longest time."

"Really?" James started laughing, too. "I figured that must be a requirement or something—you know, 'must like church.'"

Rev wiped his eyes, shook his head. "Shoo, not me. I tried anything I could when I was a kid to get out of it. We went to a pretty big church, and my older sisters, they all helped in the nursery, so my mama used to drop me off in the kids' wing. When I got older, I wised up, started walking myself. Walked myself straight out the door and onto the playground!"

"Wha—?"

"No joke! Me and my friend Troy, see, there was a school on the other side of that church, and we used to sneak out the side church door and run as fast as our legs would take us. Spent the whole church service outside. Our choir sang big and loud, and we timed it just right so when the choir started belting out their last tune, Troy and I would creep on back. Worked like a charm, every time."

"So how'd you . . . you know . . ."

"Get from there to sitting right here?" Rev shrugged. "My buddy Troy, he got shot. Dead. Fourteen years old at the time. Could have been me, too, only that was the day my mama needed me to haul the trash for her, so instead of hanging out at the arcade with the other kids, I was grumbling and carrying on about that nasty trash and how none a' my friends had to do this nonsense, grumbled so good and well I got myself a whupping and got myself locked in my room the rest of the night."

"But—but your buddy?"

Rev sighed, steepled his hands. "Yep. While I was in my room being a big baby, some gangbanger shot up the arcade aiming for someone else. Troy was just in the wrong place at the wrong time."

"Oh, man." James couldn't imagine. "So you turned to God, started going to church then?"

"No way." Rev shook his head. "I was so mad at God I never

wanted to lay eyes on church again. See, Troy was the better of both of us. The one always keeping us out of the really deep trouble, know what I mean? And here he up and gets killed, not me. I couldn't understand what kind of God would do something like that."

James had never heard a preacher talk this way—full on real like this. Chad was real, but he'd grown up a preacher's kid, knew he'd wanted to be a preacher since he was young. Rev's story was way different.

"I ran from God a good long time. Then I met the prettiest girl I ever did lay eyes on. I mean, she was flat-out, drop-dead, you-gotta-be-kidding-me gorgeous."

James couldn't help it. He laughed.

Rev laughed, too. "That's right. A woman led me to God. I started going to church 'cause she wouldn't have one single thing to do with me unless my rear end was in a church pew on Sunday morning. And you can bet that's exactly where my rear end needed to be."

"So you started going, and liked it?"

"The liking it took awhile. But that woman? She sure was worth it. Why, she even let me marry her." Rev pointed to a picture on the bookshelf of him and his wife on their wedding day. "Helped me let go of the past, realize it wasn't God who took Troy. God was there in spite of the bad, trying his best to, as the Bible says, make all things good for those who love God and are called to his purpose."

James gazed at the wedding picture. He'd noticed it but never really look-looked. He looked now.

Rev was a lot skinnier then, but he didn't look much different. He and his wife were smiling like nothing bad had ever happened a day in their life and never would again.

There were other pictures on that shelf, too. Rev, his wife, and their boy, Devon, standing outside some old house James had never seen. Devon in a soccer uniform holding a black and white soccer ball, biggest grin in the whole universe on his face. A lady and a younger Rev wearing a cap and gown. Two boys smiling, holding up some Lego things they'd crafted, arms slung around each other's necks like brothers.

"That's Troy," Rev said when James's eyes got to that last one. "His death was a bad, bad thing. But through it, I came to know good. Came to know God."

James thought about that. He'd done bad things. *That's one fat understatement.* But he shook his head, drowned out the mean voices, focused on what God was trying to show him right this moment. He'd done bad. Evil, awful evil. And look what happened? Somehow, God had found him—evil, rotten James—there in that prison cell. Used that pastor, Pastor Chad, to worm his way into James's cold and bitter heart. Helped him see hope behind bars.

Light in the darkness.

It wasn't God making him hold onto the bad, the pain, the wrongs he'd done. That all had been washed away when he made his choice, when he chose Jesus.

It was time to let the bad go and see the good God had in store.

The weight in his chest dissolved, and James blinked, turned his eyes toward the pastor.

"I think I hear what you're sayin', Rev."

Rev nodded all slow and smooth. "That's good, James. That's real, real good."

Hours later, James walked his bike back home instead of riding it. He had the day off from the pizza place, and he'd done all the work at the church Rev needed.

As he walked, James made himself notice the town like a kid would. Like he was seeing it for the first time. There on the right, he saw what looked like some rundown modern-day general store that should've been closed years ago, yet customers walked in and out, kids and moms and businessy guys and teen guys, carrying Cokes and bags of chips and plastic bags filled with stuff James couldn't see. The store was carrying on, doing its thing in spite of being rundown.

Up on the left, he saw an old house with a rusty metal gate, peeling paint, and rickety shutters, a broken-down car parked out front. Yet James also saw the lawn was cut neatly and there was a kids' swing set over by the tree, a couple of kid bikes parked by the front door. That was somebody's home—some family lived there. Happily, from the looks of it.

Carrying on, in spite.

That was what Tiff had been doing, what he was doing. Carrying on. No matter what Mama and Daddy had done to them, no matter all the bad they had gone through, somehow they were making it.

He thought about his mama then. Made himself go back in time.

For the longest time, he'd let himself think only about Daddy. The whuppings, the yelling, the fear that simmered like soup on the stove till it turned into anger and hate.

Mama was different. She'd been different, once. Tiff didn't know the early days—by the time Tiff had been born, Mama'd been her strung-out crazy self, up one day yelling at them to get up and get going, yelling how no one was gonna do for them so they'd best learn to do for themselves. The next day, she'd be slumped on the couch with a bottle of Jack tucked in the cushion next to her, not even bothering to notice she had kids.

But James remembered the early days. Him and Mama out back, her folding laundry, him running through the sheets on chunky little-boy legs laughing, making her laugh, too.

Him and Mama driving in her beat-up bench-seat car, him in the front with a soda can, his very own bought just for him, clutched in his hands.

Him sitting in her lap on the back lawn, her letting him play with her long hair instead of swatting him away.

Another memory seared through—Daddy stomping through the living room, heavy black work boots, storming over to Mama. Mama'd stood, let little James sink into the smooshy arm chair.

Daddy yelling something. Mama yelling back. Him smacking her clean across the face. Mama smacking back, just as hard.

"You get your sister and get on outta here." Mama'd shouted the words, tossing James a look like a wild animal, as though minutes before she hadn't been humming soft and sweet while he'd tangled his fingers through her knotted up, silky-thin hair.

James had done just that, scooped up baby Tiff from her play-pen, stinky diaper near to knocking him flat as he hauled her down the hall to the room they were sharing. Changed her diaper, gave her some Cheerios from his He-Man school backpack when she whined, playing blocks with her even though he wanted to be sneaking out the window.

Somewhere along the line he'd given up on Mama and put it all into protecting Tiff. Somewhere along the line Mama'd gotten sick of being beat on and decided she was gonna beat back.

Somewhere along the line it became him and Tiff.

He got home, stopping by the mailbox first for Tiff. Her car wasn't there, likely wouldn't be till evening. He opened the box, slid out the letters, and banged it shut again.

He might not have noticed the letter had it not been on top—

he didn't get mail but for once right after his release, some official something from his parole officer. This letter, too, was official looking, had the state prison name and address stamped on the top left of the envelope, James's own name typed neatly in the "to" space. Typed, not scrawled.

He ripped open the envelope, scanned the words. Read them again, his heart fluttering like a butterfly that couldn't get off the ground.

His mama.

She was dead.

CHAPTER 29

James

DEAD.

His bike had fallen forgotten to the cold winter grass, and James bent to pick it up, roll it to the back door. He turned his key in the lock and walked into the kitchen, Tiff's orange cat crying at his feet like some stray dog on his heels.

He realized the front door was still open and walked back to shut it, almost on autopilot.

Dead.

He closed his eyes there at the door, tried his best to picture her face. A face he hadn't thought of in years. Black eyes like Tiff's, only nothing like hers at all. Hard eyes. Mad eyes. Ready to take on the world like the fighter she was. Long hair making her bony face seem even skinnier than it was.

Something trickled through him, and he puzzled over it, realized what it was. Relief. Like a cool breeze rushing through his hair, rushing through as if it was in some big hurry to get past him and on toward the rest of all its breeze-friends, leaving him in the dust, an obstacle. Mama—all the thoughts, all the hurts, all the anger. It was like they'd gone and blown through his hair like the wind, rushing by on their way to freedom.

The cat was back, slipping around his legs like an eel, and he looked down at it. Peaches, Tiff called it. Him. He didn't really know what gender the thing was.

Peaches followed him to the kitchen, where he set the mail by the toaster, all but the letter and the torn envelope. Those he took with him to the kitchen table, where he sat heavily, read the words again.

There were no details, just some formal next-of-kin notification. Didn't say how she'd died, but that it'd gone and happened.

It'd gone and happened, and now she was free.

Out of nowhere, an image flashed through his mind, took hold, and wouldn't let go. A massive, building-high iceberg, some hand from above taking a hammer and smacking it right on the tip-top, the iceberg shattering into a million pieces, sinking back into the icy sea.

Now it really was just him and Tiff. The only surviving Steadmans.

Big Bro and Lil Sis.

All afternoon he sat there, sipping tea and staring at the birds outside. Finally, he heard Tiff's key in the front door, heard her shoes click-clack, heard her set her purse down on the table by the door and open and close the coat closet.

Heard a footstep creak on the stairs.

"Tiff." He said her name loud. *Don't walk away.*

The stairs creaked again, like she was considering. Then click-clack, click-clack, as her heels made their way across the hardwood floor and to the kitchen.

CHAPTER 30

Tiff

JAMES SAT THERE at her kitchen table like he owned the place, Peaches in a tight circle on his lap.

Traitor. Tiff hurled the thought at the cat, who chose to ignore her and, instead, cuddle in even tighter.

Tiff looked at her brother. He sat like a warrior defeated, arms all slack and dangling, legs somehow too long for the chair. Ancient somehow, like an old man in a young man's body.

"Hey," she said and took a seat across from him.

He waited for her to sit. "You doing okay?" He asked it like he knew, like he'd been eavesdropping on her and Bobby last night.

"Just fine." She kept her words even, forcing her body to relax in the chair, even though every muscle felt tightly coiled. A tiger itching to pounce.

They sat in silence. *I want you to leave. Now.* The words built to a crescendo in her mind, only, she couldn't bring herself to say them. Instead, she bit her lip.

"How's the parole check-in going? They're happy with the community service and the job?"

"Guess so."

"You guess?" Tiff cast a look at him. "You don't know for sure?"

185

"How would I know? I've never done this before. Far as I know, everything's good. If I'm doing something wrong, they're supposed to tell me."

"Let's hope." She worked to keep the edge from her voice, but she couldn't rein it all in.

"Tiff." He sounded hurt. Sounded . . . different somehow.

"I mean it truly. Let's hope. You have, what, ten weeks till you're through?" Nine weeks and four days, but who was counting?

"That's right." James fiddled with the mug before him, his thumb scratching up and down, up and down over the handle. Driving her batty. *Enough.*

"I—I'm sorry." Her words were hesitant, but they were enough to stop his hand cold.

"You've got nothing to be sorry about, Tiff."

"Well, I am nonetheless. I ran out of church like a fat ol' coward Sunday instead of just sucking in air and taking a breath. Truth is you surprised me."

James looked at his hands, one still fiddling with the mug. "You surprised me, too. I had no idea you went to that church."

Tiff made a face. "Thought I went to one of the fancier spots?"

"I guess. I don't know."

"Well, I like Rev's preaching. And I like that church."

"I did, too. Like it, that is."

"What do you know: James Steadman, listening to a sermon all the way through for the first time in his life."

"It's not the first . . ."

"Mm hm."

James didn't just sound hurt, now. He looked hurt. "I know you don't believe me, but I really am a Christian now."

"Guess that's between you and God. It's none of my business."

"But—but I want it to be! Your business, that is. Tiff, you're my sister!"

"I'm not your sister." Her words were a hiss, and he reeled back, blinked hard.

"You might not want to be, but you are."

She took a breath. *Just say it.* "James. You and I are just two people now who happen to be related. That's it. You helped me get through a lot of really painful times when we were young. So painful I can't seem to stop remembering them. They just want to keep pouring out and out. I appreciate that you got me through. But that door shut when you hurt that boy and went to prison. You don't get to call me 'sister' anymore."

He swallowed visibly. "I respect that."

"Why, thank you." It came out far harsher than she'd intended.

"Your anger, too."

"Excuse me?" Her blood felt like it had raced up into her face. "My anger? Your anger's the one that got you into this mess."

"Yes, it did. My anger, my stupidity, my fear, all the bad, all the junk that was drowning me from the inside out." James's eyes looked bloodshot, and he ran a hand through his hair.

"I'm glad you can admit that."

"What choice have I got? Tiff, I'm a wreck. I'm nothing. I did wrong. Awful, awful wrong. I've got nothing left in life but to start over and—and give my life to God." That last part came out soft. Trembly.

This had to be an act. Right? She folded her hands in her lap, her body rigid. The thumping in her belly worked its way to her throat, and she realized she was gripping the edge of the kitchen table so tight her fingernails were white.

"Let me tell you something, James." She forced her fingers away from the table, crossed her arms, and surveyed him. "Because we are related, because of the good you did me when I was a helpless kid, vulnerable to those—those monsters God chose to give us as parents, I am letting you stay in my home. It's my way of saying thank you and what I know in my heart I should do."

She swallowed bitterly, continued. "But when your time is up here, that's it. Not to mention whatever game you're playing with this car business in town. If it comes back to bite anyone I know, and I mean anyone, we're done."

Her words sounded cold, professional, even to her own ears. That was just fine. She needed to get a handle on her feelings. Needed to keep it all under wraps.

James just stared at her, mouth open and eyes wide.

She stared back, triumphant. *Got you, Big Bro. No one pulls the wool over my eyes. Not even you. Not anymore.*

Emotions just beneath the surface began to whirl like a mile-long cyclone. She stepped off the edge, let herself remember what it felt like to be a scared kid, like everything was dark and spinning all around her and she was entirely powerless. All she could do was hang on till the spinning stopped.

That had all ended the day she left home for good and never looked back once. She wouldn't look back anymore. Never again.

She thought about that part in the Bible when the angels were saving Lot and his family from the chaos that was their town. She'd read that part again, just last night. Don't look back, the angels had said. Focus on the future. They all listened, all but Lot's wife. She'd looked back, and see where it got her? Turned to a pillar of salt. Frozen for all time.

"Sometimes it's best to leave the past in the past." She murmured the words, looked over. Noticed his head was in his hands.

Her heart tugged, but she forced herself to stay in place. He needed to own it. Needed to know he'd done wrong.

And you just need to get it together and stop being a train wreck.

She was sick and tired of feeling weak. Desperate. Sick and tired of boohooing over her childhood, of feeling like she had to just lean in and endure. Now was her turn to fight.

"Tiff . . ." His voice was jagged.

Stay hard, Tiff. Don't cave. Tuck it all away. Seal it all up. It won't ever escape.

James was fumbling with something in his pocket, some paper. He'd probably written her another letter about his feelings, his pathetic, cowardly attempts to apologize. *Well, sorry to tell you, buddy, but it's too late for apologies.*

"Tiff."

She rose on shaky legs and pushed in the chair. Its wooden legs scraped against the linoleum with a harsh screech. She wanted, needed, to get away. Get to her room, put on her pajama pants, flick on the television set, and just escape. She'd had a hard day, a hard week. No one could blame her.

Peaches woke up with whatever James was doing with that paper, shook his tail, and jumped down, ambling to his food dish, where he eyed her expectantly.

Quickly she moved to the container of cat food and dumped crunchies in his dish. Went to the counter and filled a glass to the brim with water. Took a sip, willing her hands to steady.

No more anger. No more tears. Time for a new Tiff. A new start.

"Mama, she . . ." James took a shuddery breath.

What in the world was he talking about. Their mama? Of all things he could say—I'm sorry, Tiff. You're right, Tiff. Yes, I'll be gone the second this is over, Tiff—he was muttering nonsense about Mama.

Her heels clicked over the floor as she strode toward the living room, glass in hand.

"Goodnight, James. I'll see you in the morning."

And then the words that froze her in her tracks. Words that caused the glass to slip from her hand, hit the floor, shards exploding everywhere.

Words that stopped time.

"Mama. She's—she's dead."

CHAPTER 31

Tiff

HE DIDN'T SAY DEAD. That—that was nonsense.

Tiff's leg stung, and she bent to look. A piece of glass had some-how jabbed into her calf, and she tugged it out, limped over to the table for a napkin. She pressed the napkin tight against her leg, blood soaking vivid red against the quilted white, and watched Peaches eat. It almost felt like she was outside of her body for a moment, like she was a cameraman filming the room. Her stand-ing here, James there, cue the cat. Scene.

Mama.

Dead.

The woman she'd hated all her life. Not hated, really. Not that at all. More like—overcame. That was a better word. Like a hurdle, an obstacle.

James had risen and stood by her now.

"I'm sorry to tell you like this." His voice sounded odd, like it was underwater.

He started to put his arms around her, but she shrugged away. Snatched the paper out of his hands, scanned it.

"I don't know about this, James. It sounds like a bunch of crazy ... I mean, why would ..."

"Tiff, look at me." His voice was firm, no more trembly-shaky. "Stop."

There was something about the way he said it that reminded her of back in the day, when he'd grab her by the arms and tell her everything was gonna be okay. Only, he didn't need to be doing this now. It wasn't like she cared if Mama lived or died. She didn't even think about the woman. He had no right making assumptions, just like he had no right coming here. Messing everything up.

Upstairs. She just needed to get upstairs, get her pajamas on, get under the covers . . .

She pushed away from him.

"Hear me, Tiff. Our mama. She died. This—this letter. Came this afternoon."

She couldn't help it. The words sunk in. A flash of Mama— black stringy hair, wacked-out eyes, arms all skinny yet corded with muscle. Mama tucking her in. Mama smacking her across the face. Petting her hair. Knocking her to the floor.

Dead.

All her energy suddenly left her, like her limbs turned to jelly. She sank.

James caught her as she brushed the floor, sliding her into his own chair.

Mama.

Waves washed over her—relief? Pity? Though why she should feel pity for the woman who'd taken her childhood away was a mystery.

Anger. Finally tears, which surprised her. She swiped at her face but it was like her eyes had opened like a dam would, gushing out a full-on flood.

"Let me see." Her words were a whisper.

He passed over the letter once more.

She held it in her hands. He'd stuffed the letter back in the envelope, which was from the state prison and addressed to him. She unfolded the letter, read the words twice, then a third time.

Notice to next of kin—Margaret Reba Steadman, their mother. Gone.

On Friday, looked to be. Friday—when everything with her and Bobby hit the fan. Wasn't that the way things went?

"Why'd they send it to you? I mean, no offense." Her voice was quiet as she folded the letter neatly and tucked it back in the envelope.

"Dunno. Guess she was on record when I went in prison."

"Of course."

Still, it stung. Would they have told her? Would anyone have told her?

Then again, maybe it would be better not to know.

A thought struck, and she found herself giggling. A little at first, hidden behind a cough, then flat-out doubled-over.

James watched her, a funny look on his face, but she couldn't stop. Just laughed and laughed till the tears came, and then she was laughing and crying at once.

"It's crazy, I know." She sighed, wiped her eyes.

"He didn't know about Mama?"

She tossed him an are-you-nuts look. "When I left home, I left it all behind. I mean, all." She looked at him significantly, then gazed out the window.

At least, she thought she had.

"So Bobby knew none of this before I came here."

"You say it like I'm some kind of pathological liar."

"It's just . . ."

"Just what?"

"Just, he's gonna be your husband. That's what."

"Or was."

She heard his intake of breath, but he didn't say a word. Tiff drew her knees to her chest, the laughter gone now as well as the tears. Everything was one big, stinking mess. And it looked like there wasn't a single thing she could do about it but slog through the muck and deal with it head-on. Like she'd always done.

Enough of this running away, tucking things in a box, hoping it would all just disappear.

She was a Steadman, she saw that now. And there was one thing about being a Steadman: If there was a mess, it'd always catch up with you.

Even if it killed you.

CHAPTER 32

James

THE NEXT MORNING, James still sat in the kitchen. He'd been up most of the night, him and Tiff, talking about Mama and the old days a little, but mostly just sitting. Words still didn't feel right between them. Maybe they never would again.

They'd gone to their beds in the early hours of the morning, but he couldn't sleep. Kept dozing then waking, like he was waiting for something, though he hadn't a clue what it was. Finally he'd crept out of bed around four, comforter around his shoulders like some knight's cloak from way back when, his Bible and the paperback he'd gotten from the free library tucked under his arm.

Now, the sunlight just starting to peek through the window, light footsteps sounded on the stairs. Tiff.

"Morning," she murmured, peeking her head in the kitchen. She was dressed for work, fiddling with an earring. "Sleep any?"

He imagined he must look a sight—grown man wrapped in what must look like a giant baby blanket, huddled at the kitchen table with a half-empty bowl of sugary cereal before him.

"Not really. A little. You?"

"I think I got three solid hours. I'll manage." Tiff shrugged as she poured coffee in her travel cup. "I wouldn't go in if I didn't have to, but I've got a busy day."

He watched her do her morning thing. *Do I mention it?* Maybe better not to talk about the Mama stuff, the calls he was going to make. They were at least on better footing, even if it was a guarded better. At least she seemed not to think he was some criminal, robbing people's cars out of nowhere.

That had hurt, hearing those words from her. But he could handle the hurt. Besides, he deserved to hurt a bit after all the wrongs he'd done. She'd sounded almost happy about it, too, as if accusing him, blaming him, made her feel better. He didn't know one thing about the car situation in Dahlia, but it sounded like a kid job. Something he and his friends had done more times than he could remember—which, come to think of it, is probably why Tiff had pointed her finger at him in the first place.

The words tumbled out. "I'm gonna call around today, see about Mama's death, what they'll tell me."

She zipped her lunch bag shut and nodded. "That's good."

"Ah—great. I'm glad you're okay with it."

She shrugged. "It . . . well. It helps to know, I think." A sad laugh burst from her lips, which he saw her try to hide with a smile. "If I can't run from the past, guess I'm better off facing it head-on."

"Sounds like you're playing chicken with history," James said.

She laughed at that, and the sound was good to hear. She grabbed an apple, paused at the door. "See you tonight."

"Have a good one." *Say it.* Then the words tumbled out. "Maybe if you're off work we can have supper. I'll cook."

Tiff nodded, and he could tell she was actually considering.

"That sounds nice." Her heels clicked across the floor, into the other room, and he could hear her pick up her work bag and grab her keys from the hook. "Have a good one," she echoed back.

The door slammed shut, the key turned in the lock, and she was gone. He was alone.

Only this time, he felt the slightest glimmer of hope bubble in his belly.

Two hours later, hanging up the phone, James still sat at the table, now with a notebook before him covered in his sloppy script. All the stuff the coroner had told him—how she'd died. Where she'd died.

He gripped the ballpoint. The hope had turned to dread.

CHAPTER 33

TIFF SAT AT HER DESK at the *Dahlia Weekly*, phone cradled to her ear as she typed notes into her computer.

"Two more break-ins last night?" she asked the sheriff.

"Yes, ma'am," Sheriff Zane said, cracking his gum loud across the phone line. "Think we've narrowed down the list of suspects. We're looking into a couple'a teens, plus I hear we got a few new parolees in the area."

Tiff winced, wondering if he was trying to tell her he knew about James being her brother or if she was reading something into his words.

"Thanks, Sheriff," she said casually, saving the file. "Let us know if there's anything more."

They hung up, and Tiff made herself pick up the paper and read over the front page again. This week's edition had just come out today, and Rebecca had made Tiff's town council story the lead, with the photo front-and-center. Tiff wasn't sure if the story was that good or if Rebecca was just trying to make her feel better. She still hadn't told Rebecca all that had happened with Bobby the other night, and she didn't want to talk about what she'd learned from James last night, either. Yesterday had been production day, their busiest day of any week, which Tiff had thoroughly appreciated, both for the opportunity not to have much time to think and for the lack of questions. Her boss had tried to pull her aside this morning, but Tiff had waved it off, and Rebecca had thankfully taken the hint and stopped, her eyes full of questions.

If she had to tell a single soul about Bobby, she'd lose it. She knew she would.

The break-in story from last week was below the fold, which Rebecca had said was intentional.

"School improvements and the county council growth plan are way more positive than car break-ins, anyway," Rebecca had said. "I think we could use a dose of good news this week."

Tiff had flushed when Rebecca had said it. A day ago, she'd all but convicted her brother of the crime. He'd made a good point last night—why would he go jeopardizing his freedom for some stolen sunglasses and petty cash? Even the sheriff seemed to think it sounded like a kid thing, or at least it seemed he did.

She stifled a yawn and sneaked a quick look at her phone. Normally by this time of day there were a couple of messages from Bobby. Today, her phone was silent. Just a weather alert—nasty rain, maybe some hail, warmer temperatures. Spring in Dahlia might just finally be here.

Rebecca's chair squeaked, and Tiff buried her head in her computer, adding a few more notes to her article. Her stomach growled, reminding her of food—and dinner. With James.

She still wasn't sure dinner was a good idea, and she was tempted to cancel, tell James she had a meeting. Only, she'd be lying, which she was trying not to do. And besides, it would be good to find out what he'd discovered about their mama's death. Healing, maybe.

Either that, or like ripping duct tape off her mouth.

An image of Mama threatened—Mama, passed out cold in her dingy bedroom. Mama, too hung over to care about anything the day Tiff had left for college. The last time she'd seen her mama, seen her hometown . . .

Not going there. Tiff shook her head to clear the thought.

Out of the corner of her eye she could see Rebecca's questioning glance, her worried eyes. Tiff pretended like she didn't notice and instead pulled up her email, trying to lose herself in work again.

She was tired of feeling raw. Tired of the memories.

Bobbly wanted her to deal with the past? Fine. She'd deal with it, face it up to it.

And then tuck it away for good in the lockbox where it belonged.

The sky was dark for most of the day as Tiff worked, rain peppering the window off and on. A soft mist gathered in the air from all the rain, reminding her of the smoke from the mills back home. The mills—she hadn't thought of them in awhile. One, the textile plant, had still been in use when she'd been a girl. Most of them had closed, but that one had stayed open at least until she was done with elementary school. They could see the mill from her classroom window, could hear the bells telling all the mill workers when to start for the day and when to break for lunch, a perfect routine to the minute every day.

Tiff's aunt and grandma on her dad's side had both worked in the mill, her aunt right up until the day she died, and her daddy had in high school some, though he gave it up to be a mechanic. It was about the only stroke of good foresight he'd had. Everyone said he was crazy to leave a good-paying job, but Ray Steadman hated the mill, hated that work, hated "being stuck in a box all day," as he called it, clocking in and out and having someone tell him when to eat and when to stand and when to go to the bathroom. Though as far as Tiff was concerned, from the way he talked about the car shop he'd just traded one hateful living for another.

They'd studied it later in college—how the closing of the mills had brought poverty to communities, an "industry recession," they called it. It drove out the hope, forcing people out of the mill towns to bigger places.

Those lessons didn't much talk about the ones who stayed behind, the generations that came after the town was long forgotten, working at the laundry, the gas station, or the dollar store. Or the bars that had sprung up like wildflowers. Bars like where her mama worked.

A memory came then—she was eight years old. James had cut his leg real bad when they'd been climbing the metal fence and she hadn't known what to do. He'd wrapped it up in his T-shirt, saying it was fine and not to worry, but she was scared. They'd talked in class the day before about how if you ever get cut to where you're bleeding you needed to get a grownup and not try to handle it yourself. So she ran up to the center of town, ran right into the dark building where Mama tended bar. Dollie's.

She'd never been in Dollie's alone before, only with Mama when she was collecting her paycheck, or with James dragging her by the hand when Daddy made them go bring Mama home or there'd be all sorts of mess to pay.

The door to Dollie's had shut behind her, startling her, and it took her a moment to get used to the lighting. And the smell. It stank like bitter urine and cigarettes and dirt all rolled into one. Even though it was afternoon and Mama always said most of the parties didn't start till later, which was why she always got home so late, there were still a bunch of people lined up on chairs at the long counter, laughing with each other, or staring into their drinks or the TV screen. Some daytime talk show was blaring on one television set, and on another it looked like golf. Mama was nowhere in sight. She crept down the line of stools, heading for the back. No one noticed her.

When she got to the end of the bar, the man on the very end

turned and smiled at her. Smiled like he'd been waiting. He had shaggy hair and jaggedy teeth, like the wolf from her red riding hood book, and he leaned way down, held out his hand for her to shake, and told her she needed to have a password if she was gonna get by. The man next to him, an old man, laughed, and she couldn't tell if it was a joke or what.

And then relief washed over her as she heard Mama's shrill, scolding bark.

"Tifyni Lacey Steadman, what in blazes do you think you're doing here?"

The words had burst from Tiff's lips in an avalanche, about James and his leg and the blood, all the blood, and at first Mama'd looked worried.

But whatever Tiff was going on about must have made her mama realize it wasn't a big thing at all, James's hurt leg, and she'd finally just reared up and smacked Tiff hard on the rear and sent her home, telling her James could handle himself and he was just fine and if Tiff ever felt the need to come here again, messing up her place of employment, somebody had better be dying or worse.

Tiff had run home then, the cool air a comfort on her skin after the stale, too-hot bar and the lurking, looming people, some with crazy eyes and some with dead eyes.

Mama was right. James had been fine, had been ticked off at her for going to get Mama in the first place. He reminded her of Mama even, the way he'd pulled back to smack at her like she was some stupid idiot.

But he hadn't hit her at all. Instead, he'd hugged her and told her he understood. Told her he knew she'd been scared.

Had Mama still worked at that same bar this whole time? All those years they'd been away?

Dead.

Her mother.

The woman who'd birthed her had gone and died. *Feel something!*

Tiff knew she should, but instead of sadness or even relief she just felt . . . empty inside. It was like she felt the void of emotion more than she felt any kind of emotion itself.

There's something wrong with you, Tiff Steadman. Normal people cry when their mama dies. Even a mama like hers.

Or—maybe they celebrated. "Ding-dong the witch is dead." The song popped into her head suddenly, and she shook it away. No, she didn't feel like crying or celebrating. She didn't know what she felt.

Truth be told, she was the one who felt dead, at least on the inside. Dead and cold.

And tired.

She closed her eyes and forced herself to breathe in and out. In and out.

The bell over the door tinkled, and Tiff could hear a woman sail inside, start chatting it up with Millie, all "how's your mama" and that nonsense, when something about the woman's voice clicked inside Tiff's brain.

Tiff listened a moment, her body still and straight as a knife. Even her bones felt rigid. *It can't be.*

Slowly, Tiff turned, ears pricking at every giggle, which somehow seemed to punctuate each one of the woman's sentences.

It was.

There, in a cute Kelly green peacoat and a fur-trimmed hat, blonde tousled curls somehow laying just-so in spite of the damp afternoon.

Nat Motts.

Tiff's mouth went dry.

Their eyes met, and Tiff saw the rush of recognition flash in the woman's eyes. Immediately, Nat turned her attention from Millie and rushed around the employees-only counter.

"Oh, my word, I forgot Bobby said you worked here. Of course, how dumb of me." Nat smacked her own forehead. "Tiffany, isn't it? Tiff. You're Bobby's fiancée, right?"

She slid all we're-girlfriends-aren't-we into the little chair next to Tiff's desk.

Tiff blinked, unable to form words on her lips. *This isn't happening.* Oh, but it was.

"I'm Natalie Motts, but everyone calls me Nat. I had no idea Bobby Smathers was engaged to such a cutie. I mean, you're gorgeous!"

Help. Tiff eyes sought Rebecca's, and she sensed her boss stand, do her Rebecca-commanding-the-room thing, which Tiff had been trying without success to master since she'd met Rebecca.

"I don't think we've been introduced." Her boss's tone was sweet, and she held out her hand toward Nat. As Tiff watched, Rebecca's smile went megawatt, like Tiff was watching a darkened stage go from dim to blazing bright in three seconds flat. "I'm Rebecca Chastain, the publisher here."

Tiff, watching the interplay, was simultaneously wowed and intimidated. She still had so very, very much to learn from Rebecca. Right now, she'd give her left arm for a sliver of Rebecca's confidence.

Nat bounced up, shaking Rebecca's hand. "It's really nice to meet you. The paper looks ah-maaaazing. Seriously—it's a million times better than when I lived here."

Rebecca smiled. "Well, thanks. We try. Listen, Tiff's got a ton of work to do, and we're about to have a staff meeting. Would you mind coming back another time to catch up?"

Tiff forced herself to stand as Nat did alongside her, muster every ounce of Rebecca-confidence she could muster, look Nat straight in the eye, and smile.

Sweetly.

"Nat, it's really nice meeting you," Tiff lied. "Let's catch up later. Maybe we can have lunch."

Another lie. She was getting good at this.

Nat blinked and actually looked disappointed. "Okay, well, I sure do hope so. I can tell you all the good stories from back in the day."

Either Nat was a first-rate actress or she really was that nice. Tiff wasn't sure she cared.

"I bet you can." Tiff gritted her teeth and saw Nat to the door. "We'll talk next week."

Calmly, slowly, with every ounce of gumption within her, Tiff waved. She watched Nat drive off in her zippy car. Then, she shut the door firmly and turned to face the room.

Millie, Dinah, and Rebecca stood there, staring at her.

"Wha . . .?" Millie's face looked like she was about to spew a thousand questions—none of which Tiff wished to answer.

"Not a word." Tiff's voice must have meant business, because for the first time ever, not a single one of them pushed her. Not one bit. She could see all the questions in their eyes, and for once, she didn't care one bit. This felt good, she realized.

Millie waved her hand, shooing Dinah to her seat. Dinah sat, eyes still on Tiff as she stacked her insertion orders. The phone rang, and Millie bent to answer it, while Tiff saw Rebecca pick up the phone and turn toward her computer.

Tiff swallowed and squared her shoulders, striding across the room and into the restroom.

When she got back to her desk, the room was abuzz with activity—every one of her coworkers on the phone, everyone focused, everyone pretending the world was rotating like normal. Good. No more tears. At least not today.

She couldn't. If she cried again she was sure she would break in a thousand pieces, like a mirror someone had dropped to the floor.

Looking down, she noticed a small folded square set on top of her work bag. She opened it to find a note from Rebecca:

> I'm here for you. I love you like a sister. And if you need to take any time off right now while you're going through all this, it's yours.

Tiff folded the note and tucked it deep in her bag. She knew Rebecca was here for her. She loved her, too—more than Rebecca could imagine.

But this—this she had to handle on her own.

CHAPTER 34

James

JAMES COULD TELL from the way she turned her key in the lock and slammed her way in the door that his sister was hopping mad.

Hopefully not at him, though why she'd be mad at him out of nowhere was a mystery. Then again, he'd learned long ago that when it came to females, or at least to Steadman females, he'd best steer clear.

Tiff didn't often get upset, at least she hadn't when they were kids. But when she did, look out.

He clattered the pans extra loud so she knew he was home. His bike was parked out front, so she probably had that figured out already, but still. Did no good to surprise someone in the thick of a mad spell. He'd learned that straightaway behind bars, had sported the black eyes and busted lips to prove it.

Dinner smelled halfway decent, which made him happy. He was fixing about the only thing he knew how to cook—spaghetti, meatballs, and garlic bread. Made his mouth water to think of it.

Above him, James could hear Tiff stomping around, walking from the room to her bathroom, down the hall, and back again.

When she appeared in the kitchen doorway a few minutes later, she'd changed into soft cotton leggings and a loose T-shirt, with her hair stuck all up in a knot on top of her head. She looked about fourteen.

"Dinner's about ready if you're hungry." He said it lightly, trying not to push. Not to get his hopes up.

She surprised him with a smile. "Thanks." She looked grateful. Moving to the cabinet for two glasses, she poured them each some ice water.

They dished out the pasta into bowls and sat at the kitchen table, like last night, only this time with food. And a lot less yelling.

"This is good," she murmured past the bite.

"Thanks."

She cast him a look—a laughing look, or maybe embarrassed? "No, thank you. It was nice of you to cook for me. For us."

"It's nothing." He shrugged. It was his turn to be embarrassed.

Well, if it ain't Saint James. The voice of his cellmate, the one before Enrique, fluttered through his mind, and he remembered the guy, Paco. His big thick hands, his mocking smile. He'd called James weak for going to the church service, only he'd used a way worse word, though at first James had gone just for the cookies. Had even told the guy that, figured he'd laugh. But the guy had just poked about it, teased him for "going all Christian," getting into church and all that "weak, sissy stuff." It got to where Paco used to tear out some of the pages in James's Bible, the one the cookie-church men had given him, and toss the pieces in the air like confetti.

"Mighty convenient, finding Jesus when you got nothin' else," Paco used to say. "Next you'll be forgiving them cops, talking all like how they're doing the Lord's work when they arrested your skinny white backside. Ain't that true, Saint James?" Paco would laugh and laugh, a taunting, hard laugh. James would ignore him, like Paco's words weren't getting under his skin, making him want to just knock him one clean across the face.

Paco'd gotten in a fight not long after, got transferred some-place else, some maximum security thing, but the nickname "Saint James" had stayed, at least in James's own mind. Now here he was, cooking like some do-gooder.

James shook his head, focused on his plate. Memory lane was the last place he needed to be wandering.

"Did you find out anything?" Tiff asked, wiping her mouth care-fully.

The question surprised him, though it shouldn't have. "About Mama? I did. It—it's not good."

He saw her eyebrow quirk just a tad. "Didn't expect it would be."

It had taken him awhile to get the information he'd needed. He'd called the jailhouse first, which steered him to the coroner, which steered him to the coroner in the county where he'd grown up. The lady on the line had been rushed, out of breath, and had put him on hold a long time. Finally, the coroner himself got on and told him yes, his mama had indeed "expired," and they had her there in the freezer in the county morgue and the cause of death wasn't certain unless he wanted to pay a whole bunch of money for some autopsy, but the police said it was a stroke. That was good enough for James. Dead was dead. He didn't suppose the cause mattered much.

It was the other stuff the coroner told him that stayed with him. Picturing her alone in there, in some bed, made his heart hurt. His belly hurt.

"I guess she'd been in some assisted living place," James began, swallowing hard. "Stroke. It was her second one."

Tiff looked at her plate. "Oh." She fiddled with her fork, swirl-ing a few strands of spaghetti around and around, and finally set the fork back down. "Assisted living?"

"I think six years, maybe seven. She'd been there awhile . . ."

He could see in her eyes she was calculating like he had, imagining perhaps like he had. Wondering how long it happened after she'd left home, after James had gone in, after Daddy'd died.

"And apparently there's some paperwork we need to sign off on. For her cremation." The word, cremation, sounded so final. So . . . proper. "It's something we can do over the phone. Lady said they can overnight papers—"

"We could go in person . . ." Tiff looked thoughtful.

"Sure, we could, but there's no need—"

"A road trip." She propped her chin on her hands. "You and me."

"Tiff, we don't have to go there . . ."

His sister gave him a look he couldn't read. It was a fierce look, like she was taking all the mad and sad and crazy and adventure-y and rolling it all into one giant ball of mud. Like the look she'd given him the day they'd made mud pies after the Hanniger brothers had stolen their lunch bags, hid behind the hardware store, and waited till the brothers were almost to the church that Sunday morning. Then they'd fired them into the street, straight at them, coating the brothers in hot, sticky glops of dirt from their brown stringy hair to their loafers. The brothers didn't know what hit them or where it'd come from, but James and Tiff sure did. Probably ruined their church clothes. They could hear the brothers getting a whupping that afternoon.

Good, Tiff had said back then. She'd been so little she'd had gaps in her mouth where teeth should have been, but the look on her face that day had reminded him of a lion queen. Score. Win.

Victory.

She had that same look on her face now, nodding like she was calculating all the hows and wheres and whens. "You're right, James. We don't 'have' to. But I think we need to."

"Tiff, I don't want to go back there." He didn't. Pastor Chad and the parole officer both had told him to steer clear of his old scene. It wasn't like he expected he'd go back and immediately jump back in the crew, jack some car or find his dealer, any of that no-sense crazy stuff.

But going back . . . it sounded like a bad idea. A bad, bad idea. Like asking for trouble.

Her mouth set in a firm line. "I do."

She rose, swirling the last of her spaghetti on her fork as she did and popping it into her mouth, then stepped to rinse the rest down the kitchen sink.

"I've been running from my past long enough," she said over her shoulder. "I don't want to see you do the same. It's time we headed back and put our past to bed. Once and for all."

A burning spread from his belly to his throat. But all he could do was nod.

After all Tiff had done for him, gone through for him, how could he say no?

CHAPTER 35

Tiff

IN HER BEDROOM, Tiff pulled the little rose-gold suitcase from the top of her closet, zipped it all the way open on her bed. Something—nerves? No, she decided, excitement—bubbled up in her, and she realized her hands were trembling.

She glanced at the picture of Bobby on her nightstand, a stab of guilt threatening. She wouldn't tell him. She "needed time to sort things out," to "get her head straight," like he'd said. But while he was right, it still didn't explain all the other stuff. Like Nat. The guilt flickered, and a low boil replaced it. Good—anger was better. She was done with tears.

She grabbed a navy blouse and a pair of charcoal pants from the closet, tossed in a sweater and an extra pair of jeans. She didn't want to stay long but, well. Just in case.

Rebecca. Grabbing her phone, she texted her boss.

"Did you mean it when you said I could take time off?"

Rebecca's reply came within seconds. "Yes." Then, ". . . You okay?"

"I'm okay. Going to take a few days. I'll check in soon."

Three little buttons popped up and stayed there, telling her Rebecca was typing something in reply. Her boss was either typing out a really long message or struggling with how she wanted to reply.

Finally, Rebecca sent, "Be safe. Remember I'm here for you."

I know you're here. But some things a girl's gotta do on her own. James coming along didn't count, if he did come, anyway. Who knows—maybe he wouldn't be able to get time off work. Maybe he wasn't allowed. It didn't matter. She was going with or without her brother.

Tiff tossed the phone on her bed and finished packing. She wanted to leave first thing in the morning.

Her sleep, when it finally came, was restless, filled with dreams of the old mill, only this time it wasn't the rundown crumbly demolition site of her childhood. It was the still-operational mill from her high school textbooks, wide brick walls and symmetrical windows, workers marching in and out like ants, smoke rising from the chimney at top right. In her dream, Bobby was in the mill, working so hard and so fast he couldn't see her, no matter how hard she banged on the glass or rattled the pipes to get his attention.

She awoke in the black morning, sat straight up until she realized the dream was just a dream. *What are you doing, going back there?* She'd spent her entire adult life running in the opposite direction, and now that the going had gotten rough, what was she doing? Turning right back around and heading home, like a dog with her tail between her legs.

No, not like that. She wasn't being a coward. That wasn't what this was about. She was on a mission. Search and destroy—destroy the past, anyway. She planned to face up so she didn't have to run anymore, shine light on the ghosts so they couldn't haunt her ever again. She wasn't going home. This was home—Dahlia, South Carolina.

Even if it didn't work out with Bobby . . .

She couldn't let herself think beyond that. Instead, she forced herself to lie back down, huddle beneath her soft quilt, let her breathing go soft and calm and steady, let her heart beat slow and peaceful. Let herself sleep.

By eight o'clock, she was dressed and lugging her suitcase downstairs.

James was already in the kitchen. He had dark circles beneath his eyes and a mug of coffee in front of him. "I'm going with you. But I have to be back by Saturday for work."

"I'm glad." She meant it. The company would be nice. "I think it'll be good for both of us."

"I don't know about that, but I'm not letting you go alone."

What was that supposed to mean? She cocked her head. "I don't need your protection, James. I've been on my own a long time now."

He shook his head. "Not back there. Neither of us needs to be going back there alone."

She swallowed back a sigh and made herself pour a tall mug of coffee, poured another to-go cup for James while she was at it.

"Hope you don't mind purple." She handed the travel mug to him.

"Not at all." He took a sip as if to prove it.

She set out extra food and water for Peaches and they were out the door, her in the driver's seat, him riding shotgun, the smell of coffee and morning rain soothing as she backed out and headed toward Aberville Highway.

Straight for her past.

CHAPTER 36

James

JAMES STAYED QUIET most of the drive, the spiral notebook with all the information on Mama—the morgue, the place she'd been living—everything stuffed into the slot between the console and his seat. The plain white letter from the prison—". . . we regret to inform you . . ."—was tucked inside. He could see the edge poking out and stuffed it down farther into the notebook.

He wanted to ask his sister what she was hoping to get out of the trip, what she planned to do, why she wanted to go in the first place. But the words just settled on his tongue and wouldn't budge. He knew her reasons why. And the whats didn't much matter.

The swish-swoosh-swish of the windshield wipers was somehow calming as they drove, north and then west, across the top part of the state. She was taking mostly back roads, navigating with her cell phone.

"Hungry?" she asked when they got close to Spartanburg, and he blinked, realized they were at the big gas station. Closer than he'd thought. A thread of apprehension tickled its way through his insides.

"Not at all." He wasn't lying. He thought he might throw up if he ate, wasn't sure he'd manage to eat anything till they got back home—back to Tiff's, he corrected. Home, well, he wasn't quite sure what that looked like anymore.

It sure wasn't Walterville. It wasn't the jail cell. But it wasn't Tiff's, either.

"Home isn't a place," he remembered Pastor Chad telling them once while they were studying the psalms, something about how the man who lives in the shelter of God Almighty always has the Lord as a refuge and a fortress. And he liked that, the thought that no matter how bad things got, at least he had a heavenly home waiting for him. Hopefully God would take him. Maybe that's what hell was, he thought—living the rest of his life beating himself up for all the wrong he'd done, then spending eternity doing the same. But the Bible said it didn't matter how much he beat himself up. God's grace—

The Bible! He froze, realizing his mistake. He'd left his Bible! All the way back in Dahlia, on the table upstairs by the guest bed.

"What's the matter?" Tiff asked, and he turned to see she was watching him.

"I, uh—left my Bible . . ." It sounded stupid to his own ears, but he couldn't explain it. Some kids had teddy bears or security blankets to keep away the bogeyman. James had his own bogeyman, and reading God's Word kept it at bay.

He swallowed, wondering if maybe he hadn't forgotten it at all, or wondering if maybe they could stop, maybe borrow one from that motel on the main drag.

"You can borrow mine," Tiff offered.

He looked at her again. She had a funny expression on her face, like he had some weird glob on his chin or something and she was trying to figure out what in the world it was, but she just gestured to the trunk.

"I'm pretty sure I brought it." She said it all casual, got in the left turning lane, the click-click of the blinker steady and sure.

His chest had stopped its tight boa constrictor squeeze and set-tled back to normal again. He swallowed. "Thanks."

"No worries."

Up ahead, he could see it. Past the remnants of the original mill, past the bridge, past the junky old car lot, the big concrete sign.

Welcome to Walterville.

Oh, dear Jesus.

CHAPTER 37

Tiff

THE TOWN DIDN'T LOOK LIKE anything then, and it hadn't changed much since. Tiff drove slowly through Walterville's main street, her eyes taking everything in. Old car repair places, the grocery that looked all but closed down now, the tiny brick post office with the Walterville name and zip code posted out front. That place that sold candy, cigarettes, and comic books.

At the school she pulled in, got her bearings. She could hear little kids shrieking and laughing, and she peered over, caught a glimpse of students playing at recess. A little girl with black hair in a ponytail had her hands on her hips and was staring down at some kids from the top of the metal jungle gym, daring them to climb up after her. Tiff stared at the girl, wanting to tell her to be careful. She didn't have to worry—the girl clearly knew what she was doing. As Tiff watched, the other kids nudged each other, one after the other, drifted off. The little black-haired girl gave a triumphant smirk and sat down right on top. Queen of the hill.

Next to her, James was shuffling some papers. She looked over and saw he had the notebook out.

"Think we should go to the morgue first?" she asked him.

He nodded slowly. "Guess so."

She put the car in gear and navigated the streets. She thought the morgue was over in the county offices, up at the end of the main drag.

Her memory was correct. They parked and stood, stretching. She fumbled in the backseat, lugging out her purse.

Inside, her boots echoed on the tile. The reception guard pointed them to the coroner's office, and they took the stairs instead of the elevator.

The lady at the counter eyed them like they were strangers. Which they were. "Help you?" she said over the tops of her glasses.

"We're, ah—next of kin for, ah . . ." Tiff fumbled for the words, nudged her brother.

James pulled out the paper. "Maggie Steadman. Margaret Reba Steadman."

The woman took the paper, stared at it. Picked up the phone, pressed a button.

"Steadman, up front," she said into the receiver, waited. "Yeah, right in front of me."

The woman hung up the phone, gestured to the two narrow brown chairs beneath a framed county seal. "Feel free to take a seat."

"We'll stand." Tiff inched closer to James.

They stood there, listening to the tick of the clock, the faint scratching of the ballpoint pen as the woman made notes, shuffled papers, opened and closed drawers.

"Steadman family?" A man's voice came from the back right, after about ten minutes. He was a small-framed man, balding, with wire-frame glasses, and he looked a bit like Tiff's sophomore history teacher.

The man came over and shook their hands.

"This way." He ushered them to another office. Shutting the door, he gestured to the red and white striped candies on his desk as they all sat. "Mint?"

"No, thanks." Tiff swallowed. "You talked to my brother yesterday."

The man opened up a folder, held it toward him so they couldn't see the contents as he flipped through. "Yes, yes," the man said as if to himself. "I'm Ed Reynolds, county coroner. James and Tifyni?"

He pronounced her name with the emphasis on the y, like Tiff-Eye-Knee, and she winced.

"Just Tiff."

The man, Mr. Reynolds, nodded and turned the papers so they were flipped toward her and James. "Your mama passed away a few days ago, ischemic stroke is the expected cause. Can't know for sure without an autopsy, but I imagine you know given her health and condition, sometimes the body just gives out—"

"Actually, we don't know." James's voice was quiet. "I've been in prison the last several years, Mr. Reynolds, and Tiff here's lived out of town. We haven't seen our mama in a long, long time."

"Ah." Mr. Reynolds covered his mouth, and she realized he was smoothing down his moustache. The gesture oddly comforted her. "Well, your mama was in pretty rough shape. Her primary doctor signed off on the cause of death no question, given the first stroke and now this one . . ."

"First stroke?" Tiff asked.

"Yes, apparently the first stroke left her completely incapacitated, enough so that she had to move to assisted living, where she's been a few years." The man said, reading upside down from what looked like her health report.

Incapacitated. Completely. She'd had no idea. Would it have made a difference if she had? She wasn't sure she wanted to know the answer to that.

"She was living at Oak Corner Assisted Living," Mr. Reynolds said. "Do you know where that is?"

James looked at Tiff, who shook her head.

Mr. Reynolds wrote down the address for them. "You'll need to stop by there, sign off on things. They'll have her valuables."

Valuables. Nothing to worry about there.

"You can request an autopsy if you want." The man's eyes were kind. "It'll cost, and it takes a lot longer than most people expect, but it's well within your rights to request one . . ."

Tiff looked at James and caught the barely perceptible shake of his head. *No.*

"That's okay," she told the man. "We're just here to sign off, do whatever we're supposed to do when this sort of thing . . ."

"Certainly." The man flipped through. "As I explained on the phone yesterday, it's all pretty standard. You'll need to decide cremation or burial. Cremation's much cheaper, but we can do either. In cases of indigence there's help paying, of course, and Rita up front can help you with all that."

He showed them some figures, talking on and on—this choice or that, this method or that. Tiff swallowed at the cost. It was more than she'd expected, but she could cover it. Barely.

"Would you like to see her?" The man's question startled her.

"Ah, see . . . her?"

"I wouldn't recommend it, but that's your choice. We can pull her out, it won't take too long to set up. Some people find it easier to put things to rest when they see things for themselves."

"No." Tiff's voice was firm. The last thing she wanted to do was see the empty shell of the woman who'd been her mother. It had been hard enough looking at her in life.

Next to her, James shook his head. "Naw, Mr. Reynolds, we're good not seeing her, if it's all the same to you."

"No problem." The man checked some boxes and showed them where to sign.

Tiff signed, all the time thinking of what the man had said— pull her out. Set her up. Like she was some doll or prop there for them to look at.

By the time she'd swiped her card and gathered her purse to go, her hands were shaking. James took her arm, and the man ushered them out.

"Come by tomorrow after two. You can pick up her remains then. And James, Tiff." At the door, Mr. Reynolds looked first at her brother, then deep into her own eyes. Like he could somehow see, see all the pain and the hurt and the trouble, all bubbling and churning way down inside. "My condolences. God bless you both."

Tiff and James turned to go. Silence rested between them as they walked down the stairs, out the front door, and out to her car.

She hit the clicker to unlock the doors and slid into her seat. But instead of starting the car, she sat, keys in her lap. *What am I doing here?* This was a mistake, coming here. Saying they'd come back for the ashes. Now they couldn't even go home till tomorrow.

"You want lunch?" she asked, then regretted it. Even the thought of food made her stomach turn.

"I'm not hungry, but we can if you want."

"Let's hold off." Maybe they should go back in, ask if they could do it today. Maybe if they paid extra . . .

"We could go by the assisted living place, take care of whatever we're supposed to sign." James's voice sounded hesitant, and she glanced over at him, saw he looked as miserable as she felt. This had to be hard on him, too.

He'd pulled out his folder and pointed to the yellow sticky note, where she could see Mr. Reynolds's neat print. Oak Corner Assisted Living, along with the address.

"That's a good idea," she offered, and he looked almost grateful at the compliment. A twinge of guilt tugged at her.

The center wasn't too far, close enough that they could have walked, but for the rain that was surely coming. She drove the few blocks and parked the car in the small, treeless lot.

"No oaks on Oak Corner?" James's lip quirked in an attempt at a smile.

"No corner, either." She elbowed her brother. Humor was good. Humor helped. If they could just stay this side of it all, maybe she'd be okay.

The building was new construction, vinyl siding still fresh and clean, and the roof showing no signs of wear, but it felt sterile, she thought, as they walked up the ramp to the front door. More like a hospital than a home.

Inside, the lobby was dark, the TV on in one corner, and a bunch of chairs with magazines scattered about, but no people beyond the solitary heavyset woman at the reception desk. She was on the phone and did not give them the slightest glance as they walked up through the lobby and stood before her, waiting patiently for her to finish the call.

James cleared his throat, the sound unnaturally loud in the empty room. "Hi, uh . . . We're next of kin for Margaret Steadman."

The woman gave them a blank look.

"The coroner's office said she'd been living here?" James frowned.

The woman pointed behind her toward the double doors. "Probably Station Two is what you're looking for. Go on back," she said when they hesitated.

James led the way down the corridor. This section felt decidedly more like a hospital, but with far less medical personnel. Tiff could see a woman pushing a cart of bed sheets, and up ahead looked like a nurses' station, only nobody was there.

The doors to the patient rooms were all open, and as they passed by, Tiff peered into a few of the rooms. Two people were in one room, both flat on their backs in a pair of twin beds, seemingly asleep. In another an old dark-skinned man sat in a chair, fumbling with the TV remote. *Let's get this done and go.* Tiff pressed her lips together, walked faster.

And almost ran straight into a young nurse in crisp yellow hospital scrubs coming out of a room.

"I am so sorry!" the woman said, the tray in her hands clutched tightly.

"It's okay. I wasn't looking."

The nurse set the tray down on a cart. Other trays were there, too, with what looked like snacks. She pumped some hand sanitizer.

"Can I help you find a room?"

James and Tiff fumbled for the words.

The nurse smiled kindly. "Who are you here to see, sugars?"

The use of "sugar" from someone so young struck Tiff as old-fashioned and oddly comforting. "No one. I . . . mean our mama—our mother—was apparently living here? She recently passed away."

"I'm so sorry," the nurse said again, her eyes sympathetic. She beckoned, and they followed her to the counter, and the computers.

They gave the name, and the nurse typed something into the computer, nodded.

"I thought that's who you were talking about. She was one of ours. That was her room right there."

The woman pointed. Tiff read her name tag—Molly.

"Do you want to see? Where she'd been staying?"

"Ah, no." Tiff shook her head. "Sorry. I mean, it's okay." Out of the corner of her eye, she saw James drift off, maybe looking for a bathroom.

Molly reached out, patted Tiff's hand all girl-to-girl. "It's hard. You're not from around here?"

"I . . . live across state, south of Charlotte." It wasn't a total lie, Tiff told herself.

The nurse leaned against the counter. "Well, she was a quiet one, your mama. I've only been here a couple months, but she never put up a fight, ate her food real well for us . . ."

"Was she, ah, able to feed herself?"

"Oh, no. Miss Maggie couldn't do any of that, but like I said, she was real sweet. Didn't tussle or anything like some of our folks do. It can be a real tough adjustment for folks when they first come here, but Miss Maggie, she'd been here, what, six years or so? That stroke had done a number on her." Molly shook her head.

The picture came unbidden into Tiff's head then, this nurse spoon-feeding their mama mashed potatoes, washing her hair, trimming her fingernails.

"Here, let me get her things for you." Molly was gone quickly, sliding a set of keys from behind the counter and disappearing into a closet nearby.

Tiff could see James at the end of the hall, looking at pictures like they mattered. She waved him over. He came, slowly, sneakers making faint squeaks on the speckled linoleum.

Moments later Molly was back, a blue faded suitcase in one hand and a clear plastic bin with the label "Steadman" on top.

"These were your mama's things," Molly said. "Her personal effects and whatnot."

James took the suitcase and Tiff the box.

"Would you like to see her file?"

Tiff must've had a worried expression because the young woman patted her arm again gently. Tiff got the impression she'd done the patting thing a thousand times.

"It's not gory or nothin'. Just the basics—how long she was here, how she got here, that sort of thing. We find it's really good for the families. Helps bring closure and all." Molly flashed a smile again that also included James.

She hit a button, printed out a couple of sheets of paper, and tucked them in a file folder.

Tiff and James signed some forms, something authorizing Medicaid to do something or other with the remaining funds and paying the center or something. Then they were saying their thank-yous and turning to leave.

At the first room, Tiff glanced in, tried to look away quickly. An old woman was struggling to sit up, her gown slipping down over her shoulders. Mama. Her mama. In a place like this.

Her stomach felt all tumbly and slippery, like she just gone down a waterslide or something.

"Let's go," she muttered to James.

"That was . . . depressing," he finally said when they got to the car.

"You're telling me." Now that they were out of there, she was feeling like herself again. The slippery-sliding sensation in her belly had dissipated.

"Wonder what's in this thing, anyway," he said as she popped her trunk and he hoisted the suitcase inside next to their overnight bags.

Tiff lay the suitcase flat and unzipped it. A few sweaters, some flowery pajamas that didn't look like her mom would've worn them a day in her life, a pair of slippers. A blanket with ice cream cones on it, again nothing like she could imagine her mom buying for herself. It felt like she was looking through a stranger's things. These were a stranger's things, she corrected herself. She didn't know Mama anymore. Never had known her, if she was being honest.

"What do we do with this stuff?" James stared at the open suitcase.

"I think we should donate it."

James blinked at her. "Is that okay? I mean . . ."

Tiff zipped the suitcase back up. The unsettled feeling in her belly was starting to creep back. "It's just clothes. It's not like she would've wanted us to hang onto them or anything. I mean, what are we going to do with all this? Might as well let someone else benefit."

"Yeah, I guess." James bit his lip and reached for the other item, the plastic box. "What about this?"

"Open it," Tiff suggested.

He did. It didn't look like much—a couple of pictures, some papers, a tarnished necklace. What looked like her mama's wedding band and some other junky stuff rested at the bottom.

Tiff took the box, replaced the lid, and stowed it in the trunk. "Let's look at this later."

Her purse buzzed. *Bobby.* She tightened her lips, forcing the thought away. Sliding out the phone, she looked. Instead, it was a text from Rebecca.

"Just checking on you," Rebecca's text said.

"Thanks," Tiff typed back. "I'm doing okay. Will touch base later."

She slid the phone back into her purse, glancing up at the sky. The rain was still holding back—for now. And memory lane was calling, literally.

Tiff cocked a brow at James. "Want to take a ride?"

CHAPTER 38

James

JAMES KNEW WHERE THEY WERE GOING before they'd walked out of the nursing home, even if Tiff didn't.

They couldn't come all this way and not go there, not retrace their steps, see the place. The house. The barn. Their barn.

But as the car bumped over the gravel, splashed through a mud puddle, a low tickle of dread began to pool in his gut. *I can't do this. Not yet.*

Leaning his head back, he closed his eyes like he was tired and let the motion of the car rock him gently. Funny how a body could be gone from a place, years gone, yet know where the turns would be like he'd been there yesterday. Over the hill, left, down a stretch. Right, then left again. Every bump bringing him closer.

Bringing him back.

But James didn't want to go back.

"Probably shambles by now," he heard his sister mutter beside him. "Maybe it's not even there anymore. For all I know it's been torn down, leveled flat . . ."

He tuned her out. Not being mean or nothing, but today of all days, he'd figured out it was best to just let his mind stay right where it was. Right smack in the present. Not tumbling ahead, worrying. Not falling back into yesterday. Dead set on now.

Dead. *Nice choice of words, Steadman.* A flash of Mama, dark eyes, laughing, swatting his rear for something. Mama, sliding scrambled eggs on his plate before he was old enough to cook for himself. Mama, gray and empty in some drawer in the county morgue.

The car slowed, and James opened his eyes. It was still a ways off—Tiff had parked the car up by the neighbors' mailbox, but they could see it from here.

"Guess it's still there." Tiff said the words so dryly he couldn't tell which emotion lurked behind them.

"I didn't even know she'd had a stroke." His voice was almost a whisper.

"Doesn't surprise me any that she did."

"Still. Knowing . . . somehow . . ." He stopped, shook his head, and stared out the car window a long time. Mama'd been a wreck-and-a-half, but strokes were for old people, weren't they? Mama wasn't young-young, but surely she was too young for all that. Too young to be stuck in a nursing home, all by herself. Too young to die there.

Tiff's voice sounded crackly when she spoke. "Knowing she was . . . weak. It kinda makes me hate her less."

He looked at her, surprised she'd used the word. Hate. A dangerous word, for her. A forbidden word, or at least she'd always gotten on his case when he said it.

"Yeah." He shrugged. "I get what you mean." Only he wasn't sure he hated Mama. Wasn't sure he'd ever hated her.

She switched off the ignition and they climbed out of the car. Stood there, peering. Then, without warning, Tiff took off, making a beeline for the gate.

He jogged to catch up.

The place didn't look any different. Their name, Steadman, was still carved on the wood post.

"It looks so . . . normal." Tiff's voice was a whisper. She'd stopped at the gate, stood as if frozen. "So regular."

It did. Like some average house, where some average family lived. The roof was crumbly, and the paint was peeling, but it'd held up over time.

He could see the red and white "for rent" signs posted out front, one on the fence, one on the house. Not that anyone would be chomping at the bit to rent the place. Who'd want to rent some rundown country cottage miles out from a forgotten milltown in the middle of nowhere?

To the left were the cages where they used to keep chickens when he was small, and the barn.

He stepped past her, past the gate, toward the house. Drawn as if by a magnet.

Memories swirled. Daddy's belt. Welts on his arms, his back. Told himself he'd deserved them. Now he wasn't so sure.

Too much. It was all just too much. He cast a glance over his shoulder, saw his sister was wandering off in the direction of the barn. Good.

Pastor Chad's words were all but rattling in his ears as he made it to the edge of the house. *Let it go, my brother. Gather all the bad like you're stuffing it in a trash bag, make your peace, and chuck it, James. Following Jesus means you get to leave it all behind.*

Only right now, it felt like that trash bag was tied to his foot, and the stench was making him gag.

CHAPTER 39

THE PLACE LOOKED AWFUL. Worse than it had looked when she was a kid. Their name, Steadman, carved on the wood plank, was still there, barely hanging onto the mailbox. Little bits of white from somebody's discarded trash were strewn across the yard. Forgotten rubble on a forgotten piece of property in a forgotten town.

That's what she'd been trying to do—forget it all. Only she couldn't forget. It kept coming back to bite her.

Out of the corner of her eye she could see James wander over to the house and step onto the porch. Let him. She didn't want to go near the place. Memories of late-night screaming matches and broken glass. The stench of cigarettes on her clothes, in her shoes, in her hair just from living there. She'd never touched a cigarette in her life other than to pass one to her mama or daddy, but she'd spent her childhood smelling like a walking, talking ashtray. "Skanky Stanky Steadman." The jeers from her elementary school playground, the stupid boys pushing her and her friend Lizzie around and around on that metal spinner so fast that poor Lizzie'd thrown up all over the thing and their teacher had made them all come in from recess early. Jerks, those boys. Still, she couldn't blame them. They'd grown up in normal families. How would they know?

As she'd gotten older, Tiff had learned to read the eyes of the people in Walterville. Along the way they'd changed from "oh, that poor child" to "bet she's gonna to grow up just like her mama" to "what a shame," usually said with a wordless tsk-tsk and a shake of the head.

She'd proved them all wrong. She'd gotten out after all, gotten far away, and denied all the labels. Off at college, and later in Dahlia, nobody knew the name Steadman meant trash. To them, Steadman was just a name, the name of their nice, hard-working reporter-turned-editor who bought cookies from the Girl Scouts and went to the town festivals and put their grannies' pictures in the paper when they celebrated their ninetieth birthdays. It didn't matter, anyway. Only a few more months and she would never have to be a Steadman again.

Then her heart caught. She didn't even know if that was true anymore. Her eyes filled with tears, but they weren't sad tears, she told herself. They were angry tears. Frustrated tears. She scrunched her eyes tight, and they were gone as fast as they'd appeared, shoved back. Way back.

She stomped across the yard over to the barn, the only place she'd actually liked while growing up. Probably because nobody but her and James set foot in the place—Mama because it smelled nasty and Daddy because it reminded him of everything he'd run from.

Daddy'd hated that barn. She'd heard him say it a hundred times, just about. His own daddy had tried to get him to be a farmer just like he'd been, but Daddy would have nothing to do with it.

"These hands are too good for the mill or the fields," he used to tell them, holding up his grease-stained fingers and pointing them at her and James like they were the ones telling him what to do instead of his own memory ghosts.

Not that Daddy cared one bit about them, her and James. All

Daddy cared about was cars. Working on cars, restoring cars, talking about cars, racing cars. Cars and booze and mama. Cared about cars till the day he died, when he'd drunk too much and flipped his Mustang off the side of Wheelerton Road.

She'd thought maybe his death would make mama ease up a bit. It had only made her more miserable to deal with. By the time Tiff had left for college two months later, she and her mama'd barely said five words to each other even though it was just the two of them in the house, James in prison, and Daddy in the grave six feet under.

Over by the barn, the mud was much thicker. She stepped gingerly so she wouldn't get too much on her boots.

The barn door was open just a little, and she pushed at it, peeking through. Who knew what animals had made their home in there over the winter?

Nothing jumped out at her. She pushed the door wide, letting the cloudy afternoon sunlight stream in.

Automatically, her eyes flicked toward the ladder, and the loft. Her old hiding hole. Hers and James's.

Funny—when she was a kid it had seemed humongous. She remembered when she was so little she was scared to climb up that ladder by herself, convinced she'd break her back if she fell. Now it just looked like a bunk bed with straw.

Half the roof was missing, and the stench was awful, like some animal had crawled in there and died.

From where she stood she could barely glimpse the window, where she and James used to sit and peer out long into the night, waiting for the lights in the house to go out so they could tiptoe back to their beds. Sometimes they'd spend the night out there.

A thought struck. She went to the underside of the ladder, felt around for the little hidden board underneath.

There!

Her fingers closed around two small items, which she pulled out. In the dim light she could see them—books. Library books. There in case she got stuck out there and wanted to read. Sometimes she'd spend the whole day in that barn on a Saturday, there or in that tree down by the river.

"Tiff?"

She jumped. James.

The door creaked as he pushed through and walked over. "Thought you'd be here." He nodded toward the books. "Not a wonder why you turned out so smart and I ended up a jailbird."

"James . . ."

"Hey, it's true!" He laughed. "You always told me I needed to crack a book or watch out. Just messing with you, sis." He wrinkled his nose. "This place stinks to high heaven."

"Let's get out of here."

"Do you wanna see the house?"

"Not one bit." Her stomach turned at the thought of having to walk inside.

He stood back to let her pass. They slipped through the door and outside.

Thunder rumbled in the distance, and she quickened her pace, across the lawn, through the gate, to the car. James followed.

They got in and sat a moment as she gazed at it all—it was nothing special. Just a forgotten regular old house and barn in the country. Not even a rundown shack, the kind of place you could tell from the outside had stories. All the stories were in her head now, hers and James's. Mama gone. Daddy gone. Just them.

The ache in her belly grew, tickling up into her heart. *Don't you dare cry, Tiff Steadman.*

James cleared his throat. "I think I might could use some food now."

Food. She guessed it was as good an idea as any. "Someplace in town?"

He winced. "Maybe the next town over. I don't really want to run into . . ."

She hadn't even thought about that—who he might see. She glanced at him, realizing now how much of a difficulty this had to be for him. More so even than for her. Coming here, being in the place where his life had not only spiraled out of control but gone down the drain.

Her own self-centeredness smacked her in the head.

"I know a place," she said, starting the car and jamming it into gear. "Buckle up."

CHAPTER 40

James

IT WASN'T ANYPLACE SPECIAL, some open-all-night diner, but James couldn't remember the last time food had tasted so good.

He took another bite of burger, looked at the file Tiff had open before them. She'd brought the bin from the hospital in with them, but they hadn't bothered with any of the personal items just yet. The papers the nurse had given them were in a neat stack, and Tiff was poring over them, reading out snippets between bites.

"So it looks like she wound up at the nursing home after her boss at the bar had gone to the house when she didn't show up for her shift two days in a row," Tiff read, chewing thoughtfully on a French fry. "He found her in her bed with a half empty bottle of vodka, passed out and unresponsive, called the ambulance, and they carted her off to the hospital. Alcohol poisoning, and then it looks like she had the first stroke when she was drying out."

He didn't know how his sister could read it like that—all matter of fact, like it was some file about a perfect stranger. Then again, maybe she had it right. Maybe it was easier to read it that way.

He shook his head and finished off his burger.

"She'd missed her rent payments, didn't have any place to live, and she was in rough shape from the stroke and not really able to move much anyway, so the state put her in Oak Corner. Looks like all she brought with her was whatever her boss had gathered up—that suitcase and this plastic shoebox filled with odds and ends from her bedroom," Tiff read.

"What's in the shoebox?"

Tiff glanced beside her, where the box rested, and shrugged. "Looks like a bunch of nothing."

"Pass it over."

She did. She kept on reading as he set the box beside him and began placing the items one by one on the diner table.

A tarnished old-fashioned mirror, like what ladies would use back in the olden times. Her wedding band. A purple gemstone from some rock mining place—amethyst, he remembered the name with surprise. Her birthstone. A hairbrush that still had strands of her dark hair laced between the bristles. He swallowed back a lump.

"Guess she'd been living like that for years now, just layin' in that bed, three square meals a day, round-the-clock nurses, till last week." Tiff frowned, staring at the papers like she was searching for something hidden in the nursing home notes, something he was sure she wouldn't be able to find.

"Would you look at that." His hand closed on a small angel statue, and he set it on the table with the rest of Mama's things.

"An angel? Mama?"

"Maybe it was a gift."

Tiff snorted. "I can't imagine Mama liking angels. She hated all that stuff."

The way she said it made James feel sad. "Maybe she changed."

He felt her eyes on him. "Yeah. Maybe."

The waitress came over and topped off their sodas. Cindy, her nametag read.

"Looks like y'all are on memory lane," Cindy cocked her head, peering at the stuff.

James wanted to pull it all back, cram it all back in the shoebox, but he made himself smile up at her like it was nothing.

"You could call it that." Tiff passed over her plate. "What do you have for dessert?"

They were digging into two chocolate cream pies when James pulled out the remaining thing in the box—several envelopes, the regular letter-sized kind, all rubber-banded together.

The rubber band snapped when he started to tug it off, stinging his hand. They appeared to be ordinary-looking business envelopes, all opened, all written in what seemed to be the same handwriting. Each one was addressed to Mama from someone named Barbara Hargrave, return address someplace in Alabama.

Hargrave. He knew that name—it was Mama's maiden name.

He pulled out the contents of the first envelope, some folded up papers. A couple of photographs fell out. A younger Mama, with little James and a baby Tiff propped up on her lap. Another with a much-younger Mama and a young version of Daddy, smiling in front of some waterfall. An older picture with four pretty teenaged girls, what looked like Mama on the right, only she had braces and bangs. He could tell they were all related because they all looked like each other, all had that same crooked smile, that same dark hair. Sisters. They had to be.

He showed Tiff.

"I didn't know Mama had family." Tiff blinked.

She flipped the photograph over, and he could see Mama's handwriting on the back. "Connie, Barb, Daisy, and me," Mama'd written, with the date.

He did the math. Mama would have been about sixteen in that photo, give or take.

Tiff reached for the letter, and he passed it over. She read it as he studied the picture. Aunts. He had aunts. Maybe cousins. Were they still alive?

"Oh, my goodness." Tiff's words were a whisper.

He took the letter, read it for himself.

My dear Mags,

I know you said not to write, not ever, but I had to. He's dead, you know. It's safe to come back.

I'm missing you like crazy. So are the others. Connie's got three little ones now, and she's married to Jake Barnes—remember him?—and they got a place out past the river. Daisy's still Daisy, crazy as all get out, but her heart's in the right place. She's due any day now with her first. Finally settled down, can you believe it? I stuck some pictures in here of me and Daisy and Connie and your nephews. The oldest, Charles, looks just like you. That is, if you were a boy. He's even got your laugh.

But me, I miss you most of all. You're my big sis, my best friend, and the hole in my heart's grown to the size of a landmine since you've been gone. I get why you left, only I wish you hadn't. He put us through things no little girls should ever go through, hurting us. Doing those bad things. But he's gone now. Heart attack, in case you wondered. He'll never hurt us again.

I hope you're happy with Ray, hope he took care of you like he said he would. I bet you have a cluster of kids and a big old house and a happy life, just like you said you would. I just want you to know you're both welcome here, anytime you want. I'm living in the house still, but you know there's plenty of room. You could move in, you and Ray, have the whole place to yourself if you wanted. I know you hate Alabama, said you'd never set foot in this place again, but there's a part of me that hopes you were just talking out of anger. It'd kill me to think I'd never see my sister again.

If you won't come, maybe I could come see you. You know I'd cross a field of glass to see you, Mags. I know we had words, but I know YOU know I didn't mean them. I was just hurt. You were, too. I know you didn't mean those things you said to me, or to Connie or Daisy. It's all water under the bridge now, hear me?

Write me back soon. At least just let me know you're okay. I love you.

Your sister forever, Barbara

A sister. Three sisters. He'd never known. She'd never said.

James looked up to see Tiff holding another photo, tears in her eyes. Three young women in front of some picnic table, one on the left huge with child, the other in the center with her arms around the others, and the third on the end, three little boys crowded around. The oldest boy leaned around his mama, all protective like.

"He looks just like you, James." Tiff's voice was a whisper.

The tears tracked down her face then, silent tears, as they gazed at the picture, at the family they might have known. Family that could've helped.

He's dead, you know. The words in that letter caught his heart, swirled through his head. A father? Husband? Uncle? Had to be their father, or some parental figure . . . *put us through things no little girls should ever go through . . .*

"She told me once she ran away when she was sixteen." Tiff's words were so soft he could barely hear her. "I'd been complaining about Daddy to her, back when I thought that would help. She told me my life was a cakewalk compared to what she'd gone through when she was my age with her own daddy, said I best snap out of it and get my act together. I never knew what she meant. Now . . ." She took a long shuddery breath. "Now I guess I do."

He saw she had another letter, there with the photo. He opened it.

> To my sister.
>
> I know you're probably sick and tired of me writing you every year like clockwork. They say I'm stupid to do it, maybe you're not even living there anymore, but I figure they don't get sent back unopened, so maybe you are getting them. Anyway, happy birthday. Even if it's been twenty years, I still picture you in my mind like you left just yesterday. I bet you're still as pretty as ever. You always were the prettiest one of us all.
>
> I sure could use you back in my life. It hasn't been easy. Connie's doing okay now. Doctors said she's in remission, so maybe she will be okay. Daisy's still Daisy. That girl! She's teaching elementary school now. Her youngest just started kindergarten. Who'd have thought our baby sis would be the one who ended up the most domesticated of us all? Then again, for all I know you've got a batch of kids. Wouldn't that be a hoot!
>
> I've never stopped missing you or loving you. I pray that one day maybe you'll write me back. Until then I remain,
>
> Your loving sister,
> Barb

Twenty years and not a word. Why?

Tiff sniffled, and he saw her tears had stopped. Her eyes were just red now, raw. Like she'd been up all night.

"Come on," he said. "Let's figure out where we're gonna stay tonight."

The waitress brought the check, and Tiff swiped her card at the counter. They were out of there so quick he almost didn't notice until they were at the door.

But once he saw, he couldn't unsee—there, in the corner. His head was down, but James would know that build, that jawline, anywhere.

Big John. He could see the telltale red hammer tattoo, big and prominent on his right arm.

And next to Big John sat Mike.

From his old crew.

Oh, Lord Jesus.

CHAPTER 41

James

Go. In a flash he was out the door, Tiff trailing after him.

"What's wrong?" she asked when they got outside.

He didn't speak, just walked around the side of the building, away from their car. Pulled her close so she, too, was hidden.

"James, talk to me," she whispered, her body stiff as she tried to yank away. "Did you see someone?"

"Yes!" His voice was a hiss. "Just wait."

They waited ten minutes that felt like thirty. Watched as Big John and Mike and the other guy they were with, no one James knew, exited, climbed into a red pickup, and roared off into the night.

Only then did James loosen his grip on Tiff's arm and let his muscles begin to relax. Maybe they hadn't seen him at all. But it sure had been close.

"Ow." She rubbed her arm, and in the dim streetlight he could see her arm was red.

"Sorry. I just . . ."

"I get it." She put her hand on his arm, and he was surprised she didn't push the subject. "I'll go get the car, and you can hop in around back."

"Thanks," he said gratefully.

"We better stay another town farther," she said when they were driving again. "Play it safe. Do you think you were seen?"

James shook his head, but his heart was still pounding. "Doesn't seem like it."

"I agree." She steered with both hands on the wheel, her face set in concern. When they got to the red light, she faced him. "James, look. I'm really sorry I dragged us out here. I knew you didn't want to go, and I know I'm the one who made us. It was stupid of me, and selfish."

He waved it away. "I had a choice, sis. You didn't 'drag' me anywhere."

"You know what I mean."

"I came because I wanted to. Deep down, I needed to. Just like you. End of story."

The light turned green, and they drove on in silence.

When he spoke again, his voice sounded gruff. "The closure was just as much for me as it was for you. Besides, even if they saw me, who cares. We're not being followed, no one knows where we're staying, and we'll be gone tomorrow before anyone spots us again."

"Still, I'm going to see if my boss'll book the room on her credit card, let me pay her back."

"They're not the Mafia out to trace your card, Tiff. They're just some small-town gangbangers. It's fine."

"Well, I'd feel better."

They spotted a small motel up on the right, and they pulled in and parked. Tiff picked up her phone and dialed. He could hear half the conversation as his sister gave her boss the motel name and location.

"If you found it online it's got to be halfway decent," Tiff joked, and James could hear the woman laugh on the other end of the phone call.

They chatted a few more minutes, then he heard his sister's voice change.

"No, please don't tell him where I am . . ." A pause. "I'm just not ready. He's called a couple times, but I just need to handle this alone. With my brother."

The way she said it—my brother—felt nice.

Tiff hung up, and they grabbed their bags from the backseat. At the last minute, she grabbed the plastic shoebox, too.

He followed her inside, through check-in, and down the hall to their room, where he collapsed on his bed. He was asleep before she even got out of the shower.

And for once, he didn't dream.

CHAPTER 42

THE NEXT MORNING, Tiff awoke before the alarm and lay as still as she could in her squeaky motel bed, staring at the ceiling. She'd stayed up late last night, reading and rereading all the letters to Mama from her sister, but James hadn't budged, not even when he'd started snoring and she'd tossed a pillow over at him from across the room.

Glancing over at his bed, it seemed he was fast asleep. Good. She still felt awful—it hadn't even crossed her mind he'd be bothered about coming here. She'd been all wrapped up in her own little world, thinking her own selfish thoughts, worrying her own solitary worries. But James had lost his mama, too. He was coming back to his hometown for the first time in years, too.

An aunt. Three aunts. And cousins! It was hard to believe. Were they still alive? Would they even want to talk to her? She hoped so.

She wanted to text Bobby, tell him the news, but she made herself keep the phone where it was, on the charger, and instead thought about the letters. Three boy cousins from Aunt Connie, probably right around her age. Aunt Daisy'd gone on to have five—three girls, two boys. Aunt Barb had stayed single, from how it sounded. There was even mention of a grandbaby on the way.

All this time, she'd had family, and she'd never even known it. Why hadn't Mama said anything? Why hadn't they gone to visit, or at least invited them down?

Deep in her belly, Tiff thought she knew the answer. Her breath caught as the realization sank in.

Mama'd run from her past the same way Tiff had run from hers. Would have kept on running from hers, had what's-his-name not confessed to his role in everything and James not gotten out of prison on good behavior.

Mama's sister hadn't spelled out in exact detail what their daddy had done to Mama and her sisters, but Tiff got the picture. The thought made her shudder. How in God's holy name anyone could do such a thing . . .

From James's bed she heard a grunt.

"I think you set a sleep record," she said as she watched him slowly sit up, peer groggily around the room.

"What time is it?"

"About nine thirty. Checkout's at eleven."

He mumbled something and then buried his head back under the covers.

She bit back a smile. "I read the rest of the letters. We have aunts. And cousins!"

"That's just . . . crazy."

"Right? Go take your shower. We can talk over breakfast."

They ate muffins and sipped weak hotel orange juice in the lobby, where she showed him more photographs and told him everything she'd read.

"You read them, too, on the drive home," she said. "I think we should reach out to them, maybe try to find them on social media. I looked up their town last night. It's not a big place, maybe forty minutes from Birmingham."

James nodded slowly, staring at the pictures, his eyes blinking almost in disbelief. One of their cousins looked like a young Tiff, only she was clearly a gymnastics prodigy of some sort, all decked out in a leotard with a bunch of medals around her neck.

"We should," he said.

They took Mama's suitcase to the thrift store, then killed time at the area's sole department store until it was almost one and time to head to the coroner's office.

Mr. Reynolds smiled kindly when he saw them. "Wait here just a moment," he said, smoothing down his moustache.

They sat in his office chairs as he disappeared into the other room, then came back cradling a large white cardboard box gently in his arms.

"Your mother's remains," he said.

"Thank you," James said, taking the box awkwardly.

They stared solemnly at it. The box was bigger than she'd expected, though she didn't know why she thought it'd be smaller. She didn't know a thing about cremation, and for a moment, she regretted it, regretted not asking to see Mama once more, regretted not spending the extra money for a burial.

"Can you?" James was asking.

She started. "Sorry. What?"

"Sign. Here and here." Mr. Reynolds pointed.

She signed, and then they were standing up, shaking Mr. Reynolds's hand once more, and walking down the staircase and down the long hall out to her car.

When they got to the parking lot, they paused. She stared at the box.

"It's heavier than it looks," James said, and she held her arms out, took it from him.

Her arms sagged. He was right. Mama—her remains, her ashes, all she'd been in life, now confined to a small white cardboard box. It felt . . . wrong somehow.

She closed her eyes and felt the trees rustle around her.

"We should pray," James whispered.

And so they did—there, in the parking lot of the county offices, the remains of their mama between them, they joined hands as James spoke the words.

When she opened her eyes, the sun was peeking out from behind a cloud. They walked slowly toward her car, stowing the ashes securely in the trunk.

"I know we should get back, but how do you feel about one more stop?" James asked. "I was thinking we should sprinkle some of her ashes down by the river."

Tiff considered, nodding. The river was a pretty spot, and she could tell it meant something to James. They'd gone there on occasion when she was small, her and James. "I think she'd like that."

They left the car at the post office and walked the old trail, familiar even all these years later. She could hear the river in the distance, and to her left she could see the meadow. In the spring and summer, it was pretty, but in the winter, it just looked like old, patchy brown weeds. Still, it had been a good place. A peaceful place.

"We came here. Mama and I," James murmured when they got to the river and knelt.

"You did?" Tiff blinked. He'd never said.

"She used to be . . . different then. You were little, just a baby. She'd bring a blanket, lay it out for you."

"I have absolutely no memory of this." She shook her head.

"It wasn't all the time. Just once in a while. Then it just . . . stopped."

His eyebrows came together, and his lips thinned.

They knelt in silence, listening to the breeze rustle through the trees, the water rush through the river rocks. Finally, she opened the box.

"Wherever she is now, I hope she's happy," she said, lifting the lid to find a plastic baggie, the ashes within. "Or at least in peace."

The coroner had tucked a small scoop in the top of the box, and they opened the bag, scooped out a little of her remains.

"Rest in peace, Mama," James whispered as together they sprinkled the ashes by the riverbank. "I hope you found Jesus."

Whatever tears had been building were held at bay with the wind. She swallowed thickly, folded down the top of the bag, and closed the box up tight.

"Do you mind if . . ." James pressed his lips together, and she waited. "If we bring the rest back to Dahlia, maybe see if Rev can do a little service for us? Not right away, but when we're ready."

"It sounds like a perfect idea." It did.

And with that, they rose from the riverbank, walked back to the car, and headed home.

CHAPTER 43

Tiff

WHEN SHE AWOKE SATURDAY, the sun was high in the sky. She lay still, blinking in the morning light, for a moment not sure whether she was still in Walterville or back home, in Dahlia.

Then she felt the familiar weight across her leg. Peaches. She shifted, and he began to purr.

"Come here," she murmured, lugged the cat into the crook of her arm, where for a moment he struggled until the gentle scratch of her nails beneath his chin lulled him once more into a limp, happy mess.

Home. She gazed at the ceiling as she petted him, taking in the familiar tick of the ceiling fan above, the muted petals in the floral landscape on the wall, almost burgundy now in the pale light, but a vivid rose-pink if she were to raise the blinds. Across the room, above the dresser mirror, the words "bravery is a choice" jumped out at her.

Funny—as a kid she never in a million years would have expected to own the word "brave." Now here she was, not only living on her own and rocking her job at the paper, but she'd just driven across the state and singlehandedly stood up to the demons of her past.

251

Well, not singlehandedly. Truth be told, without James by her side, she wasn't sure she'd have attempted all they'd managed. Probably would have told Mr. Reynolds at the county coroner to take care of the ashes however he wished, driven by the old house and school without stopping, certainly wouldn't have gone through the letters . . .

Aunts. And cousins. Remembering, she peered over, saw the box was still on her nightstand where she'd left it, the letters in a tumbled heap right beside.

After she and James had gotten home last night, she'd stayed up late again, reading through Barb's words. Over and over, till she felt she knew Barb. Till she was real. Imagining the Mama she'd never known. Was Barb still out there, living in her childhood home in who-knows-where Alabama, pining for the prodigal sister who'd never come home? What about Aunt Connie—had the cancer returned? Was Daisy still teaching school and raising kids? Maybe at this point they wouldn't want to hear from her, but she'd do it anyway, reach out. To give them all closure if nothing else.

Tiff scooched to a sitting position in the bed, Peaches grumbling as she did before settling back down to his kitty dreams. She reached across to the other nightstand for her cell phone and checked the time. Almost ten thirty. She hadn't slept this late in ages.

But I feel good. Rested. Peaceful.

Bobby had texted her early, probably on his way to the grocery.

Just thinking of you, Tiff.

The words were simple, but they said all she needed to know, and her heart warmed as she closed her eyes against the tears. Whatever Tiff's own future held with him, she couldn't deny: She loved him. Maybe always would. And she'd set things right, one way or the other.

But instead of texting him back, she scrolled through her phone, opened up social media.

And typed "Barbara Hargrave, Alabama," into the search box.

There were four, but she knew right away which one had to be her aunt. Short, almost pixie-cut dark hair, grinning with her arm around a huge palomino, her fingers laced casually through the horse's mane.

Tiff clicked on the thumbnail photo, opened up the page. Her aunt clearly didn't care much about privacy settings, for almost instantly Tiff had access to all Barb's photos—Barb on a horse, competing in some race. Barb grinning with a handful other women, all decked out in riding clothes and medals. Barb smiling in a field of sunflowers, a couple of teenaged girls next to her. Barb arm-in-arm with two other ladies, one with a full head of gray, the other heavyset with jet-black orphan-Annie curls.

Her aunts. All three of them.

Tiff's heart pounded as she clicked on the little blue "message" icon and typed out the words. She hit send before she could lose her nerve.

Then she stared at the screen, at what she'd written and couldn't undo, even if she wanted to:

> My name is Tiff Steadman, and my mother's name is Margaret Reba Hargrave Steadman. I found some old letters and think you might be my aunt. Can we talk?

Tiff spent the day in a haze of memory, cleaning the house, paying some bills, painting her toenails. James was working all afternoon and evening at the pizza place, and on a whim she called

Rebecca, invited her over.

Of course, she wasn't quite ready to show her face at Smathers Grocery, but she needed groceries, not to mention toilet paper. She couldn't avoid Bobby forever, but she wasn't quite ready. Yet.

Instead, she zipped over to Village Pizza, a place she'd successfully avoided since she'd discovered James was working there. No time like the present.

She pushed the door open and gave a little wave to the owner. "Hey, Alana."

"Well, hey, stranger." The dark-haired owner crossed her thick arms over her chest, but she had a twinkle in her eye. "Ain't see you in, what, ten years? Don't tell me you've gone carb-free."

"Ha." Tiff stuck out her tongue. "Can I get a large mushroom and a salad?"

"Coming right up." Alana shouted the order to her husband in the back, then leaned against the counter. "So how's the paper goin'? You gonna cover any more 'a that business about them car thieves?"

"I think my boss has been handling most of that." Tiff shrugged and peered toward the back, where she knew James would be. Unless he was on break. "Ah . . . is James back there?"

The question slipped out before the thought to ask it even formed in her mind. *Where in the world did that come from?* But she couldn't take the words back now.

Alana gave her a look, one eyebrow slightly raised. "James? What you want with him? You and Bobby aren't . . ."

Tiff's cheeks reddened. "No, no. James, well." She took a breath and let the words tumble out. "He's my brother."

Alana's mouth hung open, then she blinked. "Your . . . hey, James!" Alana called out. "Your sister's up front." The restaurant owner put enough emphasis on "sister" that it was clear to Tiff she wasn't quite sure of the truth.

James appeared in the opening that separated the front from the back, his expression at once confused and surprised. "Tiff."

Maybe this was a mistake. She shrugged all no-biggie. "Stopped by to grab a pizza, thought I'd say hi."

"Glad you did."

Alana was still watching them. "For real? You two are, like, actually for-real related?"

James looked at Tiff, and she nodded, trying not to grin. "For real."

Alana's husband, Lou, came around the corner just then, sweating like it was July instead of February and carrying a couple of boxes of to-go orders.

"I wondered," Lou offered.

"Lou." Alana put her hands on her hips and stared the man down. "They look nothing alike! She's got black hair, he's blond. She's all tiny as a toothpick, he's like Thor without the hammer—"

Lou shook his head and sailed back to the kitchen, but not before giving his wife the tiniest of pinches. "Alana. Hello—same last name?"

Alana huffed, but he was already in the back before she'd muttered, "Not like it's an uncommon name. Plenty of people I know have the last name Steadman."

James just shook his head, and Tiff bit back a giggle.

"Anyway, just figured I'd say hey and all," Tiff told him. "Maybe I'll see you later?"

"Sounds good, sis." He winked, and she could see the pride—and maybe a touch of good-natured ribbing—behind it.

When Tiff left ten minutes later, it felt like someone had attached two enormous red helium balloons to her shoulders, like she suddenly weighed twenty pounds less without the secret she'd been carrying. A smile played on her lips as she drove the two miles home. That old saying, you don't know how heavy your burden is till someone lightens your load? One hundred percent true, she decided.

He's my brother. The words—her words, from her lips—echoed in her head. Owning it felt good. Right.

Later that evening, Tiff and Rebecca were curled up on her couch, finishing off the pie her boss had brought for dessert.

"Josh made this? From scratch?" Tiff's eyes were big as she took another bite of the apple pie Rebecca's boyfriend had made that afternoon.

"With little JJ! I could hardly believe it myself, but his son's been teaching him. JJ might be ten, but the kid knows a thing or two about the kitchen."

"I don't know whether to be impressed or start buying stock in JJ's future restaurant," Tiff managed behind another bite.

That earned a laugh. "Well, he's already talking about helping with the catering when we ... ah ..." Rebecca stopped, her cheeks suddenly flushed.

Tiff raised a brow and cleared her throat. "Catering?" That could only mean one thing.

Rebecca looked like she either wanted to disappear into the couch cushions or stand up and sing, or both. "Ah, I mean, one day ..."

"Rebecca." Tiff made her voice all scolding, but she was grinning from ear to ear. "Let's have it."

"Okay!" Rebecca all but chirped the word, sounding more like a schoolgirl than a full-grown woman. Her flushed cheeks were now an all-out red. "Josh and I have been talking about getting married."

Tiff squealed and threw herself into Rebecca's arms. "I'm so excited! Oh, Rebecca, this is wonderful news! When? How long have you been talking about it? Tell me everything!"

Rebecca shrugged all coy, but Tiff could see the shine in her eyes. It wasn't too long ago she'd seen her boss on the other end of heartache. Watching her boss's formerly cool façade melt away, watching her relax into love, had been one of the best parts about the last year. Better almost than experiencing it herself, with Bobby.

A stab in her gut came then as Tiff remembered her own reaction, her own squeals of joy, when Bobby'd proposed to her last year. She took a bite of pie, determined not to let Rebecca see the pain, and gestured for Rebecca to spill.

"It's not official-official, but I think we're going to take it slow, maybe plan something small for next spring. There's a lot going on this year."

"Spring? That's more than a year away!" And a good six months after Tiff's own wedding. If that was even going to happen anymore.

Rebecca gave a small smile. "I've waited my whole life for this. I'm not going to rush it now."

"Aren't you the voice of maturity," Tiff teased. "So when did you two decide?"

"A couple weeks ago—"

"A couple weeks!" Tiff blurted. "How could you keep something like this to yourself for a couple of weeks?"

"I didn't want to say anything with all the other stuff going on right now." Rebecca didn't elaborate, but Tiff knew what she really meant—the stuff going on with her. Her and Bobby. Her and James.

She'd been a wreck, plain and simple. And completely oblivious to how that was impacting the lives of everyone around her.

Tiff's voice softened, and she set her plate and Rebecca's on the coffee table, took her friend's hands in hers. "I am so incredibly happy for you. From the bottom of my heart. You truly are a sister to me, and there is nothing in this world I want to see more than you and Josh get your happily-ever-after."

Tears pooled in Rebecca's eyes, and Tiff felt her own well up in turn.

"I feel the same for you," Rebecca said, her voice a whisper of emotion.

"I know." They hugged.

Rebecca looked like she wanted to say something but wasn't sure whether she should.

Tiff eyed her gently. "Are you going to ask about Bobby?"

"Yeah." Rebecca wrinkled her nose. "I know how much you two love each other. I feel . . . helpless watching you both go through all this alone. And guilty for also being so happy."

"Well, I haven't talked to him yet. But I plan to. Soon." As soon as I can muster up the courage.

Rebecca looked relieved. "Good."

"And on a happier note, guess who's decided to own the fact that she has a brother?" Tiff batted her eyelashes exaggeratedly and held up a hand.

"Do tell!"

Tiff described what had happened at the pizza place, and then all about their trip, even about the ashes and the idea of a memorial service here in Dahlia.

"I think that's a wonderful idea," Rebecca said about the service.

"My mama wasn't a praying person. Never set foot in a church my whole childhood, best I can recall. But somehow, it feels like the right thing to do for her." Tiff brought her knees to her chest thoughtfully. "We could do it at Dahlia Community Bible Church, nothing big, maybe just close friends, and me and James."

Rebecca smiled at her.

Tiff blinked. "What?"

"I like the sound of that. 'Me and James.'"

"We've come a long way this week," Tiff said slowly, realizing the words were completely true. "We started out barely talking. I guess it was finding out about Mama and her sisters that brought it all home for me, made me realize I needed to stop looking at myself as the victim here. Not unless I want to be miserable and always looking backwards the rest of my life."

"Wait." Rebecca was frowning. "Sisters?"

Tiff covered her mouth. "I completely forgot to tell you!" She snagged her phone, scrolled through and opened up social media. "I have an aunt! Three aunts! And cousins!" She pointed at the picture of Barb and the gorgeous palomino and knew she was grinning like a weirdo.

"Not to mention a horse cousin?" Rebecca offered.

And then they were giggling, scrolling through Barb's online photos and pointing out resemblances. That's when Tiff noticed the little blue "message" icon was lit up. She thumbed over and opened the app.

"Is that her? Your Aunt Barbara?" Rebecca peered closer.

Tiff gasped, her heart pounding. "I think she replied back!"

Chapter 44

Tiff

TIFF SCOOTED SO SHE AND REBECCA could read the words together.

What if it was the wrong person? What if Mama's sister had moved someplace far off, or even died?

Or worse—what if she didn't want to hear from Tiff? That, Tiff didn't think she could bear.

Peaches chose that moment to jump up on the couch between the women, purring loudly as he settled his body across them.

Tiff ruffled his fur as she forced herself to click on the message, ignored the slow thread of fear working its way down her spine.

"Tiff sugar, if your mama's my sister Maggie, I sure as blue blazes am your aunt," the message began, and a breathless laugh escaped Tiff's mouth as she gripped the phone so tight the pads of her fingers turned pink.

> And you got two other aunties, too, bound to be jumping for joy the second I tell them we found Maggie and her babies after all these years! You're her daughter? Does she have more kids—do you have brothers and sisters? My gracious, girl, you are an answered prayer, let me tell you!

Enough of my rambling. Can we talk by phone? Please
call me!

The message closed with a phone number and a bunch of elec-
tronic hearts.

Tiff cast a guilty look at Rebecca. "She doesn't know Mama
passed."

"It's okay. She's still going to be happy to hear from you."

A lump settled in Tiff's throat. "Yeah, but how do you tell someone the long-lost sister they've spent their lifetime waiting to find
up-and-died last week?"

Rebecca sighed. "Gently." She looked at her watch. "Where'd
you say she lives, Alabama? The time is an hour behind there. We
could call her now. Though you probably want to wait for James."

Tiff bit her lip. "Good point."

"Here." Rebecca held out her hand, and Tiff passed her the
phone. Rebecca clicked it off, set it on the coffee table next to their
finished pie plates, then thought a moment. "Tomorrow's Sunday.
I think you should talk to James about it, and then give her a call
after church tomorrow. It's getting late. I've got to get going."

"You don't suppose you want to call and break the news to her
for me?" Tiff hammed a pretty-please face, and Rebecca swatted
at her.

They heard Mrs. Crenshaw's little white dog yapping from
next door, and then the unmistakable sound of James's bike tires
crunching over gravel.

Minutes later, his key turned in the lock and he walked in.

"Hey, sis . . . oh, sorry. Didn't know you had company."

Rebecca stood then, a warm smile on her face.

"Hi, Tiff's brother James." She held out a hand, which James
shook. "I'm Rebecca, and I'm headed home, so you both have the
house to yourself. Nice to finally meet you."

"Nice to meet you, too." He seemed almost shy.

Rebecca collected her purse and keys and gave Tiff a big hug. "See you tomorrow. Save me a seat at church? You know I'm always late."

"You've got it."

The door shut, and James stared out the window till Rebecca's car had backed out of the driveway and sped off into the night. Then he cast Tiff a gaze.

"Tiff's brother James?"

"What's the expression, 'Go big or go home?'" Tiff shrugged.

He laughed and sank down next to her on the couch. Peaches shifted to give him room, and the three of them sat there a moment, letting the buzz of the day wear off, listening to the tick of the wall clock. James smelled like garlic, tomato, and cheese—like he was a walking, talking pizza. The thought made Tiff smile.

"You know, if I worked there I'd probably gain three thousand pounds," Tiff said.

"Nah, if you worked there you'd want anything but pizza."

She giggled. "You're probably right."

Peaches stretched, and James scratched him under the chin, then looked warningly at Tiff.

"Just because I'm petting your cat doesn't mean I like them now. I just like this one."

"Don't worry. Your secret's safe with me."

He rose, checked the front door locks, then paused by the stairs. "I'm beat. Going to shower and head to bed. Need anything?"

"I'm good."

He paused a moment longer. "You sure you're okay with all this? This 'being all out in the open with your brother' thing."

She looked at him, and for a moment she no longer saw him as her big brother James, her childhood protector, or James, the skinhead gang member she'd tried her level best to make herself hate for seven years.

Now he just looked like James. Single, solitary, lonely James. Starting over in life the only way he knew how.

Her heart ached a moment, and she swallowed past the lump in her throat. "You are my brother, James. No matter what happened in the past, we are family. Can't deny that."

Why had it taken her so long to realize that? The words, once out, hung between them, a salve. A grace.

A truth.

He closed his eyes at her words, but not before she saw a glimmer of moisture in his eyes.

"Goodnight, Tiff."

The next morning, Tiff started to tiptoe down the stairs to make coffee when she saw the light under his bedroom door.

Before she could lose her nerve, she stepped to the door and knocked gently.

"I'm leaving for church in about forty minutes if you want a ride," she said as if it were the most natural thing in the world, like they did this every Sunday morning there'd ever been.

She didn't wait for a reply, just headed downstairs to the kitchen to make coffee.

By the time she'd showered, done her hair and makeup, and slipped on a cute sweater and skirt, he was dressed and in the living room, waiting for her.

"Who'd have thought—two Steadmans going to church together on a Sunday morning," she cracked as she backed out of the driveway.

His laugh cleared the air, and by the time they got to church, Tiff knew: One way or the other, it was all going to be okay.

She wondered if Bobby would be there, or if he'd start going to his mama's church again. Maybe that's where Natalie goes. The thought crept up and smacked her, and she gritted her teeth.

But the first person she saw when they walked up the path to the church was Bobby. Her heart did a little tumble. It looked like he was waiting for them. For her.

Bobby blinked as he saw James at her side, but he recovered quickly. "How's it goin'?"

They did that guy handshake thing like James being there, all public and whatnot, was no big thing. That was one of her favorite things about Bobby Smathers, she realized—his ability to take things in stride, to roll with life whatever it tossed at you.

Not like Tiff, who tended to flail and toss like a person drowning.

James went in, but Bobby gently snagged Tiff's arm, led her to the alcove, where people stashed coats and umbrellas.

They stood a moment, staring at each other. A thousand thoughts vied for the chance to lead, but Tiff pressed her lips together, forced herself to just be. *Are you okay? Do you still love me? Are we . . . ?* The alcove was warm, and she caught the barest whiff of his soap as they stood there.

He opened his mouth to speak, but words wouldn't do. Instead, she threw her arms around him and pressed her lips close to his ear.

"I miss you," she whispered.

"Me, too." His breath was hot against her hair, and they clung to each other. For a moment, time stood still.

Then the music started, and she pulled away, stepping into the sanctuary. There, up on the left, sat James. Toward the front, she could see Marla with little Devon. Marla caught her eye, motioned to the spot next to her, but Tiff winked and nodded toward her brother.

When she slid in next to him, James looked momentarily surprised, then happy. Bobby joined, too, and at the last minute, Rebecca, Josh, and JJ crowded in, and then they were all on their feet, singing and clapping and letting church take over.

After, Bobby walked her to the car. She wanted to ask him about everything—Natalie. His mama. If he still wanted to marry her. But she held her tongue. *Take it slow.* The thought washed over her like a balm.

"Think you're free for lunch this week?" he asked, opening her car door for her.

"I think definitely."

He smiled. "Good."

Bobby wandered off, toward his own car, and Tiff could see James talking with Rev and his foster son, Devon. Rev gave James a high-five, and then James was headed her way, slipping into the passenger seat, and they were driving home.

"Rev said he'd be happy to do a service for Mama whenever we're ready."

Tiff looked over, impressed that it was him, not her, who'd thought to ask. "Thanks for handling that."

James shrugged. "He already knew. About Mama. I guess Bobby or your boss or somebody said something."

She wasn't quite sure how she felt about that—the idea of people knowing their business, telling their preacher, then decided it was probably a good thing. One of the best and worst things about living in a small town was that most secrets couldn't stay secrets long. If she'd wanted it otherwise, she suspected she would have ended up someplace like Charlotte or Atlanta and not Everybody-Knows-Everything-About-Everyone Dahlia.

"Well, that's good," she said finally.

When she told him about Aunt Barb, he grinned. "Let's call her now. Right when we get home."

"But what about the news? About Mama?"

"The very least we can do is tell her. She's not gonna want to break ties after waiting for some speck of news all these years."

He had a point.

They made the call from the living room, both of them gathered around her cell phone, which she'd put on speaker.

"Oh, my gracious, you sound just like your Mama did when we last spoke!" The words, spoken by her aunt, warmed Tiff from her head to the tips of her lavender toenails.

James cleared his throat. "Aunt Barb—do you mind if we call you that?—we have to say until two days ago, Tiff and I had no idea we had an aunt, or any family beyond our mama, for that matter."

Barb sniffled. "I'd wondered. That does sound like Mags, up and starting over with a clean slate and no ties. Is she . . . still around?"

The words caught in Tiff's throat, but James pressed on.

"I'm sorry, but she's not," he said. "She's passed on. We were going through her things when we found a big pile of letters from you she'd saved over the years. All of them kept in their original envelope, rubber-banded together and stacked all neat in a special box."

The way he said it made it sound nice, like Mama had cared. In her own way, Tiff imagined Mama had indeed cared, had loved her sister. Sisters. Only the pain of the past was just too deep to get over.

Tiff surely knew what that felt like. Only, she didn't care to repeat Mama's life—or her mistakes.

"I had a feeling." Barb sniffled again. "Well, go on and tell me all about you two. Where are you living now? Did Mags ever carry out her dream of owning that hair salon? She always did have a knack for hair . . ."

By the time they hung up forty minutes later, Tiff felt exhausted, but it was a good exhausted, as though she'd just been on a speed-date with the man of her dreams. Not that she knew what a speed-date felt like, but she imagined it was just as overwhelmingly exhilarating and simultaneously draining, like winning the lottery and going on a shopping spree. She also knew a gazillion more facts about horses and horse racing then she ever thought existed.

"We'll talk again next Sunday same time, if it's all right with you. I'll gather the whole family, and we can do a video call," Barb promised, talking a mile a minute. "And we'll start working on plans to get you two out here pronto for a visit!"

They hung up, and Tiff looked at James.

"I like her."

James nodded. "So do I."

"James—we have an aunt. Actual family."

"Weird, huh?"

"Truly!"

A feeling ran through her, like an unsettling hum out of the clear-blue nowhere. *Too good to be true.* Mama's words echoed through her mind: Anytime something lands in your lap like a present from above, look for the strings. They're always there.

Tiff couldn't see any strings. At least, not yet.

CHAPTER 45

James

AFTER HIS LUNCH SHIFT AT VILLAGE PIZZA on Monday, James rode his bike to the church and checked in with Rev.

"How are things, my friend?" Rev boomed, coming in for a bear hug. Chilly February was easing toward spring, and today the preacher wore a T-shirt and basketball shorts.

James wasn't quite ready to shed the hoodie—still too cool outside, and besides, there was the question of all the ink. Especially that one. But the time was coming. Maybe a big bandage would do, at least in the short term.

Stupid, he thought. All those years of petty theft and selling car parts for cash, and he'd spent it all on booze and tattoos. Now, he was working to have those same tattoos removed. It was one big waste. Like his life had been, really, up till now.

But it wasn't too late to change that.

"What can I help with today?" James asked the preacher.

Rev led him to the back, where a giant beam of dark wood lay in the alley.

"I'm thinking I want to cut this down a bit, then fashion a big old-style cross," Rev said. "Something we can display out front during Lent."

Lent. James frowned, trying to remember what Pastor Chad had told them in prison. "That's the time that leads up to Easter?"

"Yup. Starts this Wednesday, in fact, with Ash Wednesday, leads all the way up to Easter in April. Thought the cross could tie in real nice with the Bible study I'm leading Wednesday nights. I'm gonna hand out these nails on Wednesday and this Sunday, invite the whole congregation to hammer them into the cross as a way to represent sin, then cover them all over good as new with white lilies on Easter Sunday. Marla's idea about the flowers." Rev winked.

James glanced over at the nails and saw the big container filled with cold black metal. He shivered.

"It's a good idea," James offered.

Rev grinned. "Thanks!"

They got to work, cutting the timber to size, then sanding it down smooth so little hands wouldn't catch on any splinters.

Then they hoisted the shorter beam so it set nice and even on the longer one, took a long rope Rev produced from inside somewhere, and wrapped it over and under, figure-eight style, almost like they were crafting the mast of a sailboat or something.

When it was snug, they got the discards, planks and leftover beam, and fashioned a sturdy base.

"Don't want it blowing over if we get a spring storm," Rev explained.

They finished the job just as evening was setting in and carried the cross around to the front, where they set it on a flat patch of grass outside the church where every car driving by wouldn't be able to miss it.

"That's a big cross!" said a kid's voice.

James looked over to see Rev's son, Devon, and his wife, Marla, ambling down the street. Devon carried his basketball and a water bottle, which he set carefully against a tree before running up to Rev for a hug.

Marla, her crisp cream work bag bright against her long purple dress, wandered up, too, and planted a kiss on her husband's cheek.

"Hey there, James." Marla smiled at him, then looked at her husband. "I'm glad you agreed with my idea."

Rev shot his wife a look. "Now, the cross was my idea, if I do say so myself, Mrs. Bryant," he teased. "You came up with the flowers."

"Mm-hm, if you say so. Only, who's been talking about that cross since, oh, three years ago, when we went to visit my mama and daddy up in Cincinnati?"

"I think God gets the credit," Devon broke in, and they all laughed.

"Right you are, sweet boy." Marla peered down at the boy, gave his head an affectionate rub.

James got a twinge of something—jealousy? Envy? Or deeper still, wonder—as he watched their easy exchange. He and Mama had been like that once, he was sure he remembered. Before life and fear and drink and disappointment all conspired to get in the way.

Before wrong choices landed him behind bars and, ultimately, here.

His new home, for now. Dahlia. A town named after a flower that was somehow, fittingly, helping him grow.

James gazed up at the moon, just starting to show in the early twilight. "I best get going. Need a hand tomorrow?"

"That'd be great. Same time?" Rev asked.

"See you then."

"Careful with that bike," Marla called after James as he pedaled slowly down the street toward home. "Best lock it up tight tonight. Rumor has it whoever's been doing those car break-ins are messing with bikes and such, too."

"Will do."

At the corner James realized he'd left his water bottle at the church and decided he'd swing into the corner store for a fresh one.

The girl at the counter gave him a nervous glance when he walked in, but then she relaxed, chatting it up with a couple of older men about the weather. A police officer came in just as James was paying, gave him the once-over nod all friendly-like, and continued to the back.

Outside, James took a long swig from the bottle, then hopped on the bike, prepared to pedal home, when he heard a voice from behind.

"Hey."

James whirled. It was the cop from inside, only now the friendly was gone.

He swallowed. *You didn't do anything wrong. He's just doing his job.* Only it reminded him of the old days, back in Walterville, when the cops would mess with him just for kicks. Reminded him of the seven long years he'd been locked up in prison.

"Yessir." James took his feet off the pedals, turned to face the officer. Made sure his hands were in full view.

He was more than an officer, James could see now. His badge was larger, and now that he was looking at it, James could see another word there. Sheriff.

"What's your name, son?"

The "son" made him bristle, but James kept his head down all humble, tried to smile politely. "James Steadman, sir."

The sheriff looked like he was mentally running James's name through some brain computer, sorting things out. He also saw the man eyeballing his tattoos, the few that poked out from beneath the hoodie.

"Steadman. You from around here?"

"No, sir. Moved here about a month or so ago. Up from Columbia." Should he have said state prison? His heart thumped, and he tried to recall what Pastor Chad and the parole officer had told him to do if ever he were to encounter a police officer. Nothing much, as far as he could remember. Just to keep his nose clean and stay in good graces with the authorities. He tried to smile again. "Nice night."

The sheriff blinked. "Sure is a nice night. You work around here?"

"Yessir, I do. I work at Village Pizza, and I've just come from Dahlia Community Bible Church, where I attend and volunteer." All he wanted to do was go home. Just go home and sleep. His palms felt all sticky-sweaty, like it was the middle of summer and not the end of winter. He wanted to rub them on his jeans, only he didn't want to draw attention, make the sheriff any more curious than he already was.

"Dahlia Community . . . that's Rev Bryant's church."

James nodded. "Yessir."

"He's a good man. You go to those Friday night giveaways they hold?"

James knew what he was asking—was he poor, did he go for the free stuff. "No, sir. I haven't yet, anyway."

"Hm." The sheriff's radio chirped, and he spoke some code mumbo-jumbo into it, then looked at James. "See you around, James Steadman."

"See you around, Sheriff. Have a good evening."

James gave a casual wave. A block away, his hands were still shaking. He pulled over, caught his breath.

Would it always be this way? Would he always feel like this— second-rate, some thug lowlife criminal two breaths away from lockdown? Or would it get easier with time?

He pedaled home in a daze, no longer hungry, wishing only he could disappear.

CHAPTER 46

Tiff

AT TEN A.M. TUESDAY, Tiff was putting the finishing touches on a last-minute story Rebecca had assigned her—a cutesy profile on a local kid who'd made it all the way to Los Angeles for one of those televised singing things and gotten cut just before the final round.

"I didn't like it much out there, anyway," the girl had told her, but Tiff had seen the disappointment in her eyes, seen how badly she'd wanted it, if only for the grand prize or the recording contract.

It was the first paper since she'd started that Tiff only had one story. Her boss had meant it when she said she was giving Tiff a breather, only Tiff didn't much like how it felt. Like she was an afterthought, just taking up space, not even contributing properly.

"Fine, just one," Rebecca had finally relented after Tiff begged for an assignment. She needed something to occupy her brain right now besides Bobby, the new dynamic with James, her surprise bonus family two states over, and memories of Mama, which were now starting to wake her in the night.

It was a younger Mama who haunted her dreams at night, though, not the Mama she'd known. A Mama her age, ripe with child and desperate to put a wall between her and her sad, abusive past, a Mama who didn't yell but only cried. Cried and yearned—for her sisters. For Alabama.

For love.

From what Tiff could tell, Mama'd run from one bad situation straight into the arms of another: Tiff's daddy. The combination had cost Mama her dreams, and ultimately her life.

Last night, she'd woken up shushing and rocking something, only to realize the only thing she was shushing and rocking was herself.

"Got time to proof the front page?" Rebecca was asking, and Tiff shook herself back into the present.

"Absolutely."

Tiff scanned the text, noting Rebecca's lead story—Police Zero In on Suspect as Rash of Break-Ins Explode. She scooched her chair closer as she read, poring over the words. While she and James had been in Walterville, five more cars were hit, the last in the wee hours Friday at a business that had one of those video surveillance monitors. Authorities now had a good idea of the suspect and were "actively investigating leads," according to Rebecca's story.

A stab of guilt settled in Tiff's gut as she remembered sneaking through James's room not so long ago, convinced he was up to no good. Remembered her accusations, just days ago. She was relieved to know the police had leads—and even more grateful to know those leads had nothing to do with her brother. If all this happened while they were out of town, there was no way James could be involved. Not that she'd suspected him anymore, but still. The sooner this business was settled, the better.

"How close are they to naming a suspect?" Tiff asked.

Rebecca shrugged. "Who knows. But I'm guessing we'll have something by Friday."

"It's about time," Millie hollered from across the room.

Tiff looked at Rebecca, brows lifted.

"Millie's brother-in-law got hit while you were gone," Rebecca explained.

Tiff made a face. "I'm so sorry."

"Brian had stashed half the cash for their mortgage payment in an envelope in their console and forgot about it." Millie shook her head. "Thieves got that and a pair of those fancy headphone things, too. Trish is hoppin' mad, though I'm not sure whether she's more mad at the thief or her husband for leaving cash in his car."

The rest of the stories were far more tame—some new development zoning thing, plans for an anti-bullying task force in the schools, some stink about election recounts, and Tiff's feature on the singing girl.

A yawn escaped, and the phone rang just as she finished her edits and handed the paper back to her boss.

"Tiff, line two."

She answered.

"This is Sheriff Zane calling, Tiff." The sheriff's normally friendly voice sounded decidedly cool. "Do you have a minute?"

"Uh, sure. What's up, sheriff?" She cradled the phone, opening up a new document on her computer so she could take notes. "Have some news on the break-ins?"

"Funny you should ask that." Something about the way he said it prickled her senses. She wasn't sure why—James was in the clear, that much she knew.

The sheriff took a breath. "Anything you want to tell me?"

Tiff frowned. "About what?"

He sighed. "About a certain brother who's suddenly come to town?" His voice was clipped, all trace of friendliness gone. "A convicted felon brother? Who just happens to show up right around the same time we've had a crime wave hit our county?"

A flare of rage zipped through her. Tiff gripped the phone. "Excuse me?" She could feel the eyes of her coworkers on her, and she gritted her teeth, sat up even straighter. "Exactly what are you sug-gesting, Sheriff Zane?"

"I'm saying we caught your brother on camera Thursday night ripping off some of our local citizens."

"That's not possible—"

"Your brother has tattoos, doesn't he? Wears a light-colored hoodie?"

"Wha . . .?"

"Tall guy, right? Most importantly, he's got a record. The juvee stuff was sealed, but he's got at least three petty theft misdemean-ors to his name. Not to mention a robbery and aggravated assault conviction."

"Sheriff Zane, we weren't even in town Thursday . . ."

"Is that so." He said it like his doubts were sky high.

"We weren't!" She could hear the shrill in her voice now, but she couldn't keep it at bay. She stood, still gripping the phone. "This . . . this isn't fair!"

Rebecca was standing, too. Tiff cast a desperate look in her di-rection.

"That's enough," Rebecca ordered. She slipped from behind her desk, took the phone from Tiff. "Sheriff, this is Rebecca Chastain. What in the world is going on here?"

Tiff's heart was pounding so thick and hot in her throat she feared it'd bubble up and out, and she could suddenly taste the breakfast she'd eaten three hours ago. She put a hand on her belly, forced herself to breathe. In and out. She'd been with James in Walterville the whole time Thursday night! There was no way he had anything to do with this!

As she breathed, she could hear Rebecca's side of the conversa-tion.

"They were right outside Walterville Thursday night, Sheriff. There because their mother passed. Trust me, I know. I put the room on my credit card . . . No, I wasn't there with them . . . No, I didn't see James with Tiff, but she told me . . . No, she is not covering up for him. You can check it out yourself."

The call ended abruptly.

By now both Millie and Dinah had clustered around them.

"What is going on?" Millie asked, hands on her hips.

Rebecca pressed her lips into a thin line and looked first at Millie and Dinah, then at Tiff.

"Tiff has a brother who's just moved to town," Rebecca said, cheeks flushed with anger, "and the police have named him as their prime suspect in the car break-ins."

Rebecca took a breath. "And Tiff, he wants you to talk to James. To tell him to go to the station for questioning—or they'll pick him up themselves."

CHAPTER 47

James

WHEN TIFF TRACKED HIM DOWN at the pizza place and told him the news, he'd thought it was a prank.

But the truth soon settled into his bones, making his knees shaky. He'd mumbled some excuse to Big Lou about being sick, it was half-true at least, and stumbled out the back door, not even bothering with his bike.

Then he walked, his stride long and fast and furious, down Main Street, down Church Street, and over to Aberville Highway, no clue where he was headed. Only that he had to walk. To keep walking.

Otherwise he was liable to fall and never, ever get up.

Why-why-why-why-why. The word reverberated off the pavement in time with his footsteps.

Shoulda known last night, the way that cop had looked him up and down. Known when he'd first read the news.

Couldn't expect to be a full-on criminal in a small town and not be the one the police focused on the moment anything went wrong.

Tears stung the back of his eyelids as he walked, but they weren't tears of sadness or even self-pity. They were tears of rage. Frustration.

Because at the end, he knew there was nothing he could do or say that would convince them otherwise. If the police thought he did it, he was a goner. That's how it worked now. Everyone on the inside had told him that. Forget probation—he'd be back in the slammer by nightfall.

Only, he was just starting to get comfortable again. Was just starting to live like a normal person, spend time with his sister, go to church, work a regular job. Was just starting to get excited about his new family, about how he might live this second chapter in his life.

Now, in the time it took to snap his fingers, the rug had been pulled out from under him. Just like that, he was done for.

He looked up to see he'd somehow made it to Dahlia Community Bible Church. Rev, he thought—maybe Rev could talk to them, tell them what happened. Tell them it wasn't him.

But how would Rev know? For all Rev knew, James had been the thief all along.

Karma—what goes around comes around. That's what his mama'd always said. Pastor Chad said karma was a bunch of nonsense, that the message of Jesus was most decidedly not rooted in karma but in grace, but didn't the Apostle Paul say something like it in one of his letters? You reap what you sow.

Every bone in his body felt like it was turning to mush. *You're a piece of trash, James Steadman. Always have been, always will be.*

He started to go in, then sank onto the stoop a moment, his head against his knees. Realized he still had his Village Pizza apron on. Great—he hadn't even clocked out. Now he could add that to his list of sins. Labor fraud.

Tiff must be going crazy, he knew. Or maybe not—maybe she was relieved. Maybe deep down she still suspected it, too.

James took a slow, centering breath. Then he forced himself to his feet, twisted the handle, and stepped inside.

He found Rev in the back, reading. He didn't know what expression he had on his face, but he must've looked a wreck because the preacher went to him at once.

"Hey, hey." Rev had his arms around him now, patting his back. "I got you. I got you, son. What's going on?"

At the "son," James lost it. He sank to his knees there in the center of Rev's office.

And sobbed.

It felt like hours before the tears had spent. Maybe it was. The story had come out in between. The whole time, Rev hadn't said a word, just sat close by and listened, patted his back here and there.

"I didn't do it, Rev." James's voice cracked in the quiet room.

"I know you didn't."

It shouldn't have mattered, but it did. That somebody—somebody like Rev—believed him.

James pulled a tissue from the box Rev had set close by and blew his nose.

"Now what?" he asked softly. "Do I just go to the police? Turn myself in?"

Rev sighed. "If that's what they're asking, yes. I can call a church member who's an attorney, see if she can meet you there . . ."

"It won't do any good."

"It might. James." Rev put his hand on James's shoulder and looked him in the eye. "Jesus never said life would be fair. Sometimes we face trouble for stuff we've done. Sometimes, there's trouble even when we didn't do a thing."

James knew what he meant—little kids who got cancer. Hurricanes and tornados that leveled a house at random. Drunk drivers who walked away without a scratch, while the guy minding his own business in the other car was left paralyzed, or dead.

"It just . . . stinks."

"It does!" Rev snorted. "But you know, you're not alone. Did I ever tell you about how Marla and I got together?"

Something about college, and picnics in the square, and driving eight hours straight to meet her parents in the snow and ice, tumbled through his memory. "A little."

"Did I happen to mention the student union money gone missing?"

That got James's attention. "Not that I recall."

Rev pursed his lips, shook his head. "Junior year of college, I was elected treasurer of my student union. Marla was in it, but we weren't friends yet, though I sure did know who she was, that's for certain. Now, I have zero talent for figures, part of why I went into preaching, but they didn't have anyone step up to be the treasurer, so my buddy volunteered me."

Some friend. James rubbed his eyes, forced himself to listen.

"When checks started bouncing, guess who they started looking at? Yours truly. A couple of the kids knew I was on scholarship and couldn't barely afford the cost of used books, so in their minds, it made sense. I was the one with his hands on the cash. I was the logical suspect. Only, I didn't do it."

James blinked. "So what happened?"

"Marla, who happens to be a whiz with numbers, was a freshman at the time, and she and a few of the other kids went down to the bank to investigate. Turns out it wasn't my fault at all. Bank error. But guess who got himself a new girlfriend out of the ordeal?" Rev laughed long and loud. "Romans 8:28—'And we know that in all things God works for the good of those who love him, who have been called according to his purpose.' To this day, one of my favorite Bible verses."

"Still, it must've felt rotten, at least for awhile there."

The preacher sighed. "It did. It really did. I was one of the only Black kids, too, and it was tempting to blame it on that, too. But you know what? I thought about Joseph, from the Bible."

"Mary's husband?"

"Nah, the other Joseph. He was the favorite son of Jacob, but he was no saint. Always having these grandiose dreams about his brothers bowing down to him, serving him, then rubbing those dreams in their faces. At least that's how they took it. His brothers got so ticked off they sold him into slavery."

"Ouch. And yet he became the right-hand man to the king later, didn't he?" James knew the story. Pastor Chad had led a study on it right before his release.

"Yep, but not before some married woman wanted him to herself, and when he rejected her, she got good and mad and falsely accused him of some nasty business. He got thrown in he dungeon and forgotten about for years."

James nodded. "Oh, yeah, and then he stepped up and was so good at whatever he did in jail that he got put in charge of the other prisoners, and eventually he interpreted the pharaoh's dream so well he was released and put in charge of the whole kingdom."

"Exactly." Rev gave him a pointed look. "God has a way of working things out."

"But he doesn't always."

Rev gave a sad smile. "No. He doesn't always. Sometimes, his will is that an innocent person take the fall."

"Like Jesus."

The words hung there between them. He was no Bible expert, not by a long shot. But there were others in the Bible, too, who got the wrong end of the deal for no reason at all. Job, who lost his whole family 'cause the devil played a cruel tug-of-war with God over him. David's best pal, whose only crime was having a gorgeous wife who turned the head of the king. And there were plenty who did get what was coming to them—maybe not at first, but eventually. It wasn't about deserving or not deserving. Things just happened.

Besides, like Pastor Chad had told him all those years ago when James had first opened his eyes about the Lord—not a single one of us deserve what Jesus did for us. And yet here we are.

"I hear you, Rev." James said finally.

He knew what he was going to do now. Always had. But at least now he felt peaceful about it. He'd go to the station, tell them what happened. If he got locked up again, so be it. If he didn't, so be it.

Either way, God was in command. That's all that really mattered.

Still, the sound of Tiff's voice, the low thread of panic, echoed in his ears. For her, especially, he hated what he knew was gonna come next.

"I know you do, my friend. I know. Can we pray?"

Rev led him to the chairs by the window, and they bowed their heads, gave it over into the hands of the One who had it all under control, no matter what.

"Here," Rev said as James turned to go.

He'd grabbed one of the extra Bibles from his shelf, flipped through until he got to a section, then snagged a yellow sticky note from his desk, stuck it right inside.

"Philippians. If they book you, they'll usually let you bring a Bible once they clear it. If not, they'll have some in the prison library you can borrow. Paul wrote a lot about finding joy even in tough spots."

"Thanks, Rev."

They hugged once more.

"I'll call that attorney who goes here, see if she can meet you down there," Rev said. "Want me to come with?"

"Nah. I got this."

And with that, before James could lose his nerve, before he could let the little trickles of fear and anger and frustration work their way in, James turned on his heel, strode toward the front of the church, and stepped outside.

But it wasn't a cop car that made him freeze in his tracks. Wasn't a line of police, weapons drawn.

Cruising slowly by was a red, older-model pickup.

A pickup he'd seen across the state just a few nights ago.

And inside the truck, turning his head at that precise moment and spotting him dead-on, was Big John Rourke.

CHAPTER 48

James

No.

James wanted to shake some sense into his head, tell himself to stop seeing things. Or run—that might've been a better call.

But it felt as if his sneakers were super-glued to the sidewalk. There, right smack in front of the big wooden cross he and Rev had hoisted up just the day prior, the truck came to a sudden lurching stop.

"Would you look what we have here, Mikey. If it ain't the narc. James Steadman. Or should I say, 'Deadman.'" Big John's voice was ice cold. "Get him."

James backed up, toward the church, but he wasn't about to go in. Rev might be a big guy, but he was no match for these two and the others, who he could now see climbing out of the pickup bed, heading his way.

Too late, he turned to run back toward the town center. Might have made it, or at least gotten someplace more visible . . .

Only right behind the red truck, another vehicle had pulled up.

Sliding out of that car was DJ, and next to him, DJ's brother, Dex. It was like a nightmare reunion.

Mike caught him by the hoodie when he froze, yanked him so

James fell flat on his backside on the hard cement.

A right hook caught him square in the temple. The world spun. *I'm done for.*

He should've known it would end this way.

He knew what they thought. Hadn't really considered it till a few weeks ago, but he knew how rumors flew like bees knocked from their hive, homing in on the threat. He was a snitch—that's what they thought. Only he wasn't. Tommy'd fessed up on his own accord to his part in the beating—that was why he was behind bars. James didn't know why, didn't know what had prompted it. For all he knew, Tommy's confession was tied up in some other case, but whatever the issue, James never had to say a word. Wouldn't have, truth be told. It hadn't made a difference to the public defender back then, anyway. He'd known it was a group jump, not just James, but James was the one they'd caught. James was the one they made pay.

Besides, no one ever took kindly to snitches. Disloyalty in giving out any incriminating information about another member of the Hammer Crew—even warranted—was punishable by death.

It wasn't me! He wanted to shout it, make them understand, but it wouldn't matter. They thought what they thought at this point.

"We've been looking for you, snitch." Big John yanked him up by the collar of his hoodie, squeezing the neck tight.

James couldn't help it. "I didn't say anything."

They all laughed, a low, sinister laugh. "Hear that, men?" Big John glared deep into his eyes like he wanted to pluck them out one by one. "He 'didn't say anything.' We believe you, don't we."

"Oh, sure." Mikey. Who'd brought him into the crew, who'd known him since the second grade. They'd been friends through it all.

Not anymore.

Down the street came the whirr of a garbage truck as it crept closer.

"Get 'im into the pickup," one of the new guys muttered, and then they were pushing and prodding him forward.

Last chance. James went limp, sank downward, like he was giving in.

Then with all his might, he shot his leg out, jammed Mikey smack in the kneecap.

He was free! Racing down the sidewalk!

"James!"

At first he thought it was Mikey, shouting at him. But it sounded like a kid's voice. It was a kid's voice. Headed toward him from the opposite direction.

No!

He knew that voice. Didn't want to look up and see. *No, no, no . . .*

But there was no stopping it now.

Barreling into him, right there in front of the church, basketball dropped forgotten to the street, was little Devon, Rev's kid, Marla looking worried and trailing close behind.

All decked out in his basketball gear, Devon wrapped his arms around him, grinned up. "Hey James, where ya runnin'?"

"Well, now looky what we have here. James has got himself a little buddy." Big John had caught up to them, and now a couple of the guys had James in a tight grip.

Big John had one beefy hand squarely on Devon's skinny shoulders.

"Will you kindly take your hands off my son?" Marla's voice was steady as she stood on the steps of the church, but James could hear the raw anger behind her tone.

He could also hear the fear.

Oh, dear God. What have I brought here?

Big John didn't bother to say a word, just nodded at the church door. One of the guys grabbed Marla, the other opened the church door. She started to yell, but he clamped a hand over her mouth. Tight.

Terror snaked up James's spine. "Just let them go. They didn't do anything. I'll go with you!" He struggled, but they were holding him too tight.

"Nope, I think any friend of James is someone we need to get to know nice and personal. Right, guys?" Big John drew the words out slow and sweet, but his eyes were like daggers. "In."

They were in the church and locking the door in moments, pushing the three of them toward the corner of the room.

"Mack!" Marla managed to scream toward the back, toward Rev's office. "Help!"

Rev dashed out, a look of horror on his face.

"Hold it!" Mikey snapped.

Rev froze.

James could see Mikey was holding something, something pointed right at Rev, but he couldn't see what it was.

Rev slowly backed away, hands up. "Easy, buddy."

Mikey sniffed. "I ain't your buddy."

A gun. James could see it now—that's what Mikey was holding. *Oh, Jesus. Help us.*

James closed his eyes, as if he could will every ounce of his body up and out in prayer.

"You. On your knees," Big John motioned to Rev, who complied, his face a mask of fear. "You friends with this piece of filth? With James the snitch? Answer me!"

Rev looked from Big John to Devon and Marla, and finally to James. He looked James in the eye. *Don't do it.*

"Yes. I'm his pastor and his friend."

James's heart sank. *No.*

"His pastor and his friend. Well, ain't that precious." Big John mimicked. "I think it's time to have a little fun with your friends here, James. Maybe make them pay for what you did to *our* friend."

"Please. Let them go!"

Big John laughed again. "I don't think so. Tie 'em up."

One of the guys disappeared outside, returning a moment later with what looked like a line of parachute cord. By now Mikey had the gun trained on all three of them—Rev, Marla, and Devon, who DJ was busy herding into some of the chairs they'd already set up for Bible study the next night. The start of Lent, Rev had told him, when he'd hand out all those nails to folks.

Please, God.

Marla was crying, and Rev didn't have any expression on his face that James could tell, but Devon just stared at the men, looked them one by one in the eye. Just do what they say, James wanted to shout to the kid. They'll let you go eventually. Just stop staring!

Only he didn't actually know if that was true.

Once the Bryants were secured, paracord wrapped around their wrists and then firmly around all three of them, one solid lump, Big John clapped his hands and motioned for the guys holding James to usher him front and center.

"Okay, snitch. Time to fess up. We've been looking for you since you ran outta that diner. Should've known better." Big John gave a false tsk-tsk, shook his head dramatically. "Didn't take much effort for us to convince the waitress to give the name of the woman with you, off the credit card receipt. Your snot-nosed, skinny little sister, all grown-up now and gorgeous. She wasn't hard to track down, not in the least. Maybe we should visit her next."

Dex laughed, but DJ just slowly pulled out his pocketknife, started fiddling with the blade.

One of the guys kicked James, hard, and he landed smack on his hands and knees.

"I'll do whatever you say." James gasped up at Big John. "Just don't hurt any of them. Please. I'm the one you're after, not them."

Big John loomed over him, as if James were a meal and he was deciding where to start gnawing.

"DJ," Big John said finally. "Hand me your knife."

Chapter 49

TIFF WANTED TO PANIC. Wanted to march right down to that sheriff's office and give him a piece of her mind, go "full-on Steadman" on him, as Mama used to say.

But she'd been in journalism—and worked with law enforcement—long enough to know emotions were the last thing she needed to wield right now. What she needed was proof.

Together, she and Rebecca printed out the hotel bill from Thursday night, which clearly showed two guests and two full-sized beds, and downloaded Rebecca's current charges from the credit card website.

"I'm going with you," Rebecca said, grabbing her purse and her car keys and leaving Millie in charge of the office. "My car."

They were at the small county station in minutes.

"We need to see Sheriff Zane, please," Rebecca told the officer at the front desk. "It's urgent."

The officer, who Tiff thought might have been Bobby's second cousin, widened her eyes at the sight of both the editor and the publisher of the town paper standing before her, and buzzed them back.

Zane was just coming out of his office when they rounded the corner.

"It's your brother I need here, not you." His arms were crossed.

"He'll be here," Tiff said, working to keep the quiver from her voice. "I called him, just like you asked. But we need to show you something first."

Zane sighed heavily. "What's that," he asked, arms still crossed.

"Proof." Rebecca spoke up.

Her boss reached into her leather bag, slid out a file folder, and passed it over.

Zane gazed at its contents a long moment. "Still doesn't tell me anything."

Tiff huffed out a breath. "How can it not? It shows clear as day we stayed at this hotel in this city Thursday night, just like I told you. See? Two beds. Two guests. It's her card, and you can see my name right there."

She started to jab at the page with her finger, then swallowed. *Cool it, Tiff.*

"Two guests, but how do I know it was you who stayed? And how do I know your brother was there with you? You could have told them two guests at check in and they never would have known otherwise. Face it, Tiff. There's probable cause, and you know it."

"But—but I have more! Dinner!" Tiff fumbled with her purse, ratted around until she pulled out her slender pink wallet, opened it to find the receipts from their trip—including that night at the diner. She grinned triumphantly. "See?"

"Again, two dinners at a no-name restaurant tells me nothing. Besides, how do I know it was James who went with you? For all I know it was Bobby."

"It wasn't Bobby!" She wanted to scream.

"Sheriff, please." Rebecca started to put a hand on his arm, but his glare stopped her cold. Instead, she clenched her hands at her sides.

This was impossible. Tiff racked her brain. "I know. The coroner! You can call Mr. Reynolds. Ed Reynolds. I don't have his number offhand, but I can look it up on my phone, let you talk to him . . ."

The sheriff just gave her a long, sad look. "Tiff, stop. Just stop. I know you want to protect your brother. But enough evidence points to him that it's my obligation to bring him in. We've got a man on camera in a hoodie that fits your brother's description, breaking into cars, and he's our only solid lead to date. The truth will come out eventually, one way or the other."

Tiff gritted her teeth, willing the tears back. *You will not cry, Tiff Steadman. You will not give him the satisfaction.*

"Here." The sheriff guided them to a waiting room, brought them both bottled waters. "Just sit tight a moment."

He disappeared, then returned minutes later. This time, his face was red.

"Where is he?" Zane growled.

Tiff blinked. "At work?"

"No. He left. A good hour ago. His bike's still locked out front, but he's nowhere to be found."

Oh, James. "Maybe he went home first to get something?"

"We'll go together."

Rebecca spoke into her ear then, something about an attorney friend in New York. Tiff brushed it away. *This isn't happening.*

"You'll let us in, let us search?" Zane asked when they got to her house.

She was tempted to say absolutely not. But what did she have to lose? She might as well cooperate. It'd go easier on James if she did.

But there was no sign of James at the house.

Peaches stared at them accusingly as they walked in, first Tiff and Rebecca, followed by the officers. Then he meowed his discontent and disappeared beneath the sofa. Sorry, kitty, Tiff thought in his direction. She and Rebecca sat down on the couch, Rebecca texting furiously with her legal contacts.

"Where else could he be?" Zane asked, after he'd tromped through every room.

A knock came on the door then, and everyone froze.

"Tiff?" a voice called, and then the door creaked open and Bobby stuck his head inside. "Tiff, you home?"

"Bobby!" Tiff jumped from the couch and barreled across the room.

His arms went around her. "Millie called me at the grocery. Told me what's going on. How can I help?"

"Where else does your brother spend time?" Zane demanded.

"Nowhere. Home, work, church. Community service."

Zane looked up at the last one. "Where does he do his service?"

"Dahlia Community Bible Church. With Rev Bryant."

Zane signaled, and the officers headed for the door.

"Let's roll. It's time to see a preacher."

CHAPTER 50

James

JAMES LAY THERE, afraid to move, but afraid if he didn't, they'd stop messing with him and start messing with Rev.

"Get up, big shot," somebody taunted, nudged James with a boot, then called over toward Devon. "Yo, little kid. You wanna be next?"

James grunted, balling his hand into a fist. One of his ribs was broken, maybe more than one, that was for certain. His left eye felt like it was swollen to half its size, and he wasn't sure he had any teeth left. All he could taste was blood.

The arm was the worst. Big John had started there, going to work on the tattoo—the gang one, a red and black hammer, the one they all got when they joined the crew.

Behind the laughter and the taunts, he could hear the low murmur of the Bryants praying.

Quiet, he wanted to tell them. You'll only make 'em madder. But it was no use. He knew they'd keep on praying. Even to their deaths if they had to.

Help them, God. He didn't care about himself anymore. But if one of them got hurt, if someone laid a hand on Rev, Marla, or Devon . . .

295

The kicking started again, and the air was getting fuzzy, thick.

"Looky what I found," one of the guys called. "A box of nails."

Nails. He pictured them, the cold black metal—the same nails Rev was going to have them all hammer into the cross tomorrow, on Ash Wednesday.

James knew what was coming now. Knew he was powerless to stop it. He just hoped it'd be over quick.

Random snippets from the Bible raced through his mind.

. . . Even though I walk through the valley of the shadow of death, I will fear no evil, for you are with me; your rod and your staff, they comfort me . . .

. . . Peace I leave with you; my peace I give to you. Not as the world gives do I give to you. Let not your hearts be troubled, neither let them be afraid . . .

. . . And behold, I am with you always, to the end of the age . . .

In a corner of his mind, he could hear the prayer Tiff used to say when she was tiny, every night, all the way up till he'd left home. "Now I lay me down to sleep, I pray the Lord my soul to keep, if I should die before I wake, I pray the Lord my soul to take."

All around him, the air grew thicker. And then shouts—shouts from Big John and Mikey, shouts from others, what sounded like a roomful.

"Thank God!" he thought he heard Marla cry in joy, but that couldn't be right. "Oh, thank you, Jesus!"

Then someone was crouching by his head. James took a breath, prepared his soul. He'd never felt more peaceful in his whole entire life.

But instead of the kick he expected, ending all the pain, he heard a yell.

"We need a medic in here pronto! Here, help me lay him down."

Someone's cool, gentle hands were on his head now, brushing the hair back, telling him to hang on, help was on the way.

Help . . .

. . . on the way . . .

Then everything went black.

CHAPTER 51

Tiff

TIFF SAT IN THE TINY HOSPITAL ROOM, chair scooched as close to her brother's bed as it could possibly get, her head bowed and eyes closed. Beside her sat Bobby, his gentle snores and the steady beep of the machines keeping her company.

Thank you, God. Whatever will be, just . . . thank you.

It could have been so much worse, she knew. Still, eyes closed, she forced her mind to calm, to settle not on her worry and fears for James but on God, on this moment, on resting peacefully in his plan.

"Sis." James squeezed her hand.

"You're awake!" Her head popped up.

"H-how long?"

She glanced at the clock. "Long."

It was full-fledged night now, far past visiting hours, but the night nurse was related to Bobby somehow and was kindly turning a blind eye to the fact that they were both still there.

"Are they . . . ?" His voice was raspy from the painkillers and whatever they'd given him for the surgery, but Tiff knew what he was asking.

"They're completely fine. Marla's hopping mad, and I'm pretty

298

sure Devon's crowned you a superhero or something. Rev twisted his back helping lift you on the stretcher—"

"Stretcher?"

"Well, they had to get you here somehow. But he's okay," she caressed his hand with her thumb. "And so are you."

"I thought I was a goner." James's voice was so quiet she had to strain to hear him.

"They hit you pretty bad, but the MRI is clear, thank God. A couple broken ribs, and they might have to do a skin graft where they did some dirty work on your arm, but for now that's still up in the air. Oh, and you had oral surgery. The good news is your teeth are gonna look amazing after this."

They chuckled, and Bobby stirred.

"Welcome back, man." Bobby leaned forward. "I'm glad you're okay."

"Thanks."

The nurse came in then, shooed Tiff and Bobby out so she could change some bandages and take care of other things.

Tiff and Bobby wandered down to the vending machines and bought a pack of crackers and a can of soda to share.

As they wandered, they could see an officer in the waiting room, half an eye on the television and the other on James's door. He's not going anywhere, she wanted to tell him, but it was fine. Her brother was safe, her pastor and his family had been rescued, and the bad guys were behind bars. Time would fix the rest. She was sure of it.

They reached the window, and Tiff stared out into the dark night. There was no trace of moon, and in the distance, she could see lightning on the horizon. They were calling for a big storm, but at least it would be rain, not snow.

"I got you a present," Bobby said suddenly, and Tiff turned to him, surprised.

From his pocket, he pulled two long strands of purple and green beads, slipped them over her head. "Happy Mardi Gras."

She giggled, then wrapped her arms around him as tight as she could.

"I'm really sorry about everything," she said, pulling back to look into his eyes.

"Me, too." Bobby knelt down, all serious now. "Will you still marry me?"

She smiled at him. "Scars and all?"

"Trust me, my beautiful love. You are not the only one in this family with issues. Yes—scars and all. Forever."

She liked the way he said that—"this family." She could see it suddenly, her and him, children at their feet. Dinners with his parents and brothers. Happy. Peaceful. Fulfilled. And spanning out, too. Visits to Alabama. Teaching her kids to climb trees with their uncle James.

Gazing into his eyes as he rose once again to his full height, she smiled.

"I most certainly will. But there's one caveat." Her eyes twinkled.

He raised a brow and grinned. "What's that?"

"How do you feel about bringing on James as a third grooms-man?"

EPILOGUE

TIFF STOOD IN THE CHURCH ALCOVE, peering at the guests below, her heart pounding so hard she was sure everyone could hear the dull thud. *Breathe.* Her wedding dress felt entirely too tight, her lipstick was already coming off, and if one more person asked if she was nervous she thought she'd scream.

But it was all worth it. In just about thirty minutes she'd officially be a married woman. Mrs. Tiff Steadman Smathers. She'd decided to keep her maiden name in there, after all. Owning the past and all.

"Ready for the honeymoon?" Rebecca poked her.

"Am I ever!" A breathless giggle escaped her lips. Tiff kept her voice low. "Remind me why I invited this many people?"

"Bobby's mama?" They both laughed.

"But seriously," Rebecca told her, gazing at her with soft eyes. "You look stunning."

Tiff looked down—she'd decided to wear Mrs. Smathers's wedding dress after all, enlisting the help of her Aunt Connie out in Alabama, who'd turned out to be a master seamstress. Connie had transformed the dress into a glorious, simple, yet gorgeous creation, somehow exactly all she'd wanted. She felt like a princess, only better.

Between getting to know Mama's sisters and her endless list of long-lost cousins, not to mention how neat it was watching her brother and her fiancé become true friends, this wedding was really just the icing on what had been the most incredible summer of her life. The only off-note was having her brother move two states away. Now that his parole requirements had been met, Aunt Connie and Uncle Jake had invited him to come live in the apartment on their land, which was vacant now that their youngest had gotten married the summer before. Jake was planning to teach James to farm, help him learn the trade. Aunt Barb had even promised to teach him to ride horses.

"It'll be good for you two lovebirds to start your new marriage without your older brother lurking around, anyway," James had told her, but he'd hugged her and promised to visit often. It was only a six-hour drive, and they'd already done it twice since they'd connected with Mama's sisters back in February.

"There's my daughter-in-love." Bobby's mama bustled up from behind carrying a giant box of bouquets, planting a kiss somewhere in Tiff's hair. "This one's yours."

All Tiff's favorites were clustered together—daisies, tulips, dahlias, and lavender, with a triplicate of roses in the center. Red for love, yellow for friendship, and white for faith. "Everything I hope and pray our marriage will always be rooted in," Bobby'd said.

"Thank you, Mama." Tiff drew Mrs. Smathers close for a hug.

"Oohh, I just love it when you call me that!" Mrs. Smathers tittered and headed off, passing out bouquets to the bridesmaids.

Tiff and Rebecca locked eyes and smiled. The best advice she'd gotten from Rebecca, who had just last year reconciled with her own mother, was to let the past go and love who's here. Mrs. Smathers might be bossy, loud, and opinionated, but she was a good woman, and she'd raised three stand-up boys. Tiff could learn a lot from her—she knew that well.

Below, the music changed, and Tiff peered down to see her Aunt Daisy at the church piano, easing into what she knew were the prelude songs.

Footsteps sounded on the stairs. Aunt Barb.

"Five minutes! Is that enough time? We can delay if you need. Your Aunt Daisy's got a long list of wedding classics up her sleeve." Barb looked worriedly at Tiff, who gave her a reassuring smile.

"Five minutes is perfect."

They put the finishing touches on hair and makeup, then carefully made their way downstairs, tucked out of sight, but with a full view of everyone inside. In the pews she saw a host of friends and family—her new cousin Jaymie and her fiancé, Ethan. Jaymie's younger brothers. Alana and Lou from the pizza place, Alana's hair done up in the most massive bun Tiff thought she'd ever seen. Sheriff Zane, there with his pretty wife.

Aunt Barb and Mrs. Smathers slipped off, into their seats, and Tiff's bridesmaids—Millie, Dinah, and Marla, with Rebecca as her maid of honor—gathered close. Bobby's daddy stepped from the wings, where he was waiting with Devon, who would serve as the ringbearer.

"You look prettier than a movie star, Miss Tiff," Devon said, peering up.

"You still got those rings, Son?" Marla peered down at him.

Sometime between the adoption finalization and now, they'd taken to calling each other "mom" and "son," and it still gave Tiff a rush of joy to hear it.

"Sure do, Mom!"

Tiff peeked through the window, where she could see the groomsmen lining up—Bobby's brothers, Zach and Ben, and his cousin, Rich, with James as best man. Rev in his dress robes at the center. James looked handsome, she decided—and happy. He shot a glance her way, locked eyes with her through the tiny church window. They grinned. The farm would be good for him, she knew. Good for them all.

And then her heart caught as Bobby, her husband-to-be, stepped into place.

"He looks nervous," Mr. Smathers said, taking her arm as they prepared to walk down the aisle.

"Not as nervous as I am," Tiff admitted.

Mr. Smathers smiled down at her. "Well, I know I've won the daughter-in-law lottery. I'm prouder than anything to get to be the one who walks you down the aisle. So let me tell you something my own daddy told me on my wedding day thirty years ago." He winked. "Give it to God, and keep your mind on the after-party."

And then the doors swung open and she walked toward her future, smiling to the left and the right, toward all the people gathered to help them celebrate their new adventure.

Her roots might be unorthodox, but with God at the center and her husband at her side, they certainly were a beautiful tangle.

The End

About the Author

Jessica Brodie is an award-winning author and journalist with thousands of articles to her name and a huge heart for people and their inspiring redemption stories. She holds a master's in English and a bachelor's in communications. A native of Miami, Florida, she now makes her home in South Carolina with her husband Matt, four children, three misfit cats, and one giant German Shepherd. Find her at JessicaBrodie.com.

Book Club
Discussion Questions

1. Tiff concealed her past and her brother's existence from everyone in Dahlia, including her fiancé Bobby. Do you think she was justified in keeping these secrets, or should she have been more honest from the beginning? How do family secrets impact our ability to form authentic relationships?

2. James has genuinely found faith and remorse for his past crimes, but he still faces suspicion and prejudice. What does the novel suggest about society's willingness to accept that people can truly change? Is James's transformation believable, and what factors make redemption stories compelling or unconvincing?

3. When Tiff and James discover their mother's history of abuse, they begin to understand her behavior differently. How does learning about generational trauma change our perspective on people who have hurt us? Does understanding someone's pain excuse their harmful actions?

4. The novel explores different expressions of faith through various characters—James's prison conversion, Rev's welcoming ministry, and Tiff's struggle with forgiveness. How do the characters' different relationships with faith influence their actions? What role does forgiveness play in healing?

5. Dahlia represents a "wholesome" small town, but it also shows how communities can be both welcoming and exclusionary. How does the setting influence the story's themes? What does the novel say about who gets to belong in a community and under what conditions?

6. James tries to hide his tattoos, particularly the swastika on his wrist, which represent his shameful past. How do we carry visible and invisible marks of our history? What does the novel suggest about the relationship between our past selves and who we become?

7. The story presents multiple instances where characters must choose between demanding justice and extending grace—from James's early release to the community's response to his presence. How do these two concepts work together or conflict throughout the novel? When is each approach most appropriate?

Acknowledgments

I'm fascinated with Christian redemption stories, the way that deeply flawed people undergo a profound, miraculous transformation as they see the proverbial light and begin to walk God's path for their lives. Perhaps it's because I myself am a redemption story, and I've seen the powerful and beautiful ways God works in our lives. At its core, that's where this book originates—in the notion that no matter how far away someone seems from Christ, no matter how many wrongs they've done or how bad a sin they might have committed, no one is exempt from the saving grace of Jesus Christ. No one, no matter what. There is room for everyone at God's table.

Thank you foremost to God—for your love and your grace, your mercy and your forgiveness, and your patience for those of us who sometimes take years to fully comprehend the truth of your mysterious and extravagant love.

Thank you to my family for your patience with my sometimes overly long and detailed storytelling, which always winds up far better in the pages of a book than at the dinner table. Thank you to my amazing and incredibly supportive husband, Matt, for your consistent and steady love, friendship, and encouragement. I'm blessed to be yours. Thanks to my kids, Cameron, Avery, Allison, and Will; to my mom, Kathleen, who has always been my biggest cheerleader; and to my sister, Sara, who reminds me that no matter what, our sibling relationships are one of the most complicated and extraordinarily beautiful that we'll ever experience and are to be cherished for always.

Thank you to Phyllis Brodie and to Katy Haddad for your encouragement and support, and to all the writer friends who have nurtured me over the years, especially my old conference-call group (Diane Thomas, Gene Wright, Donna Warner, and Marilyn Staats—you all helped me grow in ways I cannot begin to express) and Lexington Word Weavers, led by Lori Hatcher and Jean Wilund, whose members have been constantly positive and helpful in their feedback about this book.

Writing can be lonely, but we writers don't create in a silo. To all who shaped me and are still shaping me—thank you. I love you more than you can imagine.

THE DAHLIA SERIES

The Memory Garden: Book One

The Memory Garden, the Amazon-bestselling first book in the Dahlia Series, is a gripping Southern novel following a broken journalist who finds unexpected purpose in a small town when a troubled boy's dangerous secret puts them both at risk.

Tangled Roots: Book Two

In *Tangled Roots*, Tiff Steadman thought she'd escaped her shameful past—until her recently paroled brother James arrives in Dahlia, threatening the respectable life she's carefully built. As wedding plans and buried secrets collide, these two siblings must confront the truth they've both been hiding and decide if redemption is worth the cost.

Hidden Seeds: Book Three

Returning to Dahlia after tragedy exposes her fiancé's betrayal, Natalie Motts rebuilds her life through art and unexpected friendship with Laney, a trafficking survivor hiding a dangerous past. When Natalie's teenage sister vanishes, Laney must choose between protecting her hard-won safety and stepping back into darkness to bring the girl home.

Book Four: Coming 2027

Marla's story . . . to be continued.

Paperback, e-book, and audiobook available.

Sign up for Jessica's Dahlia Email List and stay notified about her latest releases. Visit JessicaBrodie.com/Dahlia

www.ingramcontent.com/pod-product-compliance
Lightning Source LLC
Chambersburg PA
CBHW070916260626
47162CB00007B/2695